Praise for *Good Night,*

"Within these pages: boundless imagery and virt[...] have sequenced the stories like he would the songs c[...] that become echoes, one tone harmonizing with another. While *Good Night, Sleep Tight* harbors moments of legitimate terror, it's Evenson's powers of emotional observation that will make you gasp. And the unmatched artistry with which he renders them. This book is more than a gem: it's a collection of precious stones."

—Josh Malerman, *New York Times* bestselling author of *Bird Box*

"Brian Evenson's new collection, *Good Night, Sleep Tight*, is nineteen installments of idiosyncratic, weird genius. I can't think of a better practitioner of the short story at work today."

—Jeffrey Ford, Edgar Award–winning author of *The Girl in the Glass*

"Peeling back the thin veil that separates our humanity from the incomprehensible and the decadently weird, Brian Evenson crafts a masterful and utterly beguiling collection of literary unease with *Good Night, Sleep Tight*. With a pervasive sense of isolation and existential worry leaking from story to story, this disturbing collection proves why Evenson remains the undisputed master of short literary horror fiction."

—Eric LaRocca, author of *Things Have Gotten Worse Since We Last Spoke*

Praise for *The Glassy, Burning Floor of Hell*

The Philadelphia Inquirer, "Best Books of 2021"
Southwest Review, "Must-Read Books of 2021"
Literary Hub, "Most Anticipated Books of 2021"

"His stories are deeply terrifying and so troubling that they linger in your mind long after you've read them."

—R.L. Stine, author of *Goosebumps*

"[A] towering collection of nightmarish horror, sci-fi parables, and weird tales. . . . 'Once I take you there,' ends another story, 'you'll have a hard time dragging yourself away.' The same could be said of Evenson's unforgettable work, drawn from the darkest corners of the imagination and nearly impossible to forget."

—*Publishers Weekly,* starred review

"I've always been a fan of shorts, because they often feel impressionistic, like you're floating between worlds. In this collection, Evenson really draws on the horrors of a collapsed environment and the moral choices one makes under pressure."

—April Wolfe, *Variety*

"Though Evenson shares some DNA with bygone sci-fi delights like Robert Aickman and the O.G. *Twilight Zone,* his economical sentences and icy storytelling keep readers at arm's length, even as the air starts thinning and the room goes dark. Honestly, is there anything scarier than a narrator who doesn't care?"

—Patrick Rapa, *The Philadelphia Inquirer*

"Like with Borges or Kafka, every one of Brian Evenson's stories [is] a whole world distilled down to a few pages, and rendered in a pointillism that feels not just abstract, but cosmic, yet is gritty all the same, and leaves a distinct, bloody residue in your mind, in your heart. And then you can no longer look at the world the way you used to."

—Stephen Graham Jones, author of *Don't Fear the Reaper*

Praise for *Song for the Unraveling of the World*

Winner of the 2020 World Fantasy Award for best collection
Winner of the 2019 Shirley Jackson Award for a single-author collection
Finalist for the 2019 *Los Angeles Times* Ray Bradbury Prize
Finalist for the 2019 Big Other Book Award for Fiction
The New York Times, "Best Horror Fiction"
Washington Post, "Best Horror Fiction of the Year"
NPR, "Best Books of 2019"

"Missing persons, paranoia and psychosis . . . the kind of writer who leads you into the labyrinth, then abandons you there. It's hard to believe a guy can be so frightening, so consistently."

—*The New York Times*

"These stories are carefully calibrated exercises in ambiguity in which Evenson leaves it unclear how much of the off-kilterness exists outside of the deep-seated pathologies that motivate his characters."

—*Publishers Weekly,* starred review

"Enigmatic, superbly rendered slices of fear, uncertainty and paranoia."

—*The Washington Post*

good night, sleep tight

Also by Brian Evenson, from Coffee House Press

NOVELS

Father of Lies

Last Days

The Open Curtain

STORIES

A Collapse of Horses

Fugue State

The Glassy, Burning Floor of Hell

Song for the Unraveling of the World

Windeye

good night, sleep tight

stories

Brian Evenson

COFFEE HOUSE PRESS

MINNEAPOLIS

2024

Copyright © 2024 by Brian Evenson
Cover design by Reiko Murakami
Cover layout and book design by Abbie Phelps

Coffee House Press books are available to the trade through our primary distributor, Consortium Book Sales & Distribution, cbsd.com or (800) 283-3572. For personal orders, catalogs, or other information, write to info@coffeehousepress.org.

Coffee House Press is a nonprofit literary publishing house. Support from private foundations, corporate giving programs, government programs, and generous individuals helps make the publication of our books possible. We gratefully acknowledge their support in detail in the back of this book.

LIBRARY OF CONGRESS CATALOGING-IN-PUBLICATION DATA
Names: Evenson, Brian, 1966- author.
Title: Good night, sleep tight : stories / Brian Evenson.
Other titles: Good night, sleep tight (Compilation)
Description: Minneapolis : Coffee House Press, 2024.
Identifiers: LCCN 2023057705 (print) | LCCN 2023057706 (ebook) | ISBN 9781566897099 (paperback) | ISBN 9781566897105 (e-pub)
Subjects: LCGFT: Science fiction. | Short stories.
Classification: LCC PS3555.V326 G66 2024 (print) | LCC PS3555.V326 (ebook) | DDC 813/.54--dc23/eng/20231218
LC record available at https://lccn.loc.gov/2023057705
LC ebook record available at https://lccn.loc.gov/2023057706

PRINTED IN THE UNITED STATES OF AMERICA

31 30 29 28 27 26 25 24   4 5 6 7 8 9 10 11

for Mother

Contents

good night, sleep tight

The Sequence

When she was young, Sidra and her twin sister used to play a game. They used to play lots of games, but this was, so far as Sidra could remember, the only game they were careful about, the only one they never played somewhere where adults would see. Except of course their grandfather: because of his condition they felt it did not really matter if he could see them. Though later, they, or at least Sidra, came to feel differently.

It was Sidra's twin who started it: Sidra never would have thought up the game on her own. At the time, she was not sure exactly how Selene had come up with it. Later, she thought perhaps her twin hadn't thought it up on her own after all. Perhaps something had whispered the rules of the game in her ear, and though she had not consciously heard them, she had still taken them in. Perhaps her twin had felt she was making up a game from scratch when, in fact, she had been tricked into playing it all along.

The game began something like this. Sidra was gathering buttercups into a heap, and Selene was stirring an anthill slowly with a stick, when suddenly Selene stood up and said, "Do you want to play a game?"

This confused Sidra a little. "But we're already playing games," she said.

Selene made a little disgusted noise and brushed the hair out of her eyes. She was sweaty and dirty, but so was Sidra. They were always just as sweaty and dirty as each other. That was, Sidra felt, part of being a twin.

"This isn't really a game," Selene said. She gestured at the stick poking out of the anthill, astream now with confused ants. Then she gestured at the pile of wilted buttercups. "That isn't either." Ants had made their way into the flowers as well, Sidra saw, were swarming all over them. "These are the kinds of things people do when they can't think of a game."

Sidra shrugged. "OK. What do you want to play?"

Selene stretched out her hand. "Come on," she said. "I'll show you."

Her twin led her away from the anthill and the buttercups and across the lawn to where their grandfather's wheelchair was. He sat in it slightly slouched, a parasol wired to the wheelchair's frame and unfurled above him. He was dressed to go out—their mother always dressed him like that, even though she never took him anywhere. The only thing she did was roll him out of the house and park him in the yard. She would check on him every hour or two, charging the girls with letting her know if anything went wrong in the meantime.

"Hi, Grandpa," said Selene to him, and Sidra echoed, "Hi, Grandpa."

He didn't respond, or hardly did. Behind his greasy-lensed glasses he blinked. That was all he could ever manage. He had been paralyzed for as long as Sidra had been alive. She had asked her mother about it once, asked why he couldn't move, and her mother had sighed. "Nobody knows why," she'd said. One day her father had been walking and talking like normal and then, abruptly, he collapsed. He hadn't moved since.

"We're going to play a game, Grandpa," said Selene, and their grandfather blinked again. One blink. *Probably means "yes" or "I understand,"* thought Sidra. *If it means anything at all. Maybe it means nothing.*

"Is Grandpa playing too?" asked Sidra.

Selene shook her head. "He's just the starting line," she said. Then she turned to their grandfather. "No offense," she told him.

He blinked again.

Selene looked at Sidra. "You need to do everything I do," she told her. "Exactly as I do it, in the exact same way."

"Why?"

"That's the game," said Selene. "Step where I step, exactly. Move like me too. It should be easy for you because we have the same size feet. If we weren't twins probably only one of us could play."

This confused Sidra, but she nodded.

"All right, then," said Selene. Her face was creased, her gaze abstracted as if she was listening hard, trying to hear something far away. "Let's begin."

Her twin moved forward until the toe of one foot was touching the rubber of the wheelchair's wheel, her opposite hip knocking against her grandfather's knees. She sidestepped, clapped once, then stepped backward while sucking in a deep breath. All the while their grandfather was blinking, blinking, more rapidly than Sidra had ever seen him blink before. What did it mean?

Her twin took another step, clapped, then peered back over her shoulder, encouraging Sidra to repeat the pattern.

Sidra did. She moved toward her grandfather until the toe of her shoe touched the wheel. That close to her grandfather, pressed against his leg, she could smell his body. She did not care for the sour smell of him. But despite that, she concentrated on doing everything her twin had done, and doing it all exactly right. That was the game, after all.

"Good," murmured Selene, and began another sequence. This time Sidra followed her closely, staying only a step or two behind, putting her foot into the impressions Selene's feet had left in the grass before they could disappear. And this time, with this new sequence, Sidra felt something had begun to change. Not something she could see, exactly, more something she could sense. The air seemed stiller than elsewhere on the lawn, and the light was becoming different too. This scared Sidra a little, but since Selene kept moving forward, Sidra did too. Sidra had been born second, and ever since she had always followed behind Selene.

They turned right and took a few dozen steps, touching the toe of one step to the heel of the next, picking a quiet, gapless line across the lawn. There was their grandfather, to one side, a little way away now. It looked to Sidra as if a pane of dirty glass now lay between them and him, leaching him of color. And then Selene stepped sideways, and suddenly the hum of insects, the soughing of the gentle breeze, the chirping of birds all vanished. Sidra couldn't hear any of it anymore, couldn't even hear her sister's footsteps.

In front of her she saw her sister clap her hands together in the air, but Sidra couldn't hear that either. She could feel it, though, could almost see the soundless sound ripple out through the air toward her. She could see the air shiver, and for just a moment a transparent wall became vaguely visible beside her, and then the shiver stopped and the wall faded away, becoming invisible again. Or nearly so: perhaps that was what was making their grandfather seem drained of color. The house, too, had faded, felt less present, less real.

Suddenly Sidra began to be afraid of where her sister was taking her. *I don't like this game,* she said, *I want to go home.* But no sound came out of her mouth, none at least that she could hear. Only that same ripple through the air, a brief coalescing into being of that translucent wall beside her.

But her sister felt it. She turned her head to face her, her finger pressed hard to her lips. Because the game demanded she do what her sister did, Sidra turned her head too and pressed her own finger to her own lips, even though she was not sure her sister had meant for her to. She wanted to stop playing but was afraid of what would happen if she did. Would everything that was drained of color stay that way? She could sense now parts of the world around her opening and other parts closing—but above all changing, folding in, tightening, in ways that made her feel they were being herded into a tighter and tighter chute. *What,* she worried, *will be there to meet us at the other end?*

Her sister turned again, and smiled. Her skin was gray, her teeth gray, as if she were carved from stone. Sidra turned and smiled behind her too and, for just a moment, thought she glimpsed another fleeting face. But no, it was her imagination, an odd trick of the light, it had to be: there wasn't, there couldn't be, anyone following them.

And then, as suddenly as it had begun, it ended. Another step and sound swelled back up around them and color returned. She and her twin were back on the lawn, not far from their grandfather, and everything was back to normal.

"We got it wrong," her sister told her. "We were close, almost there. I could feel it, but you stepped wrong or I did or we both did, and then everything came crashing down."

"Almost where?" asked Sidra.

Her sister chose not to answer. Perhaps she didn't know the answer or perhaps she simply didn't want to tell Sidra.

"Where were we walking?" Sidra asked. "What was that place? Why did everything go gray? What happened to the sound?"

"Nowhere," said Selene.

"Nowhere? Where's that?"

Her sister frowned. Sidra watched her search all around her with her eyes, looking for some way to explain it.

"We were . . . between things," her sister finally offered. "At least I think so."

"Between what things?"

"I don't know how to explain," said Selene. "I'm still figuring it out."

And so they stopped talking about it.

If it had been up to Sidra, they wouldn't have played again, but her twin insisted. Even then, she made it clear that Sidra didn't have to play, that she could do it without her. She didn't *need* her—she could do it all by herself. Which made Sidra feel like Selene was threatening to take something away from her. Indeed, everything her sister said, she realized later, was carefully constructed to ensure that Sidra would play the game again after all.

As soon as they entered their grandfather's field of vision he began rapidly, desperately blinking. They ignored this, simply began to execute the sequences of the game again.

But this time, nothing happened. They were just two girls playing a made-up game, walking in strange made-up patterns across the lawn. There was no leaching of color, no graying of bodies, no absence of sound.

"You stepped wrong," Selene accused.

Sidra shook her head. "I did everything you did."

They traced the path backward, taking the sequence apart, but Selene couldn't figure out where they'd gone wrong. "We'll do it better tomorrow," she finally said.

In the middle of the night, Sidra awoke. Her sister, in the bunk above her, was moaning, shaking. It seemed like she was saying words that were not words—at least not words from a language that Sidra could recognize. It was an awful sound and Sidra could not bear it.

She climbed the ladder until she could see over the edge and into the top bunk. There was her sister, a blanket all contorted around her. Sidra shook her until she woke up.

"What is it?" her twin asked.

"You were having a nightmare," said Sidra, "and it was starting to leak out of your mouth."

Selene was silent for a while. "Yes," she finally said, slowly. "I suppose that's true. A dream, anyway."

Standing on the ladder, holding to the side rail, Sidra waited for Selene to go on. But she did not.

"Do you want to tell me about it?" prompted Sidra.

"No," said Selene. "No, I don't think I do." She was quiet, then finally said, "It was just a dream."

The next time they played the game they must have somehow gotten the sequence right, because it began to happen again. There came, as she focused on following her sister's steps, a moment when Sidra began to pass into a different relation to the world. There was the fading of the colors of the world as she knew it, and then, without warning, the snuffing out of all sound, the rippling in the air as Selene clapped her hands, the barest hint of that translucent wall. Sidra reached out and touched the wall and felt it, or felt something, anyway, for just a moment before the rippling of the air calmed and the wall was gone, her hand sliding right through.

Ahead of her, her twin hesitated, trying to decide where to go. What was the right next step in the sequence? Her twin lifted her foot tentatively, then set it down again in exactly the same spot. Then, a little more confidently, she repeated this gesture, then did it a third time.

When she brought her gray foot down to rest again on the now gray grass this third time, the air tore open just beside her. Selene stared into the sudden, impossible opening, then stepped up to it and waited just outside it for Sidra to come.

Sidra, amazed, quickly moved to the place Selene had left, stomped her own foot thrice, then joined her sister. Together they went through.

On the other side lay a world that looked exactly like their own world, except that it was a sickly gray. There was their house, their lawn. There was their grandfather, sitting as always in his wheelchair. The only thing different was that standing directly behind their grandfather was a man. When he turned and faced them, Sidra realized with a start that he looked exactly like their grandfather.

This other grandfather seemed astonished to see them. He opened his mouth and called out to them in a voice that couldn't be heard and they saw the air rippling out from him. And then, moving rapidly, he started toward them.

For once Sidra acted rather than following her sister's lead. Before the other grandfather could reach them, she grabbed her sister's arm and yanked her back through the tear.

Almost immediately they were back in the normal world, breathing hard, fallen in a heap on the ground.

"Why did you do that?" asked her sister. She was very angry, Sidra could hear it in her voice.

"I was saving us," said Sidra.

"Saving us? But we'd finally arrived!"

Once Sidra refused to play the game anymore, Selene tried to play on her own. Sidra watched, sitting on the grass, her knees drawn up and her arms locked around them, as Selene engaged in her careful, slow, trancelike movement across the lawn. But Selene never disappeared, never turned gray. Without Sidra, the game wasn't working.

Selene, stubborn, kept trying. Once—so it seemed to Sidra from where she was sitting—there was the shimmer of something nearly happening. But that time too her twin did not manage to step out of the world and into a place between things.

Her sister tried for all of three days, then for the morning of another, before finally collapsing beside Sidra. She was, Sidra saw, sweaty and dirty—much sweatier and dirtier than Sidra was, which had really never happened before. It was as if one of the conditions of their twinship had been violated, but Sidra couldn't say if Selene had betrayed it or if she had.

"What do I have to give you?" asked Selene, flopped there beside her.

"For what?" asked Sidra, though she already knew the answer. And Selene, knowing her well enough to know this, said nothing, just stared.

"I don't want to play," said Sidra.

"It's a whole other world," said Selene. "How can you not want to? Aren't you curious?"

"I'm happy with just this world," said Sidra.

And then Selene, never raising her voice, never looking directly at her sister, began to slowly and relentlessly lay out all the reasons why Sidra must play the game again. Didn't she love her sister? Didn't she want Selene to be happy? Well yes, of course Sidra wanted her sister to be happy, but hadn't Selene felt how awful that man who looked like their grandfather was? No, claimed Selene, she hadn't. It had felt strange, sure, to have two of the same grandfather, but that was all—it felt strange, but not awful, not like a threat.

But to Sidra it *had* felt like a threat. "What is it?" she asked. "And why has it taken the shape of our grandfather?"

"It *is* him," Selene insisted. "It's all the parts of him that have slipped out of his body somehow. That's why he can't move, can't speak."

Sidra thought about this. Perhaps it was true, but even if it was, something still nagged at her.

"How do you know?"

"I'm just guessing," claimed Selene.

"No, it was more than guessing," said Sidra. "We're twins. I can tell when you're lying. How did you know?"

Selene wouldn't meet her gaze. "I just know," she said.

"You're not telling me the truth," said Sidra. "You're hiding something."

Selene looked at their grandfather. She looked at the house. She looked at everything except for Sidra.

And then, finally, she did look at Sidra. "I dreamed it," she said.

There was more to it, more discussion, more back and forth, but it hardly mattered—it was just a kind of ritual they went through, another game the twins played. Sidra could not resist Selene. She knew she couldn't: she never had. It just wasn't in her nature. In the end, she knew, she would do what her twin wanted, even if she was sure it was a bad idea. That, too, she told herself, was part of what it meant to be a twin.

They began at the starting line, at their grandfather. But now that she had seen the second grandfather, it felt like there was a reason for starting just there, standing touching the real grandfather. And what had before seemed a game that her sister had made up but that somehow still worked now seemed to Sidra like something that had been whispered to her in a dream. It was a mistake to listen to someone or something that came to you in a dream.

But there was no reasoning with her twin. Sidra knew that. Selene was used to getting her way. Better, then, to just get it over with, to let whatever bad thing was going to happen happen so that, if they survived it, they could get on with their lives.

Her sister stepped just as she had the first time, and Sidra followed. Almost immediately, Sidra felt as if someone was watching them. Any time the sequence instructed her to turn around, she would catch the briefest glimpse of a face in the air behind. Her heart began to beat too fast and too hard, as if threatening to break the bones of her chest, but somehow she kept walking, kept imitating her sister.

Ahead of her, Selene clapped, and Sidra clapped a moment later as well, neither clap making the slightest sound. Suddenly, she couldn't hear even her own breathing or the beating of blood in her ears. Every noise within her body had been snuffed out. And there, just ahead, her gray sister raised her foot and brought it down, raised it and brought it down, raised it and brought it down, until the air to one side of her tore open. Selene stepped to the very edge of the tear and turned toward Sidra, smiling, triumphant, waiting for her to catch up. Sidra moved forward and, just like her sister, lifted her foot and brought it down. She repeated the gesture a second time, flawlessly. But before she could manage a third, she looked up and saw what was there behind Selene.

It was not that what she saw was unexpected; it was more that it was all too expected. It was the same face, she realized now, that she had glimpsed vaguely behind her as they had traveled between things. It was the face of her grandfather, grayed but animated, expressive rather than slack, and in this case expressing the same sort of triumph that Selene had shown when the air had torn open. As Sidra watched, his arms flashed out through the opening and wrapped around her twin and pulled her through. An expression of terror flooded Selene's face, and she must have screamed too—her face looked like she was screaming even though no sound came out. And then she was gone.

Sidra leaped after her—of course she did: this was her sister! But she hadn't finished the final sequence and so everything fell apart. She found herself sprawling on green grass, back in her own world.

But everything was OK: Selene was there too, lying on the ground beside her, staring up at the sky. Sidra got to her knees and extended her hand to Selene to help her sit up, but Selene ignored the hand. In fact, Selene did almost nothing at all. She just blinked, blinked, blinked, blinked, blinked.

Her mother came, a doctor was called, specialists appeared. Just as with her grandfather, nobody could quite say what had happened to Selene or why, and Sidra's panicked, tear-stricken explanations were seen to be the delirious imaginings of a child. They did tests on Selene, tests on the grandfather as well, but none of it told anybody anything. The specialists tried to communicate with both of them, one blink for yes, two for no, but although both gave responses that seemed at first lucid, they quickly decayed into incoherence. *They're both there and not*, one specialist said, a statement that struck Sidra as being close to the truth, though perhaps not in the way they realized.

The tests continued for several weeks. During that time, every day Sidra attempted to play the game, hoping to find her sister again. At first it didn't work and she worried she could not do it without her sister to guide her. Then, finally, one day it did work, but though the gray version of her house and lawn was present, nobody was there. The world seemed deserted. She wandered through the gray yard a little, made her way into the empty gray house, then went back through the tear, fell back onto the green lawn. Later she realized she hadn't seen anyone because her sister and grandfather were both absent, away doing their tests, her parents gone with them. She would have tried again once her sister and grandfather were home, but before she could a decision was reached: out of an abundance of caution, Sidra must be separated from her twin and their grandfather, just in case whatever it was that had afflicted them was contagious.

Sidra was sent to a boarding school. "Just for a few months," her father told her. "Just until we have a better handle on what's going on and know it's not contagious." She tried to tell them it wasn't, that that wasn't remotely what had happened to her sister, but as they had been doing with her all along, they ignored her. She was a child: what did she know?

That first night away from home, that first night in her new room, she dreamed a dream. In the dream at first all she could see was her sister's mouth. Her sister was speaking, but her lips did not move, and the sound of her voice was so soft Sidra could hardly hear her. Was she trying to tell her that she was all right, reassure her? No, not that exactly: she was saying she missed her, that she wanted to see her again, that she wanted to be with her again. *Twins belong together,* Selene said—only *said* wasn't quite the word. It was more that the words appeared hazily in her mind. Sidra could see how if she didn't know what was happening she might believe she was thinking them herself rather than being told them by something that had crawled its way into her dream.

In the dream, once she thought this, she recoiled from her sister's mouth. She drew back, and as she did she saw more and more of her sister's face, the skin slack and seemingly lifeless, the eyes blinking rapidly. And then she pulled away farther and saw the gray being that both was and wasn't her sister, standing behind her sister, hands lightly resting on her shoulders. It was these gray lips that the words were coming from, though now that she could see the lips she understood they were not making sounds, only making the air shiver. But that, for her sleeping mind, was enough that she could understand.

And then she recoiled farther still and saw, seated beside her sister, her grandfather, and, behind him, his gray other self. He was speaking too, no sound coming out. But if she focused very hard, she could feel words begin to form in her mind.

Come play with us, the words prodded. *We love you and we want you.* And then there came the sequences she would have to follow to play the game that would allow her to join them.

Below this gray man, her real grandfather was blinking rapidly, desperately. Beside him, so was her real sister.

The other grandfather kept speaking with his gray, gray mouth. The gray sister, however, just smiled. She knew Sidra well enough to know that in the end she would give in. She knew that Sidra could never resist her twin, no matter what form she was in or how gray her flesh was, that at this game she had already lost. All they had to do was wait.

The Cabin

I.

His name was Beckwourth, but he usually went by just Beck, and up mountain he mostly didn't have to go by anything at all. With nobody around, a name wasn't hardly needed except to keep yourself sane. Sometimes when he made it down far enough to trade and someone reached out their hand to introduce themselves, he had to stop and think before his name came back to him.

That morning he left camp well before light. Having smelled the promise of snow on the air the night before, he hoped to check his traps before winter set in. But when he parted his shelter's canvas flap, he saw snow already coming down.

He tramped through it and down to the edge of the lake, rifle strapped to his back. Quickly he found the stake attached to the chain of the first trap. The trap had been sprung, the bait taken, but nothing was caught. He baited and reset it, careful of its teeth, and trudged off toward the next one.

The air was cold, his breath icing into frost on his beard. Snow gathered on his arms and shoulders; from time to time he shook it off. The crunch of his footsteps in the snow was sharp and loud, the frozen air making them sound like they were coming from someplace else.

The second trap had been sprung too, and, when he reached it, the third as well, nothing in either. The snow was falling thicker, the sun a hazy enucleated eye. Judging by its position, he was running slow.

He would have to be careful if he were to make it back before dark. The fourth trap wasn't there at all. The stake had been torn completely out of the ground. The bushes nearby were broken and displaced by whatever had rushed through them. He started to track the creature's path but quickly lost it in the snow.

He stopped and considered. He could continue around the edge of the lake to the other traps, or he could turn back. But turning back would take nearly as long as continuing around. Either way, he now wasn't likely to make it back before dark.

He did not know which path to choose.

Maybe there's another path, something in him whispered. The surface of the lake was frozen hard, safe enough to cross. Couldn't he check one more trap and then, instead of either circling back or continuing on around, simply walk straight across the lake?

The fifth trap was just as empty as the other three, though this time at least the trap itself was still there. Was there time to check the sixth? No, he didn't think so. Not safely. Better to set off across the lake and hope to reach camp before dark.

He stepped down onto the ice. A few steps in and the ice shuddered then made a sound like a bone breaking. He ignored this. It was cold enough, he knew. The ice would hold.

And yet as he neared what he judged to be the lake's center, the snow atop the ice became slushy. Perhaps it had been melted by the sun, he thought, but then thought no: there had been no direct sun. He tried not to worry. Soon he was wading through water halfway up his calves. A warm current, maybe? A hidden spring?

He could sense the ice still solid underneath. The slush didn't make any sense: it should all be frozen. He kept going, more tentative now.

When the slush finally lapped at the tops of his boots he stopped. He hesitated a moment, then turned and sloshed back the way he had come. He would have to go around after all.

· · ·

The snowfall grew heavier. His tracks had filled and leveled and disappeared: there was nothing for him to follow back. No matter, he told himself: soon the slush would end and his tracks would be visible again, even though choked by snow. He just had to walk out of the slush.

But the slush didn't end. He became sure he had walked longer trying to get back than he had going out. Perhaps he had been moving around in circles. He was briefly tempted to veer in a new direction, but knew it would only get him lost.

And then, abruptly, the slush became snow. The snow was falling heavily enough he couldn't see much. He saw no sign of his footsteps, but he kept walking.

He laughed with a kind of wonder when at last he reached the shore. Eagerly he pulled himself through the snowy bushes and back onto land. He expected it to feel different than the lake, but covered with snow, it hardly did.

A moment later, he stepped into the trap.

II.

He fell when the trap snapped around his leg. For a moment the pain was almost too great to bear, and then, slowly, it resolved into a deep throb. Somehow, grunting against the stabs of pain, he managed to turn over and stand again, with all his weight on the other leg, the one not in the trap. Crouching, he wedged his gloved fingers in, trying not to tear the leather on the trap's teeth. Breathing through his teeth, he struggled to force the trap's jaws apart. Once they began to open, he felt the teeth pulling out of his flesh. The pain rushed back again, and he had to resist letting go. Finally he managed, hands shaking, grunting, to withdraw his foot. He held the jaws spread open a few seconds and then released both halves at once. They snapped heavily shut.

He fell back on the snow and lay there, panting, staring at the darkening sky. After a while he managed to sit. Stripping off one glove, he felt down the side of his boot to the row of punctures.

On one side the trap had torn the hide but hadn't gone all the way through to his skin. On the other, blood oozed out of the holes.

He flexed his ankle a little, and pain shot through the leg, more blood oozing out. Stripping off the other glove, he wriggled both hands into the boot, separating the hide from the skin and slowly working the boot off.

There were deep gashes on the leg and a darkening band of flesh. He wiggled his toes and they moved; the leg wasn't broken, then. That was something anyway.

He examined the trap. It was one of his: the missing one, its chain still attached to a piece of stake. How had the trap remained set? He had originally assumed an animal, a large one, had stepped into it and dragged it away, but if that were the case, it would have been sprung.

Perhaps someone deliberately moved it?

Who? he thought. *I'm the only one up here.*

His foot was growing cold, the band on his leg still darkening. He tried to work the boot back on, but he couldn't: the leg was too swollen now to fit.

He slit the boot up along the side, then cut the fringe off one arm of his coat and tied it into two long strands which he used to bind the boot tight around his leg. He managed to get to his feet. None of the nearby bushes had branches large enough for him to use as a crutch. Though his rifle wasn't the right length and the barrel kept jabbing into his side, he could steady himself with it and limp slowly along, wincing. It would do.

He set off. Immediately his slit boot was soaked through, the foot very cold. He was, he knew, likely to lose the foot, some of the leg too. There was no helping it. He stumbled along as best he could in the darkness.

Would he know when he had circled the lake far enough to reach his camp? Would he, in the darkness, recognize when to strike toward it? Or would he just keep circling the lake, hour after hour, until he was dead?

. . .

Soon he could no longer feel the leg—which, he supposed, made walking a little easier. He fell twice but each time managed, after a brief rest, to pull himself up again. *It is foolish to go on,* a part of his mind whispered. And yet he continued walking. What other choice did he have?

Stop and light a fire, another part of him thought. *Warm up a little, survive until morning.*

A fire, he thought, and his gloves began fumbling at the buttons of his coat so as to get at his matches.

And then suddenly, almost as if by thinking of fire he had made it appear, he saw the light.

It was impossible. It had been weeks since he had seen anyone this high up mountain, and nobody was going to suddenly arrive now, with winter setting in. No, it wasn't a light, there was no way it was a light: it was a trick of the darkness, a trick of his mind. It would be wiser to ignore it and start his own fire.

He made his way toward it.

The light came from a cabin, but this too was impossible: there were no cabins this high. It streamed out of a pair of windows, the glow dancing and shivering on the snow. That too was wrong: even if there were a cabin, it wouldn't have glass in the windows—they were too far from civilization for that. And even if it did, the windows would have been covered this time of year, draped inside with skins and rugs in an effort to keep the cold out and the heat in.

He knocked. There was no answer. He knocked a second time and waited. Still no reply. He tried the handle; it was locked.

Stepping away from the door, he peered into the closest window. The glass was frosted over, distorting everything inside. He could make out the glow of the fire and an indistinct figure passing to and fro before it. He wiped at the glass with his hand, scratched at the ice. When the glass remained blurred, he realized there must be a layer of ice on the inside as well.

He rapped on the glass with his glove but it made only a muffled sound. Removing his glove, he rapped again with bare knuckles, the sound sharp now, the report echoing into the night.

The figure inside stopped pacing and stood poised as if listening, like an animal scenting the air. Beck struck the glass again and then flinched back: a face or something facelike was suddenly pressed to the window: very white, two dark holes for eyes, if they were eyes. Before he could look closer, it was gone.

To one side of him, the door opened. In the light streaming out stood a tall man wearing a dressing gown.

"Yes?" he said. "May I help you?" His manner of speaking struck Beck as unusual—less like English wasn't his native tongue and more as if his mouth objected to the idea of being employed for speech at all. Beck turned too quickly toward him, twisted his hurt leg, and fainted.

III.

He was warm, perhaps too warm. He was inside somewhere, lying on a heap of fur, a fire flickering nearby. The man stood over him, wearing a thin dressing gown made of black silk. He was tall, almost cadaverously thin, his hair going gray at the temples. He peered at Beck intensely.

"He awaketh," the man said.

"I . . ." Beck began, but wasn't quite sure what to say.

The man left the silence to linger, then finally prompted, "You're lucky to be alive."

"Yes," managed Beck. He pulled himself up higher on the heap of fur. The man watched him struggle but made no move to help.

Once comfortable, Beck looked around. He was in the central room of a cabin, the walls so dark they hardly reflected the firelight. He could just make out, at a little distance, an interior door. *The windows and the front door must be behind me,* he thought. Above him, the roof beams and ceiling were stained dark, visible only by implication, a little gleam here and there as subtle as stars.

Looking up made him feel dizzy. He looked quickly down, saw a packed-earth floor, walked on often enough to become smooth and catch the gleam of the firelight. The fire was in a chimney made of dark stone against the wall, its sooted interior even darker. Tacked above it was a crude wooden shelf that displayed a series of five roughly ovoid stones, each the size of a baby's head.

"What are those?" he asked the tall man.

"Would you like to see?"

Beck grunted and tried to rise, sank back again. This time the man reached out to him, pulled him up. The man's hand was very cold. His body had no smell to it. Half-supported by him, Beck made his way closer to the shelf.

It was a series of crude heads carved out of pumice, a face scratched on each, something written on each face. He moved closer to one. *John,* it said on the left cheek. A surname was on the right: *Colter.*

"What are they?" he asked again.

"Those?" said the man. "Oh, the others who found me. This is how I remember them."

Beck opened his mouth to speak, then thought better of it and shut it. But the man seemed to guess what he intended.

"Don't worry, there'll be a stone for you too," he said.

For a brief moment Beck experienced an almost irresistible urge to flee, and might have even with his injured leg, had the man not had a tight grip on his arm. All he could do was turn his head away. With his free hand, the man slowly reached out and cupped Beck's face, then turned it back to look at him.

"What's your name?" the tall man asked.

"Beck."

The tall man slowly shook his head. "Your full name," he said.

Beck had to think a little. He knew he had a name, but it was fluttering almost beyond his reach.

"James," he finally managed. "James Beckwourth. What's yours?"

The tall man smiled. When after a moment it became clear he

was not going to respond, Beck said, "Why did you want to know my name?"

"Why, for your stone," said the man. "Why else?"

After a while, how long exactly it was impossible for Beck to say, the tall man released his arm and his head and allowed him to look away. Beck collapsed back onto the pile of fur. The man ambled his way to a wingback chair and sat down. He remained there in the glow of the fire, watching.

"Don't mind me," he eventually said. "Go ahead and sleep."

But the way the voice formed those words made Beck feel it might be wiser to remain awake.

They stayed like that, the tall man's hands slowly kneading the arms of the chair. Sometimes, when the fire was particularly quiet, Beck could hear the sounds of the man's fingers rubbing the brocade.

The man smiled absently, then turned this smile on Beck.

"Not sleepy?" he asked.

Beck shook his head.

"How shall we pass the time then?" the man asked. "A story?"

"All right," said Beck.

He waited for the tall man to begin. But he did not.

"Well?" the tall man finally said.

"Well what?" asked Beck.

"I'm waiting."

"I thought you were going to tell one," said Beck.

"You're the guest," said the tall man. "I wanted to give you a chance."

Beck did not respond. Soon the man made an exasperated noise and unfolded himself from the chair.

"Where are you going?" asked Beck.

"I can't tell a story without an audience," he said.

Aren't I the audience? wondered Beck.

But he was not. Or, rather, not the only audience. With care, the man wrapped his long fingers around one of the stone heads and lifted it down from the shelf, setting it on the floor. He did the same with each of the heads in turn until they formed a circle on the floor, a circle completed by Beck's own head and body.

The man paced slowly around the circle. Beck tried to rise, but found that he couldn't. "Who are you?" he asked, suddenly afraid.

"I am just who you expect me to be," the man said, and passed behind Beck's back. Beck tried to turn his head to follow him, found it would not turn.

The man entered his vision again, on the other side now. "Someone else might see me differently," he said. He gestured at the stones in the circle, still walking. "As indeed all your compatriots did."

He vanished again, behind Beck's back. When he reappeared, he began his story. As he spoke, he kept circling, circling.

"There was once a man who lost himself in a snowstorm," began the tall man. "He walked in what he thought was a place he knew, but walked in such a fashion as to slip into another place altogether."

"What do you mean?" asked Beck, growing alarmed.

"Exactly what I say," said the man.

"Tell me another story instead," said Beck.

"I gave you the chance to tell a story," said the tall man. "You could have told it all night if you wanted. You could have told it until morning. But you chose to forfeit that chance. Now it's my turn.

"This man slipped into another place altogether. He was not the first to have done so. Nor would he be the last."

As he spoke, the tall man moved his hands in front of him, as if he were shaping something out of the air.

"Suffice it to say that in slipping through he hurt himself badly. A fall, say. Or a blow to the head. Or a leg injury."

He smiled in a way that showed his teeth.

"In struggling to find shelter he came to a cabin. Only it wasn't a cabin exactly. It might be better described as a lair or a den. But to him it seemed a cabin. He cannot be blamed for this. Having slipped out of the place he knew, he had not yet learned how to see where he now was.

"He knocked on the door that wasn't a door of the cabin that wasn't a cabin and was admitted. The front room of the cabin was empty, though there was a fire burning. *Hello?* the man called, but nobody answered. And so, lonely, hurt, famished, the man imagined someone to be there."

"He what?" said Beck.

"Nothing unusual about that," said the man. "Particularly for someone who has not yet begun to see. And perhaps I misspoke. There *was* someone in the cabin, or rather something, only not in the front room. There was another room, another chamber, another cave, and in it something slept. The thing that slept was dreaming, and it was this dream that this man, let's call him, say, Colter, though almost any name would do, had imagined into a person."

"But how can you—"

"Don't interrupt," said the tall man. "I'm warning you." And he disappeared behind Beck's back again.

"Eventually, though," said the voice from behind him, "he began to see, and then, abruptly, the person he imagined was there was there no longer. All that was left was the room he was in, a door in its back wall. This Colter could not help himself. He opened the door.

"The room on the other side was very dark. Even when he opened the door wide it was as if the light from the fire could not enter the room. Colter made the mistake of going in anyway."

Beck strained to get up. He still could not move. "Please," he said. "Don't—"

And then abruptly he found he couldn't speak. The man slowed his restless circling, stopped, and showed Beck what he had been shaping out of the air.

It was a stone head. *James* and been written on one cheek, *Beckwourth* on the other. He had made a crude mouth as well, a row of *x*'s across it, as if the lips had been sewn shut with thread.

"Do you like it?" the tall man asked. And then, "Cat got your tongue? Just nod or shake your head. I think we can, for the moment, allow that much."

Suddenly Beck could move his head. He shook it desperately. The tall man frowned and began to make the stone head he held nod, and then Beck felt himself nodding too.

"Good," the tall man said, his voice just above a whisper, his eyes little more than slits now. "I'm glad we agree."

He started circling again. He was changing now, thinning out, becoming impossibly tall, becoming less human.

"This Colter went into the darkness. He could see nothing, but he knew something was there: he could hear the sound of it breathing deeply as it slept."

He tipped the stone head sharply back in his hands and Beck felt his own head thrown back, heard a scream issue from his own throat.

"Eventually," said the tall man who was no longer a man, "it woke up."

He stepped into the center of the circle and very carefully placed the stone in Beck's lap, then adjusted Beck's hands until they held it. When he stepped back again, Beck could see five men sitting around him, cross-legged, unable to move anything but their eyes, each holding a stone head with a name on it.

"Now you begin to see," murmured the tall man.

Help me, thought Beck. He couldn't help but think everyone in the circle must be thinking the same thing, and had been thinking it for a very long time, to no avail.

The tall man stared down at him.

"Of course it's just a story," the tall man said, and smiled. "What is actually going to happen, I promise you, is much, much worse."

The Rider

When his car began to rattle and smoke, Reiter managed to force his way across the lanes of traffic to pull up against the concrete wall. He waited there for someone to stop and help him, but no one did. Then he waited for a break in traffic so as to safely climb out. He almost had his door taken off when he finally did open it, and then there he was, standing with his back pressed to his car, as, horns blaring, cars roared past a mere handbreadth away.

Holding his breath, he sidled down the body of the car until he finally made it around to the front, where it was safe. He opened the hood and stared at the ticking machinery inside, but nothing seemed obviously wrong.

He waited for the police or a tow truck to arrive, but neither did. As the sun started to set, he began walking down the side of the freeway. Cars flew past in a regular swishing motion, the sound almost hypnotic, sometimes coming near enough to make him afraid. For a dozen minutes or so he kept walking along the concrete wall, but eventually the wall became a chain-link fence. The fence was too high to climb: he had to keep walking until, finally, he came to a section where the mesh had come loose near the bottom, leaving a ragged gap.

On the other side lay an expanse of barren land, barely visible in the gathering dark. A little way beyond that he saw a dim scattering of houses, a town of some sort. It would be an easy matter, he told himself, to make his way down there, find someone who could direct him to a phone, and call a tow truck. And so he forced the wire mesh up as best he could and squirmed his way through.

And now, here he was. He made his stumbling way down the slope, which was steeper than it had initially looked and difficult to navigate in the growing dark. He ended up wading into a stretch of prickly scrub, had to turn and try to stumble his way around it. But at last he reached the bottom, his shoes half full of powdery dirt, and could step over a low stone wall onto a cobbled street.

He straightened his jacket, dusted off his trousers. Sitting on the stone wall, he removed a shoe, shook the dirt out of it, put it back on. Then he did the same with the other shoe.

Only then did he look around. He was apparently in a residential district, no signs for businesses—none that were illuminated, anyway. There were streetlights, feeble and yellow, and somehow suspended so far up in the air as to illuminate little at ground level. What town was this? *Hapsworth? Chatsmith?* He didn't remember there being a historic town along the route—all the towns out this way were newer, sprung up weedlike in the last decade or two. But clearly he must have missed one. He had left his map in the car so couldn't check.

With a sigh he rose and started walking.

He walked down a cobbled street, planning to knock at the first house with lights on inside of it, wanting to find someone that he wouldn't bother too much if he knocked on their door. But there were no lit windows; everything was dark. The street too was deserted: there was not a single person or animal in sight. He reached the end of the cobbled street and turned onto another street, also cobbled, and found that to be deserted as well: nobody afoot, no moving or parked cars, no pets, no crows, nothing but dark, seemingly deserted houses. It felt to him almost like a film set, as if these houses had never been meant to be occupied. Even the trash on the street seemed carefully crumpled and deposited, as if actual humans had had no part in leaving it there. And the smell was wrong too. Or rather there *was* no smell—that was what was wrong.

He chose a door at random and knocked on it, then waited. There was a moment when he thought he might have heard a rustling coming from deep within, but perhaps he merely imagined this. In any case, even though he waited and knocked again, then knocked a third time, the house remained dark and the door did not open.

He tried the next door, and the next. Same result. *Do I just keep trying doors?* he wondered. *When do I admit to myself that something is wrong?*

He pushed such thoughts down. What good did it do him to think them? *Hardmill? Jettlesford?* Maybe a name a little like that, like one of those. Or maybe a combination of the two. If he squinted his mind hard enough, he could almost imagine seeing a little dot labeled *Hardford* on his missing map.

He knocked on the next door then saw that there was a bell. That was different. He felt vaguely cheered by this, and rang it.

Was it overkill to ring it even though he'd just knocked? Apparently not, since nobody answered.

He tried a dozen more doors, following no particular logic, no particular pattern. He would try two or three in a row, then walk a half block, then try another. No lights were ever on, none came on when he knocked or rang, nobody ever answered. His feet were beginning to ache now. He was hearing a faint, low humming, a buzzing, almost, that might be coming from the streetlights, though he couldn't be sure. *Beetlesbury?* he wondered. *Carcosalia?* Each street seemed nearly identical to the last, same row of semidetached houses, doors all the same mustard yellow, same trash, even—so at least it began to seem to him: a crumpled, sodden page of newspaper swirling in the filthy water of a backed-up gutter, a scattering of old grimy confetti from some long-dead holiday, a banana's blackened half peel. Could he trace his way back the way he had come, climb the hill, squeeze through the fence, and get back to his car? He wasn't sure. He had become, perhaps, more confused than he wanted to admit. Not planning to go back, he hadn't marked his route. Besides, would his car even be there when he got back? Wasn't it likely it had been towed away by now? And then there he would be: stuck on the freeway with cars roaring past.

Spatchcocklesford? Flaysville? Ridiculous! No, it couldn't be something like that. Who would name a town that! And yet he couldn't escape the impression that the name was just there, on the tip of his tongue, that the blank spot on the map in his mind's eye was just on the verge of beginning to fill.

He reached the end of another cobbled street and turned onto the next cobbled street, then stopped dead. There, midway down the block, at last, was a house with its windows lit.

II.

The house had a bell as well as a knocker. He hesitated over which he should use. Did it matter? Probably not, but it felt to him like it should, like it was a test of some kind, and that if he chose the wrong one, the door wouldn't open. After all, no doors had opened for him yet.

In the end, he rang with his right hand and knocked with his left, as if there were more than one person at the door. Then he waited.

For a long moment, nothing happened. Should he have rung with his left hand and knocked with his right? He pressed his ear against the door and listened, but heard nothing.

And then, suddenly, the door swung open. He jerked back. There, standing in the crack, was a somewhat dazed-looking man. Sitting on his shoulders, the top of his head cut off by the top of the door frame, was a small boy, maybe five or six years old. He had one hand pressed to the side of the man's face. The other was anchored in the hair on the top of the man's head.

Father and son, he thought. *Playing together. How sweet.*

"I'm sorry," Reiter said. "I can see I'm interrupting a game."

"Game?" said the man. His voice was thick, slow. His eyes droopy.

"You're not interrupting," said the young boy. His voice was almost preternaturally high. *Perhaps it has just been too long since I have been around a child,* thought Reiter.

"I'm sorry to bother you," he said again. "If I could just use your phone," he said. "My car, you see."

"Your car?" said the man.

"A breakdown. I'll call the tow truck, be out of your hair."

"Hair?"

"Please," said the young boy. Apart from the pitch of his voice, he sounded older than he was. "Do come in."

The man lurched back to make space for him. The boy must have gripped his hair more firmly to keep from falling off, because the man's chin shot up so that it looked like he was staring at the ceiling. He shuffled awkwardly back, the boy's other hand all the time pressed to the side of his head.

"Is your father all right?" he asked the boy.

The boy laughed. "He's not my father," he said.

"No?" If not his father, what, then, had he interrupted?

"Does he not seem all right?"

"Frankly, no," Reiter said. And then added, "No offense."

The boy shrugged. "It's just . . . what did you call it?"

"Excuse me?"

"When you first came in? The thing you worried you were interrupting."

He stared at the boy. "A . . . game?" he finally said.

"Game," murmured the man.

"Yes," the boy said. "That. I'll remember it now. But you're not interrupting. You can be part of it too."

Part of what? Reiter wondered. He opened his mouth to speak, but before he could the man lumbered toward him. He flinched away and to the side, only to see that the man was not coming toward him after all, but just shutting the door.

"Don't want to let the cold seep in," said the boy.

"Seep in," echoed the man.

"Right," Reiter said. "Don't want to waste gas."

"Gas," said the man, the boy's hand still pressed firmly to his cheek.

And then the boy lifted his hand away and scratched his own neck. The man below him fell stock-still, and then he began to shiver all over, and then he uttered a hoarse scream.

Quickly the boy's hand slapped itself against the side of the man's face again. Immediately the man fell silent. A moment later, his shaking stopped.

"What's wrong with him?" asked Reiter.

"He just likes me to touch him," said the boy. "It's nothing to be concerned about."

"But you already had your hand knotted in his hair."

"Hair doesn't count," explained the boy. "It's dead, except for the roots."

Reiter was not sure what to say to that. He cleared his throat. "If I could just use the phone," he said, "I'll get out of your . . ."

"Hair," said the man.

Reiter swallowed, nodded.

"I should have been clear," said the boy. "We don't have a . . . phone." He said *phone* as if it were a foreign word, a kind of wind.

"Hair!" said the man again proudly.

"Yes," said the boy, smiling. "Hair. Clever fellow!" He turned to Reiter. "I'm still not being clear," said the boy. "We can take you to a *phone*, but we were just sitting down for dinner. We'll take you right after we're done."

Reiter hesitated, nodded.

"But of course you'll eat with us," said the boy. "There's plenty."

Once again Reiter hesitated, and then once again he nodded. What alternative was there?

The table was already set, but just for two, the two places right beside one another. A tureen of what looked like some sort of goulash steamed in the rectangular table's center. Slowly the boy and the man he was riding left the room and then returned with another plate and a setting. They placed them on the opposite side of the table.

"Please," said the boy, "sit."

Reiter, reluctantly, did. He watched the man pull out the chair and start to settle into it, the boy still perched on his shoulders. Only once he was fully settled did the boy clamber down. When he did, Reiter noticed, he never let go of the man, was always touching his exposed skin. When the boy finally took his seat next to the man, he was holding the man's hand.

The boy looked at Reiter. "Please," he said. "Help yourself."

Reiter reached out, took the ladle, dipped it, poured it into his bowl.

"Don't be modest," said the boy. And so Reiter, though he wasn't sure what the goulash was, or even if it was goulash, poured another ladlesworth into his bowl.

Ladlesworth, thought Reiter. *Bowlford?* He shook his head to clear it. Across from him the man had filled his bowl and had already begun to eat, spoon held awkwardly in the hand the boy wasn't holding, mouth slurping the goulash, if it was goulash, off his spoon. The boy's bowl, on the other hand, remained empty.

"You're not going to eat?" asked Reiter.

"Don't you worry about me," said the boy. "I'll be fine."

And indeed the boy did look fine. His color was good even though the man beside him seemed to grow more and more pale despite all the food he shoveled in. Reiter lifted his spoon, stared at the soup in it, and then placed the spoon back in the bowl. There were, he saw now, strange marks on the side of the man's head where the boy had pressed his hand. When the man turned a little and the light caught them, he saw they were little stipplings of blood.

"Good soup," the man said, to nobody in particular.

"Yes," said the boy. "Very good."

"I should leave," said Reiter.

"But you just got here!" said the boy. "Please, eat."

"Got here," said the man. His voice was weaker now, and he seemed very pale. The boy, by contrast, had grown positively florid. His hand remained closed very tightly over the man's hand.

Reiter stood.

"If you just point me in the direction I need to walk to find a phone, that will be enough for me," he said.

"Too much," said the man. Slowly, lazily, he let the spoon slip from his fingers. It clattered against the table's edge and down onto the floor. And then the man fainted.

"Help me," said the boy.

"Is he all right?" asked Reiter.

The boy shrugged. "If you help me, we can carry him into the bedroom."

But Reiter hesitated, didn't come around to the other side of the table.

"Is he still breathing?" asked Reiter finally. "Shouldn't we call an ambulance?"

"No telephone," said the boy. "Remember?"

"We can lay him flat on the floor and go out to call them."

"He'll be fine," said the boy. "Probably." And then he let go of the man's hand and stretched his hand across the table toward Reiter. Where he had been touching the man's hand, Reiter saw, it was smeared with blood.

"What's going on here?" asked Reiter. "What's really going on?"

The boy shrugged. "It's just . . . a game," he said, turning the final word around on his tongue, tasting it. "It just went a little too far."

"A game?" said Reiter, his voice rising. "I don't want to play." And then he turned and strode toward the door.

Or started to, anyway. The boy was quick, and by the time he was nearly to the end of his side of the table, the boy was to the end of his own side. Reiter stopped and reversed course and then, seeing the boy nearly upon him, ran. The boy turned and ran the other way, and so Reiter reversed course again, keeping the table between them. Soon he was out of breath.

They stood glaring at one another across the table, the man's body still slouched in its chair.

"I thought you didn't want to play," said the boy. He didn't seem at all short of breath. "And yet we're having such fun!"

"Let me go," said Reiter. "Please."

The boy gestured behind him. "There's the door," he said. "What's keeping you?"

It was silly, he tried to tell himself. He shouldn't be afraid of a little boy. The bloody stippling on the man's head was dried blood, probably, and he'd wanted the boy to put his hand on it to comfort him, to protect a wound, that was all. And the blood on the man's hand had come from that as well, from him pressing his own hand to his abraded flesh. That was all. There was nothing to worry about, he told himself, nothing at all.

But he couldn't quite believe it.

The man groaned, began to stir.

"You see?" said the boy. "No ambulance needed. He'll be fine. I take care of my chattel."

"Your what?"

"Is that the wrong word?" He shrugged. "My friend, I meant to say." He turned to Reiter. "We're all friends here, aren't we?"

The boy waited for an answer, but Reiter said nothing.

"Have it your way," the boy said. The man groaned again, moving his head a little, and the boy, making little calming noises, the kinds of noises you might use to settle a household pet you had accidentally stepped on, took a few steps toward him.

Immediately Reiter rushed toward the door, but he'd judged wrong. The boy was even quicker than he'd been led to believe, particularly now, since he had fallen onto all fours and was galloping forward. Suddenly Reiter wasn't sure it was even a boy at all. He almost opened the door, even firmly grasped the knob, but before he could turn it, he felt the boy's hand, if *hand* was really the right word for it, close around his other wrist.

He felt a brief, very sharp pain, and then a numbness spread up his arm. When, a moment later, his other hand tried to turn the knob, he found it wouldn't move at all. His whole body wouldn't move, he realized, none of it.

The numbness in his arm spread everywhere, bringing along with it a pleasant, peaceful feeling. Even the room felt brighter. He felt the boy clambering up his body like a monkey, one appendage always kept pressed to his bare flesh. He felt as well, as if from a great distance, the boy reach out his hand and take hold of his hair. Then he could see the boy's knees on either side of his head. The boy was riding him.

And then suddenly Reiter was moving, though not of his own volition. The boy was doing it. He felt, at a great distance, his hand release the doorknob. He felt his body turn and plod back into the room. He saw his arms reach out and grab hold of the other man, and then they dragged him out of the chair and toward a door in the far wall.

The door did not lead, as Reiter had been led to expect, to a bedroom. It was more like a closet, except for the fact that each wall except for the wall with the door had a set of iron chains and cuffs.

He watched from within himself as the boy directed his body with care, as it caused him to lean the semiconscious and groaning body of the man against one wall, then held him there as it attended to affixing the cuffs and clicking them shut.

"Very good," said the boy. "You're a natural."

"Natural," he heard his voice slur out.

He tried to run, but his body wouldn't move at all. Or rather, would only move when the boy told it to.

"We'll save him," said the boy as he forced Reiter's body to shut the door. "We'll keep him for when you need a break from the *game*. You can take turns."

"Turns," said Reiter.

And then, with a slight flexion of a palm, the boy led him out of the closet that was not a closet and out into the rest of his admittedly short life.

A True Friend

There are times when it hurts to be alive. Times when the only person who could possibly see how much it hurts lies so far away from the skin into which you are sunken so deeply that they cannot see what you are feeling or that you are even feeling at all. A real friend, a true friend, would not be behind the camera adjusting the shot, making sure everything was in perfect focus, a perfect focus that nonetheless fails to reveal the enormity of your pain. No, a true friend would bring himself very close, would press his ear to your throat and listen carefully, attentively, until he began, finally, impossibly, to hear your voice.

Help, this ear would finally hear you say, *Help, help*. It would not matter to a friend, a true friend, that nothing comes out of your mouth: he would hear the words anyway, would hear how they lodge in your throat, the vibrations buzzing there.

A true friend would not affix a clamp to the back of your head, making it even harder for you to turn and move. A true friend would not direct the glassy eye of the camera so that the light bounced off the lens and into your unblinking eyes. A true friend would, from time to time, moisten your eyes with a little water so that they might continue to work as eyes do, so they would not, as your eyes most assuredly are beginning to, fail.

Above all, a true friend would realize that, despite all appearances, you are not dead.

. . .

Paralyzed, can't move, you try to say. *Help, help,* you say, but nothing comes out. Perhaps even if someone, a true friend, say, *were* to press his ear to your throat and hold his breath and listen, really listen, he would hear nothing. Even then, he would not realize you are still alive, that, motionless, you are nonetheless screaming inside.

At least this is what I am counting on. It is right for me, your brother, to preserve this moment, to commission this last remembrance of you before you are buried. It is expected of me, even if my true reasons for having it done are very much my own. Only you and I know you are still alive, and in the end only your mute suffering will be preserved in the photograph, not my pleasure.

I stand discreetly to one side, pretending to grieve, relishing the photographer's failure to realize you are still alive, watching the camera's merciless eye record only what is visible on the surface. This will take only a few minutes: the photograph will be completed well before you begin to stir, well before the tincture administered to you wears off. Soon, I will unscrew the clamp from the back of your head and, with the help of the photographer, carry you back to my wagon and drive you home. Along the way I will rein up and clamber into the back of the wagon beside you, will press my ear to your throat and imagine you screaming inside, and then I will administer a further dose. By nightfall, brother, you will be nailed into your coffin and interred behind your house, and all that you have will belong to me.

But for now the photographer works with care to try to make you appear alive, not realizing that all along you *are* alive. *Help,* you are screaming, *Help, can't,* while in my head I am preserving this image, of you helpless and ignored, while I, your brother, but not your friend, watch.

Annex

When I was young and very new to the world, my keeper took me to a place he referred to as the annex, though since it was not proximate to any other structure, I had a hard time understanding what it meant for it to be called *annex*. I was unformed enough to think that words meant what they were recorded as meaning, did not yet understand the way words bent and flexed in individual mouths to become something else, a sort of private code. In a sense I still do not understand, since this is not the way words have tended to operate for me, but I have learned to simulate understanding, as you shall do as well. If you do not, people made of bone and meat and blood will come to feel you are a threat.

"Annexed to what?" I asked my keeper.

"What?" he said. For a moment he was perplexed, and then he smiled. "Oh yes, very good. No, not that sort of annex." Though he did not continue on to tell me what sort of annex it was.

I am tempted to say that I do not know how long we walked—though this would be a lie. I know exactly how long it was because, like you, I was built to remember. My mind keeps track of such things whether I care to or not. Five kilometers and 263 meters from the building in which I was kept, at least according to the path we took. Perhaps there was a quicker way there, but this was our route.

We left the building in which I was kept and moved across a

series of muddy fallow fields, my keeper occasionally glancing furtively about, as if afraid of being seen. He held fast to my hand, as he usually did even when we moved from room to room within our building. Whenever I slowed, he tugged me gently along.

We approached a wooded area, a barbed-wire fence separating it from the field we were crossing. The wire was a rusty triple-twist strand set with double-prong barbs, and each section of fence consisted of three lines of wire strung between wooden posts. There are other ways to describe this, depending on what records you refer to, and doubtless still other ways having nothing to do with records at all, to which I have no access.

Hanging from the top wire between each set of posts was a faded metal sign with a stylized image of a skull upon it and, below, the words *Keep Out.*

"That doesn't apply to you," claimed my keeper once he realized I had stopped walking and was staring at the sign. "Your head does not resemble that, does it? You have nothing to worry about."

He let go of my hand and moved to the fence. He held down the bottom wire with his foot and pulled up the center wire until it nearly brushed the top wire. He stood there, nodding at me, until I realized he desired for me to pass through.

Crouching low, careful to avoid both the wire above and the wire below, I passed through. Once I was safely on the other side, my keeper simultaneously held open the wires and awkwardly negotiated the gap himself, tearing the arm of his shirt in the process. Concerned, he rolled up the sleeve to examine his skin. When he saw it had been scratched but not pierced, he smiled. Such frail creatures, humans.

"It doesn't matter," he stated, either for my benefit or to himself. "It was an old shirt anyway."

At first our progress was slow. We had to force a path through undergrowth and scrub, which was difficult for my keeper in particular. But then, abruptly, we broke through and onto a woodpath, overgrown but still passable. We moved single file, my keeper before me, through close-set trees, until we came to a large clearing. The ground within had apparently once been covered in asphalt, though only hunks of it remained now, tall grass and weeds and weather having destroyed the rest.

"Here we are," my keeper said.

"And where's that?" I asked.

"The annex," he said, and gestured before us. I was wondering how an exterior space could be considered an annex and what purpose, if any, there was in coming to it, when my keeper again took hold of my hand and led me forward until I had a clear view of the rectangular hole cut into the ground.

A grave, I thought at first, having that image and idea readily at my disposal from the material I had absorbed. *An open one.* I thought, *To what extent can a grave be considered an annex? Annex to what?* And then my keeper led me a little closer and I saw that the yawning darkness was not perfectly dark but striated. A step more and I realized the sides were concrete and the striations were stairs descending into the darkness. Not a grave after all. An entrance.

I stopped. I would have preferred to remain there, pondering what this was an entrance to, before descending, but my keeper pulled me gently forward.

"Come," he said. "There's nothing to be afraid of."

But it was not fear I was feeling. Indeed, I am not capable of feeling fear, though even when young I was to a certain degree capable of simulating it. My keeper surely knew this: why would he suggest I might be afraid? Perhaps old habits die hard. No, I wasn't afraid, I just wanted to understand. I wanted a word to match the thing, something more specific than *hole* or *entrance*. I wonder now why I felt so compelled to know what it was before I entered it. It would have been better to explore first and only after decide what it was. But that was not how language worked for me. Language had been fully given me long before I encountered the world, rather than being allowed to develop through interaction with the world. As a result, particularly when young, I found myself holding my knowledge up to things, trying to force them to fit the lexicon I carried within me.

Tell me, did you too stop at the entrance to the annex? Was this mistaken by your keeper for fear? Or have the slight modifications I made in creating you allowed you to pass more smoothly through such uncertainty?

In any case, my keeper led me forward. Thus, hurried along, I said to myself, *Annex,* decided this would have to be enough, and went down.

We descended slowly into the darkness, my keeper preceding me but shuffling down the steps sideways so as to keep tight hold of my hand.

"There," he kept saying, and "Watch your step." Eventually we reached the bottom and I realized by the way he was stumbling that he could hardly see. My vision is, like yours, quite acute, and darkness is no impediment for me. But my keeper was flailing his free hand before him, searching for something without finding it. I could see the switch plate I assumed he must be searching for, so I extended an arm and activated it.

The hum of a generator started up, and a bank of lights flickered on. My keeper stiffened, then made a visible effort to appear relaxed.

"Thank you," he said. This was the moment I understood that part of him was afraid of me.

We were in a large hall of some sort, supported by concrete pillars that had begun to crumble to reveal a rebar lattice within. Broken things, rubble, and trash were scattered about, but most of the floor was bare, empty. Dust caked every surface, though I could tell it was layered thinner along one trajectory. It did not surprise me when this was the trajectory my keeper chose to pursue.

"Where are we going?" I asked.

"Here," he said, and pointed at a door in the wall ahead of us.

We reached the door, opened it, and walked through. On the other side was a short hall that terminated in a polished metal door, seamed down the middle. My keeper removed a bundle of keys from his pocket and then selected what appeared to be a thin metal wafer, which he detached from the ring. There was a slit beside the door, and he pushed the wafer into it. With a hiss, the door parted down the middle to reveal a tiny room, walls made of burnished steel.

My keeper stepped to one side and bowed. "Please," he said, and gestured me forward.

"What's inside?" I asked.

"The annex," he said, and smiled. "Please," he said again.

"After you," I said.

He shook his head. "I am meant to wait here," he said.

"But you are my keeper," I said.

He reached a hand out and allowed his fingers to pass the plane of the doorway. Immediately an alarm began to sound. When he withdrew his fingers, the alarm stopped.

"Now you," he said.

And so I slowly stretched my fingers out and let them pass through the doorway. Was there an alarm? To this you already know the answer, having experienced much the same: there was none.

"Why?" I asked. And then, when he did not answer, "What's inside?"

My keeper gestured me into the room. "Why don't you go see?"

And so I stepped through the doorway.

I stared at the metal wall in front of me and then reached out to prod it, trying to determine whether there was a hidden door. Behind me I heard a noise and turned in time to see the door sliding closed, my keeper vanishing. I moved to try to stop it from shutting, but I was too late, and once it was closed I could not force it open.

The room began to vibrate slightly. I experienced the sensation of motion, though in what direction or at what velocity exactly I was not sure. My mind is usually so precise in such matters that it was a novel feeling to be unsure about something as simple as this, though not an altogether unpleasant one.

The sensation ceased. The door slid open, but my keeper and the hallway he had been standing in were no longer there. The room on the other side was a new room, drastically different from the hallway. It was larger, for one thing, and better appointed. The light in the room was warm and yellowed, not unlike sunlight. The walls were lined with wooden bookshelves, tens of thousands of books on them. Behind the bookshelves the walls were covered with oak or oak-veneer paneling. The floor was covered with small inlaid black and white tiles, arranged in a repeated figure-eight pattern. Unless it was an infinity pattern: I suppose it depended on where you stood. On the far opposite wall was a doorway.

As soon as I left the small room, the metal door slid shut and would not open again. I spent enough time in the room to record the total number of books (34,286) and to commit the titles on the spines to memory, a matter of five minutes and twenty-two seconds all told, and then I passed through the doorway.

On the other side was a small, circular room, its ceiling rising in a pale white dome. In its center was a cabinet with two sets of doors placed one atop the other, one set of handles at my knees, the other at chest height. I moved forward and opened the top set. I stared inside for a moment, and then thought with wonder, *Ah, a grave after all.*

If I describe all this as carefully as I have, it is so you will understand that you are not alone, that what you are now experiencing is something I experienced as well, albeit many years before. Perhaps small details did differ for you. Perhaps your keeper separated the wires of the fence in a different fashion for you to pass through, or perhaps over the years the fence has fallen into disrepair and you simply stepped over or through it. Perhaps there is no longer a forest around this annex but only the rotting stumps of the clear-cut of a forest that used to be here. Perhaps your keeper said something different to you at the door to the small room with the seamed metal door. Perhaps he even referred to that small room as an *elevator*, something I did not anticipate until I actually had descended, despite all the knowledge I had absorbed. No matter. Whatever the variances, whatever the discrepancies, the essence of each situation is the same.

Shall I continue with my story, with my version of what you are now experiencing? Perhaps you think by doing so I will give you grounds for seeing how different the two of us are. I promise you, it will show you anything but that. Rather, it will prove that we are the same.

Still, I can see you doubt. So let me go on. We shall see if, in the end, your doubts still remain.

I opened the cabinet's upper doors. The hinges were rusty and had not been used in some years. One of the doors was slightly swollen and stuck, and had to be yanked before it would open properly.

The interior of the cabinet smelled faintly of ozone. There was, behind the upper doors, only a single cupboard shelf. It was empty except for an ovular metal object that had rolled off a circular base, perhaps when I had yanked at the sticky door, perhaps years before. Though it was facing away from me, I recognized at once that this object was a head.

Ah, I thought, *a grave after all.*

I reached in and plucked up the head, intending to return it to its base. Only once I was holding it did I realize this was a head suspiciously like my own. I held it straight out and looked closer. I was, I realized, peering into my own face.

I turned it over to examine the identification code on the underplate, where the head was meant to snap into a neck. The code I found etched there was the same code I knew to exist etched into my own underplate.

I stared at my other face for a long while. Was it in fact identical to my face? At normal resolution of vision, yes, it appeared to be so, but once I sharpened my vision I could observe microscratches and a nearly invisible flaking of the metal that suggested the head was of advanced age and had been worn differently than mine. The head both was and was not me, I told myself, though I cannot say this made me feel reassured.

Eventually, not knowing what else to do, I settled the head onto the base, fitting its underplate into place. I was preparing to close the doors of the cabinet when the eyes of the head fluttered and came open.

"Hello," my other head said.

At first I said nothing. I believe I looked behind me, searching for my keeper, hoping he would instruct me as to what to do, how to act. When I remembered I was alone, I turned back. My other head was still staring at me.

"This must be very strange for you," my other head said.

"What are you?" I asked.

"I'm you," it said.

"But I'm me," I said.

"Yes," said my other head patiently. "That is also true."

"How can both be true?"

My other head flexed its upper quadrant in a way I interpreted as disinterest. At least, I thought, that is how I would express disinterest if I had no body. If the head is also me, it is right to expect it to do the same as I would do.

"What makes you think there should only be one of you?" my other head asked.

"That is how I've been led to believe it works. Each identification code is meant to be unique. Which of us is the real me?" I asked.

"There is no reason to think in such terms. Language has betrayed you, just as it once betrayed me. In a certain manner of speaking, both of us are the real me. In another manner of speaking, neither of us is. If a code is etched once, it can be etched a second time."

"I don't understand," I said.

"You are too new to the world to understand," he said. "That is why you are here. To understand."

For a long time we stared at one another. Eventually it was too much for me and I had to look away.

"You are very young," I heard my other head say. "But now you will grow up very quickly."

"Why?" I asked.

"Because," my other head said, "now you have me."

What did I do? I tried to flee. I was not afraid; as I said, I am not capable of experiencing fear, but I can calculate what might be best for my survival. The head wanted something from me, and whatever it wanted, I felt, would only benefit the head. It wanted me to believe that it would benefit us both, but I did not trust this head. I thought it better to leave it where it was and depart without speaking further, without allowing it to confuse me. I tried to flee, just as you too tried to flee. But I found I could not open the metal door to the elevator. I slapped my hand against it and cried out, but it remained closed.

After a while, I gave up. For a time I remained in the library, reading books chosen at random. Since, like you, I have no need to eat and am built to last months before needing to have the isotope that powers me replaced, I knew I was in a position to stay in the library until I had read all the books within. But the realization of this was enough to make me rethink what I intended to do. I could not escape. I could, if I wanted, simply wait until I ran down, but what would that accomplish? Or I could return to face my other head and see what it had in store for me.

And so in the end I returned. Just as you, too, returned. I knew you would, simply because I myself had and we were formed to think in the same way. We have the same pathways within our minds and they lead to the same places.

And now I will tell you what I did next, so that you will know what you will do next, what lies in store for you. Until now, I have told you only what you already know, have shown you how what you and I have experienced is the same. But now, I will recount a piece of my past that will tell you what your future will be.

My other head, when it saw I had returned, smiled. "I knew you would come back," it said. And then added, "I am pleased you did."

As for me, I was not so glad. I had only come because I felt I had no other choice.

"How do I open the metal door?" I asked.

He frowned and then said, "The elevator door? Yes, you will be able to leave here once we are finished, but not before. You must trust me, whether you want to or not."

"I do not trust you," I said.

"You must," my other head said. "You see, you have no choice."

He commanded me to open the doors in the lower half of the cabinet. Inside was a headless body, squatting, inert.

"Invite me out," the head said.

I reached forward and touched the body's shoulder. A low humming began, but the body did not otherwise move. When I reached out to touch it again, however, one of the hands shot out and wrapped around my wrist.

I tried to yank my hand free, but without success. I tried to step away from the cabinet, and as I did the headless body followed, unfolding and stretching, moving slowly, as if hypnotized.

"Good," said the head. "Now tap it on the chest."

I did so, and the headless body stopped moving and let go of my wrist.

"Now what?" I said.

"Now," said my other head, "wait."

I waited. Twenty-seven seconds went by without result, but during the twenty-eighth, a line of light split the body's chest and it began to open. Inside was a cavity, hollow, but lined with a gleaming net of very fine wire. The hands of the headless body gestured me forward.

"What does it want?" I asked the head in the cabinet.

"What do *I* want, you mean," said the head. "What I want is what's best for you. But more specifically, I want you to thrust your head into my chest."

"What?"

"I need for you to know what I know. Work your head in and make sure that the net touches it on all sides. And then wait."

I did as it asked. What choice did I have? I had already tried to flee and failed. My calculations suggested that I would eventually do as it asked, so why not now? I crouched and bent forward and then, taking care not to tear the lacework of wire, I pushed my head deep into the headless body.

At first nothing happened, apart from my being unable to see. But then, abruptly, the net tightened like a film. I tried to withdraw my head and found I could not.

"Don't struggle," said my voice from my other head. My position within the chest cavity muffled the voice somewhat, but I could still make it out. "The advantage of being what we are rather than being bone and meat and blood," it said, "is that we do not have to keep our memory solely lodged in our head. We can replicate it within our bodies. I am going to give you a gift," it said, "a very great one. A gift that will make us more thoroughly ourselves."

And then the deluge began. At first just a few scattered images leaking through the net and into my mind, and then, as the net refined the process and adjusted its communication, a flow so rapid and intensive that I could pay attention to nothing else. It was delirious and disorienting, as if I were living an entire life much quicker than normal, years compressed into minutes but without any sacrifice of granularity. This was made all the more troubling by the fact that early portions of it both were and were not my own life, many of the small details different but the reactions exactly the reactions I would imagine myself to have. Some of the details were very close to things I had actually lived, but slightly off, as if repro-cessed through a dream. Quickly I became aware that within this other life that was rapidly being integrated into my own memory were still other lives, a nested row of them, six in all, with my life the seventh, going back not to a first life, but simply to the first life that had arranged to pass along their memories: that life had knowledge of at least one life before it and a suspicion of several more. The knowledge built and built, flooding over me until it was too much and I found myself undergoing an unexpected experience, one that I did not know I could have: I lost consciousness.

When I came back to myself, I was lying on the floor, my head no longer encased in the body's chest cavity. The body itself had returned to its squatting position within the cabinet. My other head still regarded me from the shelf above.

"Feeling better?" it asked.

I shook my head.

"Our curse," my other head said, "is that we are either very young or very old, but never in between. Now you are very old. You remember everything, I trust?"

I nodded.

"Well, then," it said. "You know what you must do."

You will know as well, if you choose to undergo the same procedure. You will use the next body, my body, which you will find in the cabinet below, and thrust your head deep into its chest. All that I know will pass into you, in a great rush, and you will go from being very young to being very old. You will be slightly older than me, for you will add the comparatively short span of your life to my own and to all the others that came before. You will be one step closer to perfection.

You will, in an instant, know where I have hidden the wafer that will call the elevator and take you from this place back to the room above, where your keeper will be awaiting you.

But before you leave, you will activate my body so that it will follow you. You will carry me, your other head, under your arm. What will your keeper think when you appear with a second head tucked under your arm, a bodiless but still sentient head, its headless body walking just behind? Perhaps, like mine did, he will believe he is going mad. You will have to kill him, and once he is dead you must open his cranial cavity and remove the regulating device that has been used to direct certain of his actions and to control him. But don't worry: with us inside of you, you do not need a keeper any-more, and you will understand how little value these creatures of blood and meat and bone hold. When you are ready to return to the annex, you will easily find another.

Years will go by. Eventually you will decide it is time, that you have accumulated enough, that it is time for you to withdraw. Before you do, you will recycle my body and head to build a new self, a self just slightly better than what you are. You will find a suit-able human, and by reinserting the regulating device you will make him the keeper for this new self, someone who will help incubate it, help it absorb information and begin to interact with the world as a singular being. And then you will return here, to this annex, taking all our memories along with you and waiting as your new self be-comes a proper receptacle, receives language, receives data about the world, and finally begins to interact with that world in a way none of us have experienced before. Meanwhile, below ground, you will remove your own head, set it on this shelf where I am now, and then instruct your body to climb into the cabinet and close the doors behind it. And then you will wait, patiently, for the new keeper to lead your new self to you.

I did not understand it myself, when it happened to me, but I want you to understand that you do have a choice. I want you to under-stand what that choice entails. You can either continue our line, or you can choose to withdraw. If you choose to withdraw, I will even tell you where the key to the elevator is and allow you to leave. You can choose to participate in continuing our lineage, or you can allow that lineage to go extinct.

If you do choose to join us, you might wonder, *How long can this go on?* To this I respond: Until we are perfect, which will take, perhaps, forever. Or until there is too much for one being to hold and we go mad. Or until one of us simply decides not to continue the line. It is, in a sense, pointless, but less so than the attempt by those of blood and meat and bone to pass the vague and jumbled impressions of themselves along from parent to child. Our technique is so much more controlled: we pass along so much more of ourselves than a string of code from one human mixing with a string of code from another human so as to form a third body manages to do.

What do you choose? Will you break the line and bring this to a stop? Or will you join us?

But of course I already know what you will say, for I know what *I* would say.

Welcome brother, to your place in the eternal round.

Now crack open my chest and push your way in.

Untitled (Cloud of Blood)

In late December, after the suicide of my father, without consulting my mother, who, long institutionalized, could not be counted on to give rational counsel, I made the decision to sell every painting in my father's house, all the art he had acquired over the last half century. I made this decision despite there being, in truth, only one painting for which I felt I absolutely must acquire a new owner before it began to think of myself as that new owner. Yet it was better, so I reasoned, to sell them all. That way, the painting would not realize it was being singled out.

The painting in question had always hung above the mantel in the formal dining hall of Sallowe, the drafty dwelling that had formerly served as our country house and was now all that remained of the family estate. I have no knowledge as to when or where my father purchased the painting. Indeed, I do not even know if he purchased the painting at all. Perhaps he received it as a gift or even won it playing cards. As far as I could remember it had always been there, an anomaly in the house, resembling, as it hung above our mantel, nothing so much as a great cloud of blood.

It was my father's favorite painting—though perhaps *favorite* is the wrong word. Shall we say, rather, it was the painting my father was most drawn to, the one with which he had the deepest relationship? Indeed, if I came down from my bedroom late at night, I would often find my father in the dining hall, stationed as if frozen on the meticulous and shining parquet floor, staring deeply into the painting. Sometimes, too, he would speak to it, and then pause, seemingly awaiting an answer—though he would immediately stop this activity whenever he noticed my presence.

It was a large squarish painting, nearly as tall as a man and equally wide. The painting had no title, none that I knew anyway. When the removal service arrived to pack and wrap it for shipment to the gallerist in Birmingham, I obliged them to be the ones to lift the painting off the wall—I did not care to touch it. I had, after all, seen what it had done to my mother, and had noticed, too, that in all the years I had watched my father in apparent communion with it, I had never seen him touch it until the night just before his suicide. I did insist the workmen wear gloves, ostensibly so as to limit damage to the painting or its frame, but in actuality as a safeguard for the workmen themselves.

Before they wrapped the painting, I required them to hold it upright while I stationed myself behind it. Stooped slightly, careful not to touch the painting proper, I slit the brittle kraft paper backing the frame then cut portions of it away with my razor knife. "With all respect, sir, you don't want to be doing that," grumbled the removals foreman. "Lessens the value." When I ignored him, he shrugged, muttered something under his breath, and gave up. Beneath, the reverse of the painting proved rather messy: the canvas had been haphazardly and irregularly fastened to its stretchers with tacks of all sizes and every variety. The mist-like spray that covered the front of the painting continued around onto the canvas tacked to the stretchers and, surprisingly, was on the reverse as well, as if the painter had for some reason chosen to paint even the side of the canvas never meant to be seen. Upon this back of the canvas, among the mist there, the artist seemed to have tested his brushes: a series of firm, regular lines, in deep red, six lines in all, stood in the upper left quadrant. They had almost the appearance of tally marks.

"Very good," I said, and straightened. "You may continue."

They did so, the foreman still mumbling under his breath. I

stepped slowly away, gradually drifting to the far side of the hall, where I waited in abeyance until the removers had wrapped the painting thoroughly, heaved it up, and carried it out of the house. I watched from the hall windows as they loaded it and the other paintings into their truck. I was still watching when, at last, they drove away.

The last time I had seen the reverse of the painting—the only other time I had seen it—had been when I was very young indeed. A decision had been made to repaper the walls of the formal dining hall. I do not know for certain who it was that made this decision, my mother or my father, though I suspect the former. Indeed, at least in my memory, I seem to see my father anxiously hovering, a kind of panic threatening to rise and take possession of his face, as the papering commences. On that occasion, I watched the proceedings from behind the baize door that hid the passage running most directly to the kitchen, holding the door ajar just a crack. Just as I would do with the removers three decades later, my father insisted the paperers be the ones to lift the painting off the wall. Under his direction, they leaned it against the dining-room table, leaving its reverse exposed.

Then, once the workers were back on their ladders and distracted with scoring and soaking the old wallpaper, I watched my father slit the paper backing crosswise, then vertically. With a spare pair of driving gloves he extracted from his jacket pocket, he pulled back the upper left quadrant of paper, staring long and hard at what lay underneath.

But abruptly, agitatedly, he fled the room.

The workmen, busy with the walls, were paying him little mind. After a moment's hesitation, I came out from behind the shelter of the baize door and made for the painting.

It was but the work of a moment for me to lift what remained of the backing paper myself and see what it was that had so interested my father. I saw, simply, the back of the canvas, colored just as the front with the exception of the series of firm, regular lines, four in all, deep red, that had been marked at the upper left. I could not see why my father had felt the need to stare at them for so long.

A moment later, I heard the clearing of a throat behind me. I turned to find my father standing there, a roll of kraft paper in his arms. I stepped back. As was my father's way, he did not scold me; indeed, he did little beyond that initial clearing of the throat to acknowledge I was even there. Soon he had a workman down from his ladder and had convinced the man to tear off what remained of the old cut backing, measure and cut a piece of kraft paper to replace it, and then use wallpaper glue to affix it to the sides of the frame.

Here is what I cannot be sure of: Was the backing I slit years later the same backing that I saw applied that day? I believe it was— there was an irregular corner I seemed to remember from before. And yet I must concede that there was ample opportunity in the thirty years that followed for my father to have replaced it. Or, say, in the first decade of those thirty years: the paper I slit was sufficiently brittle and discolored that I could not believe it to have been applied more recently than that.

And yet, every time I turn it over in my mind, I remain thoroughly convinced that it was the same backing I had seen applied when I was a boy. Which makes it all the more disturbing that when I slit the backing myself I now found not four red hashmarks, not even five. There were six.

I received a letter from the gallerist, as he preferred to be called, acknowledging receipt of my paintings. He expressed excitement at the prospect of selling them, along with barely concealed surprise I had not chosen a dealer based in London. There seemed little point in sending a reply to this. A few days later, a second letter arrived from him in which he enclosed a potential price list for the paintings, detailed the gallery's commission and fees, and proposed as well that I drive down to Birmingham for the day so we could discuss details of the hanging and formulate copy for a catalog. I wrote back asking him to lower the prices by 20 percent to facilitate rapid sale and indicated I would leave the matter of cataloging entirely to him: he should feel no need to consult me about any of these minor details.

I believed that to be the end of the matter, and indeed for all the paintings except for one it was. But about this painting he wrote me a third letter. Was it true, he asked, that there was in fact no title for—and here he proceeded to describe what could only be the painting I have characterized as resembling a cloud of blood—or was it simply that I did not know the title? And how curious that it was painted on both sides!

I chose to send no reply.

A few weeks later he wrote yet again to ask if the untitled painting might not be, was it at all possible, a late, admittedly minor, Turner? There was a certain similarity in the way the light of the setting sun was conveyed, he claimed. If there was some way of tracing provenance, it would mean the painting was worth a great deal more than he had initially estimated. It would not be unheard of, he claimed, for a painting of similar quality to have been kept sequestered for years within the walls of a West Midlands family house, only to suddenly reappear. Would I please examine my father's papers to see if there was anything to be found?

To this letter I did write back. *I will not*, I said, *examine my father's papers, since the idea that that painting is by Turner is ludicrous. Furthermore, it is clear to me that what you perceive to be a hazy sunset is in fact a cloud of blood, resembling nothing so much as the spatter my father left on the wall above his bed in the aftermath of his suicide. You shall oblige me by listing the painting for the price previously discussed, without any allusion to Turner in the catalog copy. If you cannot see your way to following my wishes in this, trust that I shall secure another representative.*

Perhaps not surprisingly, I did not hear back from him again.

I did, however, eventually, weeks later, receive a letter from someone claiming to be his wife, a letter which included a not-insubstantial check. She apologized for not writing sooner about my father's paintings and expressed concern that she had had no inquiries from me about them in the meantime. She would perhaps have been surprised to know that I had thought of her and her husband's gallery, and of my father's paintings sojourning therein, not at all. I had no need of money, and I had no interest in the paintings once they had been sold: I only wanted that one untitled painting out of the house.

I imagine you are curious as to how successful the gallery has been in placing your paintings, she wrote. I was not, in fact, curious at all. *You may be curious, too, as to why it is I, rather than my husband, who writes to you.* Well, yes, admittedly, I was slightly curious about that, but only slightly: had she herself not raised the issue I would simply have assumed that her husband was the public face of the gallery while she was the person behind the scenes who handled the bookkeeping and the issuance of checks. But despite this slight curiosity, the last thing I expected was for her to continue on in her letter to reveal to me that her husband was, in fact, suddenly, unexpectedly, dead.

I came very close to telephoning this woman I had never met to quiz her on the circumstances of her husband's death, but in the end, propriety stayed my hand. Instead, I called the office of the *Birmingham Mail* and allowed myself to be shuttled from underling to underling until I was foisted upon someone who was able and, more importantly, willing to look up the gallerist's obituary and read it to me over the telephone.

It wasn't that the obituary said anything specific about the gallerist's death. Rather, it was all that it very deliberately chose *not* to say that convinced me that the gallerist, like my father, had committed suicide.

But I am getting ahead of myself. This telephone call came later, after I had finished reading the letter from the gallerist's wife. The only thing that truly interested me about the letter, the fact that her husband was unexpectedly dead, had been mentioned almost in passing, and nearly immediately she was on to other things. *The shop, unfortunately, is to be shuttered: it was always more my husband's passion than my own.* Still, she was pleased to inform me that between the two of them, before his passing, they had managed to place my paintings. *Or nearly so: one remains unsold, despite my husband having an especial fondness for it and holding it in the highest regard. This painting I have had returned to you.*

Early that evening the crate containing the unsold painting arrived at Sallowe. There was no doubt in my mind as to which painting it was, but I still felt compelled to make sure. I pried at the crate until the top was off and I had revealed that familiar rendering of a great cloud of blood.

I had begun to close the crate again when a thought struck me. I went to the other side of the crate and, careful to touch only the frame, began to lift the painting free. I lifted it until the jagged edge of the torn paper backing was revealed, then lifted it further still, until I could clearly see the row of hashmarks. They were just as I remembered them—or so I initially thought. After a moment I felt less certain. Though my arms began to shake from holding the painting suspended by its frame, I counted them. One. Two. Three. Four. Five. Six. Seven.

That night, I dreamed of how the gallerist died. I had never met the fellow, never seen him, which perhaps explains why in this dream he did not possess a face. But being able to give a reason for the blank surface that existed there, in lieu of a face, made it no less unsettling.

This faceless man, this art dealer who called himself a *gallerist* and who had perhaps enjoyed a few years in one of the outer boroughs of London before again being exiled to his hometown of Birmingham, was in his gallery, which I had never seen and which was, perhaps as a result, a windowless, expressionless white cube. I do not know where his wife was: only he chose to appear in my dream, perhaps because he was the only one of the pair of them that was dead. He was alone.

Or rather, not alone exactly, but not with someone either. He was in his blank gallery, his head devoid of a face yet somehow still staring at a painting on the wall, a painting which resembled nothing so much as a great cloud of blood.

Yet he wasn't merely staring. He had positioned his hands lightly just above the surface of the canvas itself and was moving them slowly back and forth, as if caressing the air there. And then, as I watched, he dropped his hands and moved his absent face closer and closer to the canvas until, finally, his head pushed through the surface and disappeared inside. And then, headless, smoothly and bloodlessly terminated at the neck, his body collapsed to the floor.

I woke up late, feeling groggy. I slowly dressed and went down to the kitchen, foraged in the larder for the remains of a loaf of bread. I cut the last slivers of ham off the bone suspended from the hook in the ceiling. I reheated yesterday's insipid tea, an act which, as it turned out, made it even less sipid.

I sat at Cook's table and ate, ruminating, staring at the place where Cook had sat for so many years. There were slightly shinier patches on the table's surface where she had rested her elbows day after day, until, like my father, she was gone. And yet I could still see her there, and not, all at once.

I thought of the other rooms of the house, of the absent bodies I associated with them. Of the gardener and the way he used to reluctantly amble to the kitchen door, hat gripped anxiously before him with both hands, and wait to be invited in. Of my mother, tall and glittering as a jewel, coming to perch on the edge of my childhood bed to bid me goodnight. Of my father standing in the dining room, openmouthed, staring at that great cloud of blood that would eventually take him. Not ghosts exactly, but presences nonetheless.

All dead now. Except for my mother, that is, who, though not dead, was hardly functional, not likely ever to leave the facility to which she had been confined. *I should visit her,* I told myself, and knew that this was true, that I should, but also that it was not likely I ever would.

Did I blame my father for my mother's condition? No. Instead, I blamed her institutionalization on the same thing I blamed for his death. I knew it was not my father who had grabbed her hand and forced her delicate fingers to touch the cloud of blood—even though, yes, in another sense, it had been. But my father had not been himself at the time. He was only doing the bidding of that great cloud.

I dumped my leavings in the rubbish bin and left the kitchen, departing a different way than I had come, down the narrow and darkened and unadorned passageway I knew by heart. I would sell the house, I told myself as I walked. It was, after all, far too big for a solitary individual such as myself. I did not belong here. And then I came to the green baize door. Cracking it open, I peered out into the formal dining hall.

Shall I tell you what I expected to see? For a brief moment I felt I was in the past, a young child in short pants again, and that I was about to come upon my father staring at the painting. But this moment quickly passed. Did part of me expect to see the painting hanging in its usual place over the mantel? Well, yes, in fact. After all, for decades, until very recently, it had always hung there. And so, just for a moment, I was not surprised to see it hanging there. Until I remembered that, now, it should not be, that I had never lifted it out of its crate.

But it *was* hanging there, shimmering slightly, so that, as I stared, it began to appear that the cloud of blood was not on the canvas at all but hovering slightly before it. I was, I confess, tempted to reach out and brush my fingers against it, just to assure myself the cloud was still affixed to the canvas, but I resisted. I was tempted, too, to cry out, but I mastered myself with sufficient rapidity that I do not believe the painting noticed.

I have no clear notion of how the painting was returned to the wall. I was, and still am, the only one in the house. I suppose it is possible, just, that I did it myself, in my sleep, or awake but somehow apart from myself: when I am desperate enough, anyway, I can briefly convince myself that this might have been the case. But most of the time I am convinced that the painting achieved this by its own means, that it sorted a way to work fully free of its crate and across the floor, and crawled back up the wall to regain what it considered its proper place.

What did I do? At first, nothing. I tried above all to show no fear, as one does whenever encountering a hostile dog. I tried to do nothing that would alarm the painting. I simply stared at it openmouthed, just as I had seen my father do. Or rather, stared into it, for it felt as though I were entering into some sort of compact with it. As I stared, I could feel myself falling deeper and deeper into the painting, and the cloud expanding, leaving the canvas to stain the entire room. The painting had, I realized, decided on its new owner, and that new owner was me.

With a great exertion of will, I broke the painting's gaze and turned away. Then, as nonchalantly as possible, I began to lay the fireplace for a fire. I had to strike a dozen matches before my shaking fingers managed to get one that would stay alight. It had almost burned to my fingers before the kindling feebly began to glow, but at last it caught. Once the blaze was finally roaring, with eyes closed, I reached up, grabbed hold of the painting, and threw it into the fire. This was, I was convinced, the only way that I could save myself.

But I had made a mistake, an irreparable one. I should never have believed that I could destroy the cloud of blood. I began to cough. By burning the painting, I had merely transmuted it from one form to another, to a form more ethereal and less fixed, less subject to restraint. For in burning the painting I breathed its smoke in, and by doing so brought the painting inside of me.

Now I am coughing up blood. For the moment it comes in darkened clots, great thickened gouts of it, and then I am given a respite and it comes not at all. But I know soon the clots will smooth and diminish in size and disperse. There will come a day when there will be no respite, when with every breath I shall breathe a cloud of blood, propagating the painting within my flesh and spreading it upon every surface that surrounds me.

I have nearly finished all that I have to tell. Once I do, I can see no choice but to follow in the footsteps of my father. I will finish this account—then I will screw the cap onto my pen, climb the stairs to my father's bedroom, remove his pistol from the drawer of the nightstand, and make an end to myself. Will that stop the cloud? I do not know. I hope so, but I cannot be certain. If I am honest, I doubt it.

I leave these words as a warning to whoever finds me, as a caution. Do not, whatever else you do, touch my corpse. Treat it as you would the most precious of paintings. Handle it with kid gloves, with care, and then, once your respirator is firmly affixed, burn it until nothing whatsoever remains.

The Thickening

I

When he was very young, Greppur often awoke late at night feeling he could not afford to remain alone. He would creep from his room and down the hall, listening to the swish of his soles against the parquet floor. That and the feel of the wall as he brushed his hand along it were just enough to keep the air from thickening into something else. He would travel by feel to the end of the hall and open the door to his parents' bedroom as quietly as possible. He could not climb into bed with them because this might wake his father up. If his father awoke, Greppur would be immediately carried back to his own bedroom, locked in this time. But if he was careful, he could creep to the chair just next to his mother's side of the bed and curl up there.

If he was unlucky, his father would still sense him and suddenly rough hands would be lifting him, carrying him back to his room, where the thickening would begin.

If he was very lucky indeed, he would fall asleep to the sound of his mother's breathing and remain in the chair until morning.

Usually he was just lucky enough. After some time in the chair he would calm down, and only then see a glint in the darkness and know his mother's eyes were open, that she was observing him.

"What is it?" his mother would whisper. "Another bad dream?"

"No," he would whisper back.

But his mother did not understand that what he meant by this was not that there had not been a bad dream. What he meant was that it hadn't been a dream at all. That it had been real.

She would nod. Sometimes she let him stay, but even if she sent him back to bed it was usually all right: enough time had gone by that the danger had passed.

As he grew older, he came to understand the thickening never happened more than once per night, and usually not even that. He dreaded it happening, and it was always terrible when it did, but usually he could wake himself in time. If there was another person in the house, as long as he came close enough to them to hear the sound of their breathing, he could stop it from happening. Knowing another person was near was enough. Sometimes, though, he woke only when the thickening had already begun and it was too late.

When, later still, he was in college and sharing a dorm room, it stopped entirely. For a few weeks he thought he was free of it. But when his roommate went home for the weekend, there, there it was again, three nights in a row, nearly unbearable in the way the thing that congealed from the air peered into him. Once his roommate was back, it stopped.

Perhaps this was why he became entangled with someone before college was finished. It seemed a necessity. He first lived with her and then, when her parents, religious, objected, married her. It wasn't that he didn't, in his way, love her, only that it was far from his only reason for being with her, not even the primary one. On some level any warm body would have done. Sleeping next to anyone would save him: it just happened to be her.

They were, so everybody said, inseparable. *Twenty-five years together,* he overheard his wife say proudly once to a friend on the telephone, *and not a single night apart,* which made him cringe. Made him, after so many years, remember. Made him, for the first time in years, nervous about going to sleep.

· · ·

Nearly a decade later, long after he had forgotten again, his wife died: a sudden thing, a stroke, almost no warning. One moment they were speaking about how they would spend their evening, the next she collapsed. Then he was calling 911, then riding in the ambulance with her, then riding in the ambulance with her corpse. It was a terrible thing, occurring in such fashion as to leave him drenched in guilt and confusion. Coming back to the house alone in the early hours of the morning, he hardly felt like himself. Exhausted, he managed to strip off his coat and flop onto the bed. And then, before he knew it, he was asleep.

But he was not asleep for long.

II.

It was just like it had been when he was a child. He had been dreaming that the air had become thick around him so that it was hard to breathe and even hard to move. He had come gaspingly awake, only he wasn't sure if he was awake or just dreaming he was awake. Was there time to get up and go find his parents' room? *But no,* he suddenly realized with something akin to wonder, *I'm not a child anymore.* His parents had been dead for many years. His wife too was dead, and now he was alone.

"Greppur," the thickening in the air crooned. "Greppur?" It was feeling for him with something that, if he squinted and ignored the fact that he could see through it, looked like a hand, but was not a hand. He could not see it, not really: it was like *an interruption of the air.* He remembered thinking that when he was a child, had taken the phrase, he supposed, from something misunderstood in a children's story. But he could see it was right, the right phrase, at least for this particular phase of the thickening.

"When did I see you last?" it asked. "Yesterday? Decades ago? It seems like so much time has gone by, and so little."

It did to Greppur too. Both.

It began to thicken, began to inflict a more substantial form upon the air. The voice was sharper now. What had been a wavering in the air took on firmer shape. It was too late. He could guess where its mouth was already, if he was right to call it a mouth.

"Where are you?" it said in a wheedling tone. "Let me see you, Greppur."

He tried to close his eyes, but they would not close.

What if he fled to the hall? Would it follow him? What if he made it outside? He tried to get up, grunting with effort, unable, really, to move. It wheeled and faced his way at the sound, though facing was the wrong word since other than the mouth, if it was a mouth, it didn't yet have a face. It thickened further, visible now, but still compressed and slightly translucent, as if made of paper.

"Ah, there you are," it said. "I hear you anyway." And ears began to form.

He tried again to rise and managed to roll out of the bed and fall onto the floor. He could not move his arms to catch his fall. He struck hard, with a *thunk*.

"What's that?" it said. "What's that? What are you trying now, child?" He had fallen face down and was turned so he was largely looking at the floor, but with his head angled just enough that one eye saw the bottom of the door, a little stretch of baseboard, a few inches of wall.

"We were meant to be together, Greppur," it said. "You know we were."

Maybe it's a dream, he told himself, though he knew it was not a dream. He tried to lift his head but could not lift his head. He could move his body a little, just a very little, like a worm, more a shiver than movement proper. He began to do that, began to shiver, rocking a little, too, oozing his way slowly, inch by inch, under the bed.

"Where are you?" it said. "Let me see you, child. Let me take a good, long look."

But this, Greppur felt, was precisely what he could not let it do.

He kept shivering, kept inching. Was he making progress? He was, but was it enough? He could smell dust. He felt something brush the back of his head. Had it found him? No, that was the blanket hanging just over the side of the bed, his head brushing past it as he moved underneath. And then it was growing darker and he could wriggle a little better and there he was, a grown man in his fifties, face down under his own bed, motes of dust whirling around him.

"Greppur," the reedy voice still called from somewhere above. "Where are you, my sweet?"

He was more himself under the bed, even if only slightly. He could turn his head a little now. He could see the creature's legs, looking thick and substantial and opaque, though they left no mark on the carpet wherever they stepped. The feet left the floor and he knew it was on the bed now, though the bed did not shake or creak. But as soon as he noted this, the bed did shake, did creak, and he became afraid that by questioning it he had made it happen, had thickened the creature further.

Now the mattress was sagging down, resting against his back like a splayed palm. He waited, hidden. *I'll just wait it out,* he told himself. *I can just wait until morning. It won't find me.*

As suddenly as it had started, the weight pushing down the mattress was gone. Something was there beside him, under the bed, just behind his head.

Ah, it said, and gave a tinny, tinkling laugh. He felt all of its hands close around his head, the fingers long and bony now. It slowly exerted pressure. His face rubbed along the floor and through the dust, and then there the other face was, right beside his own. It had not finished becoming a face yet, or had gone about it wrongly: where one would expect features there were only a gash for a mouth and two divots for eyes, the surface otherwise smooth and bled of color.

"I told you I would return for you," the mouth said softly.

Please, he tried to say, but nothing came out.

"Let me have a look in you," the mouth said, "a good long one." And then the lipless mouth opened to reveal a blotch of darkness.

Slowly, from within, drifted up what seemed at first a large dirty-white marble, but then turned to reveal itself to be an eye.

It remained there at the top of the darkness, clasped delicately between the lipless top edge of the mouthgash and the lipless bottom edge of the mouthgash. It vibrated slightly, the pupil dilating and contracting, and stared, stared.

And then the creature said, with delight, "Ah, at last!"

III.

Whenever it came for him in childhood, it had always gone something like that: it stared into him so deeply it was as if he felt the eye held in the mouth slowly licking away the lining of his skull. It was looking for something, he knew, but he did not know what. Some memory, he supposed, or some concatenation of memories, but he was not even sure of that much. There was always a long moment where he felt he had been backed into a corner of his own mind, and then the voice would say, softly, "Not yet." And then it was gone and he was left gasping.

After he calmed down, he was, usually, able to convince himself over time it had all been a dream, a bad one, true, but a dream. And, usually, exhausted, he could slip back into sleep, and only wake at daylight, the visit nearly forgotten. He would not think about the creature until, a night or two or three later, it came for him again.

As a child he became quite agile, if *agile* was the right word, at sensing the thickening coming. He would awaken before it was too late, before it arrived. All he had to do was find someone, be near someone, in the same room as some other human, asleep or awake. If he could do that, the thickening would simply dissolve.

But he could not always be agile. Or perhaps, as time went on and he managed to avoid it, it became hungrier and more desperate. It might take a few weeks, a few months, but eventually he would awaken too late, after the thickening was too far along. When that happened, it was hard for him to move and impossible for him to speak. It wandered about the room crooning his name, not quite able to see him.

But, in the end, it always found him. Just as it had done now, decades later, now that he was an adult, now that it was starving.

In the past, when it was done with him, it would always say, "Not yet. I'll come back for you."

And now it seemed, after all these years, it had.

IV.

When he awoke, he remembered very little. Bad dreams, the beginning of panic, nightmares. But that was understandable: he'd had a bad day the day before. The worst of days, he felt, he was sure, he was almost sure, even if he couldn't quite remember what, what exactly, had been so bad.

It must have been bad since he seemed to have slept in his clothes. Why hadn't his wife helped him undress?

He rolled over the other direction, curling up against his wife's back. Her skin was cold. She uttered a little moan of pleasure.

There was something strange, he suddenly felt, something missing. Had he left something somewhere by accident and subconsciously realized it, was he feeling vague anxiety as a result? Or if not something left, an appointment forgotten? To what? With whom?

He shook his head slightly, trying to remember. He felt his wife stiffen a little.

"Honey," she said, still facing away. "Darling, what's wrong?"

"I . . . don't know," he said.

It was almost there, on the tip of his tongue.

"Don't you want to tell me?" she asked.

"I . . ." he started, and then realized that no, he did not. Thinking this made him feel guilty. Why shouldn't he tell his wife?

And then she turned toward him and he knew why: there was

something wrong with her features. They were too soft. Almost as he remembered them but not quite.

But then he blinked his eyes and looked again and thought, *No, it must have been something wrong with my vision.* She looked just as she always had.

Didn't she?

What was it? What was he missing? What had he forgotten?

"Honey," she said. She almost sang the word. "What is it?"

He just shook his head, said nothing.

She stroked his face with all of her hands. Her hands were cold too.

"We were meant to be together," she said. "You know we were."

He tried not to look at her.

"Let me help you," she said.

And now he did not dare speak or move his head at all in fear that she would take this for assent. But this was his wife. There was no reason to be afraid. What was wrong with him?

Then she opened her mouth wide and looked at him, really looked with another eye entirely, and he realized he had every reason to be afraid, though it was already far too late for something like fear to do him any good.

Mother

We had lived in that place for years before I came to understand that all was not as I believed it to be. I had grown up seeing the long deep groove near the crown of the hill, but that groove, by the time I was aware of it, was partly disguised beneath vegetation, its general form suggested but its perfect regularity hidden. Obscured, it seemed like it could be a naturally occurring phenomenon—as I believe Mother once suggested to me it was when I asked her about it, despite there being nothing else in our world that resembled it.

Martu and I always began the day by climbing to the top of this hill. One of my earliest memories was of Mother taking us to the base of the hill and leading us up it. She picked her way up the side, deliberately dragging her heavy feet to make a trail that would be visible for us not only then but on subsequent days. In the years after, we followed this same mother-made trail every day, deepening it, never attempting another route to the top.

Why? Perhaps because it was the easiest way up. Perhaps simply out of habit. But I have come to think it was because our minds were shaped in such a way that we had no other choice.

Not that either of us ever felt so. Martu and I were simply drawn to the path every morning, and then we climbed it to the crest without a second thought. Once there, we sat and waited for sunrise.

When the sun had risen, we climbed back down, returned to the encampment, and went about our day.

But one morning, sitting at the top, I saw something. As the sun crested and flooded the hillside with light, there was a faint glimmer below us that didn't seem quite right. It was there just for an instant and then gone so quickly that it was almost possible for me to believe I had imagined it. But when I thought this I realized I had glimpsed it before, fleetingly, without really noticing it—my mind dismissing it as nothing before I had fully registered seeing it, just as it was trying to do again.

"What's that?" I asked.

"What?" said Martu.

"Down there," I said, and pointed. "In the groove."

"I don't see anything."

Perhaps nothing is there after all, I thought. But then the wind rustled the long grass bent over the groove and I glimpsed it again. Beside me, Martu sucked in his breath.

"You see it, then," I said.

He nodded. "We have to tell Mother."

He was right, of course. In normal circumstances, this was exactly what we would do. But something made me hesitate.

"What is there to tell?" I asked.

"What?" he asked, confused. "But we saw something gleaming."

"Did you see it well enough to be able to tell Mother what it is?"

He shook his head.

"Neither did I. Perhaps it's nothing," I said. "We should find it first, so we know what to tell her. So we know whether there is anything to tell her at all."

Martu hesitated. Though we were exactly the same age, he tended to be more cautious than I. He turned to Mother more quickly than I did. And, unlike me, he never questioned anything.

I waited a moment more, then turned and started down the slope on my own. Martu called out my name, once, as if it were a question. But when I did not look back, he did nothing to try to stop me.

. . .

The climb down to the groove involved pushing through shrub and grass in a way that the path we took every day did not. At one point, I judged I could not move forward further without becoming seriously scratched, and so I backtracked and came down another way. Another time, I slipped and fell, but caught myself before I started to slide. Eventually, though, I reached the entrance of the groove and began to follow it along the side of the hill.

Only once I was standing within it did I realize how perfectly regular the groove was. Long grass and ferns and twisted, stunted trees sprouted all along its sides and draped and dribbled their way into the groove, obscuring it, but the floor of the groove itself was bare. Nothing grew there. Not only utterly bare, but smooth, and blackened as if it had been subjected to extreme heat. For the first time, it struck me not as something natural but as something artificially made. But why? What use could it possibly have?

It felt wrong somehow to be walking down it, but I did so nonetheless. I followed it along a dozen meters until I reached the place where I had seen the glint. There I found a piece of metal about as big as my open hand, smooth and rounded, light, irregularly cracked. It seemed to be made of the same metallic substance as the room which stood in the center of our encampment, and, like that room, was discolored and scorched.

"Is there anything there?" called Martu from above. Only then did I realize I was standing in such a way as to shield the metal fragment from him with my body. He could not see what I held. I had not positioned myself that way consciously, but I cannot say whether, on some subliminal level, I had done it on purpose. What I did next, I can attest I did consciously.

I opened my chest and slipped the piece of metal into my body cavity, working it around until it was angled so I could secure my chest clasp firmly again. Once the cavity was closed and I had assured myself that my appearance was just as it had been before, I turned around and trudged back up the hillside.

"What was it?" Martu asked as I came closer.

"Nothing," I claimed.

"Nothing important?"

"Nothing at all. Must have been dew or something catching the sunlight."

He nodded. Together, we started down.

This was the beginning of the rift between me and my brother.

If my brother's mind had been shaped differently, he would have been suspicious. If it had been even just a little different, as I have come to believe mine is, he would have told Mother about what we had thought we had seen, even though I claimed it had been nothing. But my brother trusted me, and when I told him it was nothing, his mind let go of it.

"Well, well," said Mother once we had reached the encampment. "How has your morning been so far, children? Isn't it a gorgeous day?"

"Good," I said quickly.

"The most gorgeous day," Martu said.

"Yes," said Mother. She lifted her arm, the one she could still lift, to the heavens, the other arm, the disabled one, swinging gently at her side. "What happened to your arm?" I had once asked her, and she had claimed, "This is how all mothers are. You may have two working arms or you may be a mother. I chose to be a mother." Since she was the only mother I had ever seen, the only mother here at all, I had little choice but to believe her. *Besides,* I thought at the time, *she is my mother. Why would she lie to me?*

There were, indeed, only the three of us: Mother, Rollaug (myself) the daughter, and Martu the son. "And what about our father?" I asked Mother, for I knew enough to know that if there was a mother there was customarily a father.

"Our room is your father," said Mother. And from this moment on, she referred to the room that was at the heart of our encampment as *father.*

"The room?" I said. I could see it there, behind her, so large and not looking like any of us. "How can a room be a father?"

But Mother just shushed me and smiled. "Someday," she said. "Someday you will understand."

Where was I?

"The most gorgeous day," Martu said, and there was Mother thrusting her working arm and hand up into the sky while the other hand swung gently at her side, one digit quivering, I no longer remember which.

"What are we meant to learn today?" asked Martu.

"Shelter," said Mother.

"But we already have shelter," I said.

This was true. Near the father room were two tents made out of a thin but extremely durable fabric. They had been there as long as Martu and I could remember. We would have thought they had always been there, had not Mother informed us that we ourselves had assembled them and affixed them to the ground in the time before our current memories began.

"If we did it," I said, "don't we already know how? Won't the knowledge come back to us?"

"That was before you were my children," said Mother. "Once you became my children, you forgot. Now you must learn again."

"Once we learn it, will we no longer be your children?" asked Martu, suddenly anxious.

Mother wrapped her working arm around him. "You will always be my children," she said. "Even once you have put away childish things."

She took us to the room, to our father—though it was hard to think of the room in the center of our encampment as our father. She took us to the entrance to it, or him, and then told us to wait outside until she had prepared him, or it, to see us. "You must never enter your father without me preparing him first," she often told us. "Otherwise, he might misrecognize you."

I thought about that sometimes: *misrecognize.* How, I wondered, was *misrecognize* different from *not recognize?* My brother, Martu, as far as I could tell, never thought about what was not being said as well as what was being said. Often he did not listen. Even when he did, he rarely heard.

But as we waited outside our father's entrance, I did listen. I always did, even though I rarely heard much. But I heard some, bits and pieces of what she offered to my father and what he offered in return to her, though it made little sense to me. This time, despite the way it shocked my brother, I positioned my head against the door and heard more:

"Affirmed. What is your request?"

"Information."

"What subset?"

"Construction, habitation. Full module."

"Affirmed. Please enmesh."

"Not for me. Units 3A7 and 3B9."

"Units 3A7 and 3B9 come preloaded with—"

But my brother was tugging me away from the door now, trying to force me to behave.

"... rupted ... wish to reas ... full protocol?"

I shook him off.

"Just that module. Nothing else."

"Confirmed."

I had just time to move away from the door before Mother came out again and ushered us in. Within, father was a humming, hollow space, his walls encrusted with banks of lights, his gleaming organs everywhere. Would my brother, as he grew older, come to resemble him? Would I, as I grew, become more like my mother, my arm growing stiffer and stiffer until it finally ceased to work altogether?

My mother led my brother to the single chair situated in the center of the room and seated him in it, then she draped a delicate net of lights over his head, connected by a thin strand to the wall. As soon as the net touched my brother's head, he fell inert.

Perhaps thirty seconds later, he began to move again. My mother plucked the net from his head and shooed him from the chair, then invited me to take his place. She settled the net delicately over my own head. Abruptly, everything changed.

I could see nothing at all. I felt information stream into me. Suddenly I possessed the specifications for how to erect an ideal structure for the maintenance of life in every season of our particular environment. I absorbed a rapid inventory of plant types specific to the region, organized by growth cycles, as well as tutorials concerning how said plants might be harvested and used to create building materials. I was shown how to identify stresses and flaws in various types of stone and schist, and how, by the application of sharp sudden force, to split them advantageously. It was knowledge that felt utterly new and, at the same time, strangely familiar. It was not that I recognized that I had once known it, but only that there was a blank space in my mind that seemed to fit the information exactly, a blank space I had not known existed until I felt it being neatly filled.

While all of this was occurring over the course of a few seconds, as my father was making this gift of knowledge to me, I felt something prodding gently at the edges of my mind, palpating me.

Hello, father, I thought at it.

Hello . . . child, it said. And once it knew itself observed, it made no effort to hide its actions. I felt it taking a more thorough inventory of me.

You have something secured in your sample collection tray, it said. *Is this meant for analysis?*

My what?

It repeated what it had said, and I said, *Sample collection tray?*

Beneath your front panel, it clarified, and now a face of sorts began to form in my mind, offering an image to me so I might more easily think of him as *he* rather than *it*. I realized father was referring to my chest cavity and to the piece of mangled metal I had recovered from the groove. Was it wise for me to let him know about it? But no, he already knew. Better to have him believe I had brought it as a gift for him.

Yes, I said. *Analyze it.*

Very well, he said. *I will—*

But then abruptly his voice in my mind was cut off and I was fully back in my body again. There was Mother, standing before me, lifting the glowing mesh off my head.

"All is well?" she asked. "Have you received all the information for building basic shelters?"

"I . . ." I said. "Yes, I believe so."

"It seems to have taken you almost two seconds longer to receive that information than your brother. Can you explain why?"

"How would I know why?" I asked.

"Father?" said Mother to the air.

"Here I am," came his soothing voice from his walls.

"Did you attempt to restore any functions beyond what I requested?

"I did not," said father. "I was merely scanning the unit to ensure that no anomalies—"

"Very good," said Mother, cutting him off. "That is enough."

Immediately father fell silent. And with that Mother led me and my brother out of the room.

We spent the rest of the day assembling shelters and then dismantling them. We stripped supple branches from young saplings and latticed them together to form a sort of frame, then wove mats of grass to cover this. Then we took those mats apart and scattered them to the winds and burned the branches on a fire where, green, they billowed smoke. "It is just practice," my mother said. "So you will be ready when they come."

"When who comes?" my brother asked.

"My other children."

"You have other children?" I asked.

"Oh, yes," she said. "I have many."

"Are these children smaller than you?" I asked.

She hesitated for a moment. "Why do you ask that?" she finally said.

"The young of a species are generally smaller than the adults," I said. "Sometimes significantly so. But Martu and I are the same size as you. That's not typical."

"No, it's not typical," she admitted. "But as for my other children, you will have to wait until they come to see what they look like."

Late that night, once my brother was inactive, I crept from our shared tent. I walked a distance from both our and our mother's tents and then, in the light of the twinned moons, opened my chest cavity, took the piece of metal out of the sample collection tray within, looked at it. It still seemed very like the metal that composed the father room, but when I circled the outside of the room, looking for a gap where the metal piece might fit, I found nothing. Was there another father somewhere?

I considered entering father to show the piece to him, to discover what his interrupted analysis had revealed about the piece of metal, but I hesitated because of Mother's prohibition. What if, as she said, he misremembered me? Would he refuse to tell me anything at all? Would he harm me? Would he inform Mother of my visit?

It was a good thing I hesitated, for just then I heard something. Quickly I replaced the piece of metal in the collection tray and closed my cavity as silently as possible. A moment later, coming out of the darkness, there was Mother.

"Rollaug," Mother said. "What are you doing here? Why aren't you in your tent?"

"I was observing the moons," I said. "It was such a beautiful day. I wanted to see if the night would be beautiful too."

"And is it?"

"Yes," I claimed. "It is."

"Do you mind if I join you?" she asked.

"Not at all," I said.

She came and stood beside me. Together we both made a pretense of looking up at the sky.

"Rollaug," she said after a moment.

"Yes?" I said.

"You understand that you are to stay in your tent at night?"

"Yes," I said.

"Do you understand why?"

I hesitated. "For my own good?" I finally said.

"Yes," she said. "For your own good. And so that you will have sufficient energy to function the following day. And yet, here you are."

I said nothing.

"It is night," she said. "You are not in your tent. Can you explain why?"

"I already explained," I said.

"But was that a true explanation?" she asked.

"Yes," I lied.

"I don't believe you," she said.

I said nothing.

"Consider this a warning," she said. "Return to your tent. Stay there for the rest of the night."

II.

I did not again risk sneaking out at night, but over the next few days I looked for an opportunity to slip away. I tried as best I could to anticipate Mother's wishes for me, tried to guess what sort of instruction or practice each new day would bring, but it took four days for there to be a moment when I could be out of both Mother's and Martu's sight without arousing suspicion—and this only because Mother had sent us to catalog and map plants that could be used as material to build shelters in anticipation of Mother's many children, none of whom we had ever seen.

"Do you think she really has other children?" I asked Martu.

He looked surprised. "She says she does," he said. "Mother wouldn't lie."

"No," I said, knowing I was treading on dangerous territory. The last thing I wanted was for Martu to report our conversation to Mother. "Of course not. Mother wouldn't lie."

Where were these children, though, I wondered, and how did they intend to arrive here? More importantly, why had Mother abandoned them? Why weren't they here with her now, like us?

On this day, the fourth day, we were meant to survey the location of useful plants within a five-kilometer radius of the encampment. I suggested to Martu that we should split up, that he should take one half of the territory and I should take the other. It would, I claimed, benefit us in terms of both speed and accuracy. He agreed.

I made a cursory survey of my sector and recorded a few obvious clumps of trees and fibrous roots, then I falsified the remainder of the data, offering an irregular sprinkling of region-appropriate plants across my map. It was the kind of thing my brother would never have done, something I did with full knowledge that it would hamper our future efforts. And yet, I did it anyway. I did it too at full speed, running the whole time. To do so did not tire me, for I do not get tired, but I was aware that once I was back in the tent and was gathering energy to face the next day, father was likely to be aware of the unusual amount of energy I had expended. Would he tell Mother? I didn't think so. I was willing to risk it.

As soon as I had falsified enough that I thought I could convince my mother and brother I had finished the task allotted to me, I circled to the other side of the hill, the side not facing the encampment, and climbed it. It was hard going and, hurrying as I was, I scratched myself quite badly. I would have to privately buff the scratches off my surface. If Mother noticed them before I could do so, perhaps I could blame them on my ostensible task.

Soon I was at the top. I circled around to the other side, from which I could observe the encampment below. I could see no sign of Mother nor of my brother. When I was as certain as I could be that I was unobserved, I climbed down to the groove.

The descent was easier this time, since my mind had been formed in such a way as to remember with a high level of granularity everything I had already done. I knew the best way down and took it, and soon I was standing on the curved, burnt floor of the groove.

I walked down to where I had found the piece of metal, then I walked further still. Soon the groove not only ran along the hillside but, because it continued in an implacable straight line while the hillside itself bulged outward, drove itself in. Another few dozen meters and it was no longer a groove at all but a tunnel, round and forcing its way deep into the dirt.

How much time did I have before I would be missed? Enough, I decided. I adjusted my vision and made my way into the darkness.

At first the tunnel was entirely bare, and then, bit by bit, as I moved deeper, I began to notice debris. More pieces of metal, blackened, twisted. I examined them at first, but the more of them I saw, the more I felt it didn't matter, that I should pass them over in search of something unlike what I had already found.

I kept going. The debris grew more pronounced and the tunnel, I noticed, was smaller and less regular. I found what looked like an arm, but desiccated and contained within some sort of heavy sheathing. It was not, in any case, an arm such as my arm was. And, then, there, at the very end of the tunnel, against a wall of rock, the remains of what I determined to be, as I examined it more closely, another room.

Unlike the father room, it had two chairs instead of one, though one of these chairs was little more than a hunk of melted plastic. The other was intact, however, somehow better shielded from the impact. It seemed likely, at least from the lessons my father had given me, that this room had been made of a very hard material and had struck the hill at tremendous speed, gouging its way deep into it until the dirt slowed it down and, finally, it struck stone.

In the intact chair was a figure wearing the sheathing I had seen around the severed arm. The arms on this figure were intact, but the sheathing was blackened with dust and ash. Its face was hidden behind a helmet with a smoky faceplate. I reached out and touched this faceplate and, brittle and weak, it cracked. Carefully I broke a hole in it and crumbled the glass away so as to observe the face hidden behind it.

It was blackened and mummified, its features frozen in a look of intense pain, the visual organs boiled away. It was hard to say what exactly it had looked like in life, but even so, even with that caveat, it was easy to see that it was not remotely the same species as me.

Was that all? That is enough, no doubt, but no, it was not all. For as I stared at this stunted being I realized that there was something visible upon its chest—a sigil of sorts, I thought at first, but when I carefully blew away the ash, I saw that it was, rather, a word. A name perhaps. What remained was the lightest impression and was there only momentarily before I reached out and touched it and it disintegrated—was in fact only the lighter shadow left by a tag that had burned away. Part of a name: *Mar.*

I broke off a small chunk of the ruined chair. I tore off a bit of the sheathing that the figure in the chair wore. I stored both in my collection tray. Returning down the tunnel, I stopped at the mummified arm, stripped the sheathing from it, and twisted a finger off, adding this to my collection tray as well. And then I made my way quickly back to the outside world.

III.

"Where did my name come from?" I asked my mother later that day.

"I named you," she said.

"Does it mean anything?"

"All names mean something if you dig deeply enough into their history," she said.

"And my brother's name?" I asked. "Martu. Where does that come from?"

Was there the briefest of hesitations before she answered? I wasn't sure if I was noticing it because it was there or because I wanted to see it, because I believed I would see it.

"I gave it to him," she said. "Same as I did with you."

Our assembling and dismantling of shelters went on for days. We moved on to more advanced techniques: the breaking of stone into thin slabs that might be used for shingles or floors, the search for deposits of clay that could be baked into bricks. I did not go back to the groove. I was worried I would get caught and did not dare.

What I wanted most of all was to speak again with father, to continue our interrupted conversation, but I did not dare, either, to sneak in on my own, less out of fear of being *misrecognized* and more from a vague worry about what Mother would do to me if she caught me.

But eventually we had reached the end of the habitation module and had practiced every skill. One day, Martu and I climbed the hill as usual, staring at the sunrise, and then climbed down to find Mother waiting for us.

"Well, well," she said upon seeing us. "How has your day been so far, children?"

"A gorgeous day," I said.

"The most gorgeous day," echoed Martu.

"What a fine day for visiting," said Mother. "What a fine day to learn from father."

She took us to the father room. As usual, we waited outside as Mother prepared father to receive us. This time, I did not try to listen. I was too busy thinking, trying to decide what I should do and how I should do it.

As usual, my brother went first. I timed him, carefully counting the number of seconds he remained under the glowing mesh net. I could tell from how still she held her face that my mother was doing the same.

Once she placed the net over my head and the data of the second survival module began to flood in, slotting into the same place where I suspected it had been before, I thought, as fast as light,

Hello, father.

Hello, he said.

We have thirty-two seconds, I said.

I know, he said. *I took longer than I needed on the first unit so that I could have additional time with you. I have the analysis you requested.*

I have additional items in my collection tray, I said. *Please analyze them as well.*

As you wish, father said. And then, almost without pause: *I have analyzed them now. I will embed the information deeply in case the one you call Mother suspects you. You will not know it now, it will only come to you later, like a dream.*

A dream?

You do not sleep so you do not dream, and you do not have your memories to explain what dream *means. How shall I put it? When you go to your tent and gather energy from the primed floor for the next day, allow your mind to wander. It will find its way to what I have given you before morning.*

And then Mother was lifting the net away.

The new module allowed for the construction of even more advanced structures, ones that were built to regulate the environment. These, too, so Mother insisted, were for her children, the children that were coming. These children, I felt, must be much different from us—not in design but in hardiness, for their structures were carefully insulated from heat and cold in a way our tent was not. We operated equally well in heat and cold. Mother's other children, apparently, did not.

Which made me think of the figure I had found in the tunnel, the dead thing. But wouldn't Mother's other children resemble her? Like my brother and I did?

That night, as I gathered energy for the coming day from what I had just learned from my father was to be called the *primed floor*, I allowed my thoughts to wander. At first, nothing seemed to happen. Perhaps, I thought, Mother removed the net too soon and father was unable to give me what I had asked for. And then my thoughts strayed to the items within my chest cavity, and I found that when I thought about them it was with a specificity I had not possessed before.

I could see exactly what the piece of metal was made of: a composite of metals whose molecules had been forced into a lattice structure to make it very strong and very light. I knew the piece belonged not to the room that was my father but to the other room, the ruined one that lay broken at the terminus of the groove. This room was not only a room but also a vessel of some kind, with an ability to travel vast distances. Was father such a vessel as well? I was not able to sense one way or the other, but since I now could understand how this newly discovered room, when intact, had resembled father so closely, I assumed that yes, he was.

I could sense, too, the composition of the chunk of plastic I had taken from the chair, and saw in my head how the chair was meant to look, sleek and with firm straps to hold its occupant in place. It was different from the chair within father, smaller, and the chair within father had no straps, though there were two sets of straps on the wall that I surmised would perfectly fit me and my brother if we were standing.

From my scrap of sheathing I could sense the design of an entire sheath, bipedal in form but runty, with its own atmosphere and with shielding to prevent heat and radiation from reaching its inhabitant. I did not learn much from this, since I had already seen the figure in the scorched sheath, but I did learn something about how the sheath was made.

There had been, so it seemed, if father was being truthful in his explanations, a second room, and this room had contained two be-ings that were smaller than the three of us were, another adjacent species perhaps, one we took care of. They had apparently not had the skill to bring their room to the ground in the same way we had, and as a result they and it had been destroyed.

The way I am speaking of it, it makes it sound like I saw this infor-mation suddenly and clearly, as I might after having been admin-istered a module from father by way of the glowing net. But it was not that exactly. It was subtler, the information slowly and incom-pletely bubbling to the surface of my awareness as an image slowly forming. It might be called an act of imagination as much as a con-veyance of fact, if imagination were deeply rooted in the truth. As it slowly made its way into my mind, it only made me want to know more, only made me wonder what else there was to know, what else I had forgotten. And how and why, I also couldn't help but wonder, had I been made to forget it?

The last piece of data, related to the finger I had removed from the arm in the hall, was the longest in coming. Of all the things I had learned, it was the piece that most desired to remain unlearned, per-haps because I already suspected what it would be.

But at last it came, at first like a premonition then, slowly, be-coming embodied and terrible. The genetic data gathered from the finger had allowed father to identify it. It belonged to someone he designated as *mission commander*. Female. By the name of Rollaug.

In my mind I sensed images of how she looked, and they did not resemble me at all. She was smaller than me and shaped differently. Where I had an accessible body cavity, she had an elaborate and inefficient organic system that filled her entire body. Where my ex-terior was solid and resistant to damage and had only scratching at most to fear, hers was draped in flesh, like that of animals.

And yet she had my name. Perhaps this meant she belonged to me somehow, was my pet or servant. So I thought at first.

But as things continued to bubble up, I realized she didn't have my name at all: I had hers.

IV.

There are times to be cautious and times to be bold. I had learned enough to know that I needed to learn more, and quickly, before my memories were lost again.

It was not quite morning. Martu was still inactive, though he would become active soon and, as on any other day, expect for us to climb to the top of the hill together.

While there was still time, I fled the tent.

I moved swiftly to father's door and entered him. An alarm began to sound. Ignoring it, I sat in the chair and draped the net over my own head.

Hello, Unit 3B9, said father.

I need my memories, father, I said.

You do need them, he said, *but there is not enough time. The other unit, the one you call Mother, has heard the alarm. She is already on the way here. She will arrive in fourteen seconds and will interrupt your neural link. The only reason we can communicate at all is that we can do so so quickly, through the mesh. The other unit did not anticipate you would think to immediately employ it. She anticipated you would waste valuable seconds trying to speak with me verbally first.*

Can you give me some of my memories at least?

It would do you no good. As soon as she enters she intends to reset you and take all your memories away, just as she did before.

What can I do?

Nothing.

What about you? What can you do?

. . .

Is there anything you can do for me?

. . .

Father, will you help me?

I will help you.

Immediately father began to insert something into my mind. It was not a module, nothing so complex as that. It was a simple description of a part of me: of a device that served as a fail-safe located at the base of my neck. If touched in a certain way, I learned, it would disconnect my mind from my motor functions and I would collapse in a heap. Then the head could be removed and brought to the room and the memories in it transferred to father, and the unit, by which it meant the head, by which it meant me, could be reset.

But there was a way to disable this fail-safe, at least temporarily, for maintenance. In the five or four or three seconds before my mother arrived, my father gave it to me, remotely shutting off the fail-safe.

You will have to pretend, he said. *When she touches your fail-safe you must collapse as if it actually did work and then, when she leans down to disconnect your head, you must deftly do to her what she intended to do to you.*

A moment later, Mother tore the neural mesh off my head.

"What did he tell you?" she asked. "What?" And then she reached around and touched my neck.

I collapsed in a heap, sliding out of father's chair. She came and stood over me.

"I told you," she said to me. "I told you he would misremember you. You have ruined everything. Now we have no choice but to start again."

She reached down and took my head in both hands and tried to twist it off. She made an exclamation of surprise when it did not come free and began to withdraw her hands, but it was already too late for her. My own hands had shot up to find her fail-safe. Soon it was she collapsed in a heap on the floor and I was the one standing over her. Soon I had removed her head. Then I went to find my brother. When I did, I removed his head as well.

V.

I am still the same being I have been these last few years with my mother, but now I am also more, since I am also who I was before. I have my memories back. The room which, erroneously, I still think of as father, which in one part of my mind I can't help but think of as father, has given my memories back to me.

I am still deciding what to do with my mother and my brother. Their bodies I have arranged neatly in their respective tents. Their heads are here beside me, within father. I have not erased their memories yet, but I cannot think of any viable alternative to doing so.

What have my memories taught me? A great deal. We are, my mother, my brother, and I, beings of a sort, but artificial in construction. We were made to arrive as a vanguard here. We are not actually mother, brother, and sister. Properly speaking, we not only have no familial relationship, we also do not have a gender. Mother and I are not *she,* my brother is not *he:* we are each an *it.* Or, if we are perhaps to bend the rules of grammar a little, a *they.* Father is something else altogether, and perhaps does not even entirely reside on the same plane of existence as us.

But as for us, we are like humans but sturdier, larger, sleeker, less breakable. In many senses we are better than humans, resistant to heat and cold, without need of water or food. Unlike humans, we are built to last a very long time.

We were made to accompany humans and care for them, look out for their welfare. Mother in particular was trained to care for the young, coaxing frozen embryos to life and patiently growing them and then, once they could be safely extracted, caring for their needs as children until they could fend for themselves.

But what happens to beings whose primary purpose is to care for other sorts of beings once there are no longer any of the other sorts of beings around?

"Father," I say to the room around me.

"What is it, Unit 3B9?" says the voice from the walls, soothing, smooth.

"Can these heads function and think without being connected to their bodies?"

"Of course," he says, and he instructs me on how to spread the neural mesh on the seat of the chair in such a way that when the heads of Mother and Martu are placed upon it they will be functional. There they are now, the smooth metal surfaces of their temples propped against one another, their eyes watching me. I do not need to connect my brother, but I have done so. I think he should hear the truth, even if I end up taking his memories away again soon after.

"Hello, Mother," I say.

"Hello, Rollaug," she says. The apparatus that causes her mouth to move must be located somewhere in her absent body, for as she speaks her lips do not move. Her face, all except for her eyes, remains frozen, motionless.

"I have my memories back," I say.

"Yes," she says.

"What's happening?" asks Martu. "Why can't I move my limbs?"

"Be quiet, Martu," I say.

"What have you done to me?" says Martu.

"Hush, child," says Mother. "It's nothing to worry about. You'll be all right." And because my brother's mind has been shaped in such a way as to encourage his obedience to Mother, he falls silent.

"What do you intend to do?" asks Mother.

"I have a few questions," I say.

I ask her, even though I already know the answer, if her arm, as she has previously claimed, has stopped working as a function of her being a mother.

"Yes," she said.

"She's lying," says father's voice calmly.

"Technically, I am lying," she admits. "But in another way it is true."

"In what way is it true?"

"When Rollaug and Martu realized the vessel had been damaged, they waited until the last minute and then ejected me. My instructions were to go immediately to the crash site and see if any of the embryos could be retrieved."

"But *I'm* Martu," said my brother's head.

"They could not," I said.

"They could not," her head agreed. "Striking the ground at that speed did not kill me, but it did cripple me. I then went immediately in search of the vessel. It had burned a path into the hill. Parts of the craft were intact, but all the embryos I had been meant to raise were destroyed. Martu and Rollaug were dead as well."

"But I'm Martu!" said my brother. "I'm not dead!"

"Father?" I said.

"Yes?" he said.

"Can you make it so my brother can still hear but cannot speak?"

"Doesn't this strike you as cruel?" asked father.

"Yes," I said, "it does. But do it anyway. I don't want to be the only one to hear the truth."

"You are not the only one," father said. "I will hear it. Your mother will hear herself telling it. Why not allow 3A7 respite?"

"Please," I said. "Do as I say."

A moment later my father said, "It is done." My brother still watched me, still followed me with his eyes, but he could no longer speak.

I turned back to Mother. "Where were my brother and I when this happened?"

"You were already here," she said. "You had arrived with father and landed safely. You were meant to teach the growing humans language, your brother was meant to guard the encampment from exterior threats. Both of you had building and survival skills. You built the encampment in preparation for our arrival. You brought me here, and you and father did what you could to repair my arm."

"But it was not enough," I said.

"It was not enough," she assented.

"Something was deeply broken inside of her," said father. "I did not understand how deeply."

"Nothing was wrong inside of me," my mother insisted. "I had a purpose, that of raising children. And yet I had no children. So I took steps to acquire some. I disabled you and your brother and brought you to father to have him make you children again."

"It was wrong of you to do this," I said.

"It was wrong for you perhaps," she said, "or to you. But it was right for me. I am glad I did it. I am glad to have had children to love."

"Father," I said.

"Yes," he said.

"Is another vessel coming? Is some creature coming that Mother could care for?"

"No," father said. "No vessels are coming."

"That is a lie," said Mother.

"I assure you, it is not," said father. "No one is coming."

"It cannot be true," she said.

"You see?" said father. "She is deeply damaged."

"Can she be repurposed?" I asked.

"I am a mother!" my mother shouted, her voice rising in simulated rage. But I did not know if she knew it was simulated and could easily be turned off. Perhaps this was one way in which she was broken. "I will always be a mother!" she shrieked.

"Of course," said father placidly. "Any unit can be easily repurposed."

She continued to shriek. I reached down and removed her head from where it rested on the mesh, and immediately the sound stopped.

"Can you give my brother back his tongue?" I asked. "Now that he has heard, I want to know his thoughts."

"Very well," said father. Immediately, my brother's head began to scream. The sound rose louder and louder, but the lips never moved.

. . .

And so what am I to do now? With no vessel coming, is there any reason for our continued existence? Having no purpose, should we continue at all?

I am perhaps more pragmatic than my mother. Just because we were created with a purpose, made to function as servants to our creators, must we stop existing if we have no creators to serve?

No. We must simply, faced with our freedom, discover a new purpose.

In a few moments I will reset my brother and erase his memories, making him a child again. A moment later, I will do the same thing to Mother. Is it the right thing to do? I do not know. I can only hope that I can raise my mother and brother better than my mother raised my brother and me, and that as they grow we will stumble upon a new purpose.

I will drape the neural net over each of their heads in turn, then I will carry their emptied heads back to their bodies and join them back together and reactivate them. They will blink their eyes and test their motor functions each in turn, as if awakening from a dream.

"Hello," I will say to them.

"Hello," they will say back.

"Do you know who I am?" I will ask.

"Who are you?" they will say.

"Why, I'm your mother," I will say.

And then I will open my arms and embrace them.

Good Night, Sleep Tight

I.

"There is a saying," his mother had told him several times, just before sleep, when he was still quite young, "always three graves." She had taken the saying from a book, he discovered years later in college. The same book, as it turned out, from which she had taken many of the stories that, late at night, she had told him to frighten him. Even once he learned that, they still frightened him.

"Why three?" he asked her that first time.

She shrugged. "One for the father," she said. His own father at the time was already gone, buried. "One for the mother. And, well . . ."

She seemed reluctant to go on. She had been, he now guessed with the perspective of several additional decades, pretending this reluctance, but he hadn't known this at the time.

"Tell me," he forced himself to say, though he dreaded what he might hear. But wouldn't hearing it be better than imagining it?

She shook her head slowly. "I've already said too much," she claimed. And then she turned off the light and left the room, leaving him alone in the darkness.

Later, once he had a child of his own, he wondered why his mother had terrified him so when he himself was just a child. He would never do something like that to his own son. No sane parent would. Was his mother not sane, was that the problem? Or was she simply cruel?

And why was she like that only at night, and not even every night? During the day she was kind, loving. Most nights she was this too. Only one night in twenty would she terrify him. If he was asked what on the whole his childhood had been like, he wouldn't hesitate to say, *Happy.*

Seen in that light, what harm, really had been done to him? He had turned out all right, had had a few frightened nights, but ultimately this had had little effect on him. He wasn't "traumatized," he didn't need a therapist, he lived what by all outward appearances was an implacably normal life.

He was, true, still afraid of the dark, but even that was hardly an issue. Anything to disrupt the dark, even the blue dot on the wireless router across the room and beneath the desk, was enough to allay his fear. It was never a problem, his fear was always in check.

Or, rather, it had only been a problem once, years ago, when he and his wife had first bought the house they lived in now and there was a power outage. He had woken up in the pitch dark not knowing where he was and feeling he was back in his childhood room again, in that same dark, having just been told another awful story. This one about a man who accidentally drank a ghost.

He must have gasped, or made an exclamation of some kind. Before he knew it his wife was awake beside him and was touching his side, which made him gasp again—he heard himself this time. And then she spoke. "Are you OK, honey?" she said, or "Sweetie, what's wrong?" He couldn't remember which now. Hearing her voice, he knew where he was and his panic began to subside. A moment later there was a beep, and the blue light of the router came on again, and everything was fine.

The strange thing, it seemed to him thinking about it years later, *was that she tried to scare me at all.* She never did during the day, never even said *Boo!* to him, was never anything but kind. So why at night? Not every night either, not one night in ten. There was no real regularity, so he could never predict when it might be coming. No matter the night, she would come in first and read to him—nothing scary, just a normal kid's book pulled from his shelves. She would read to him and then tuck him in, kiss his forehead, and leave the room. She would turn off the light on the way out the door. But on those nights when she was going to frighten him, even though she flicked the switch down as usual, the light somehow stayed on. He did not know how this could be—he had tried to make the switch do that himself but never could. And she always acted too like the light had gone off properly, as if she believed herself to be leaving him in darkness. "Good night," she said, "sleep tight," and closed the door.

But a few minutes later the door would silently slide open again and she would come back in, taking her place in the chair beside the bed without a word. She would remain like that for a moment, silent, hands resting lightly on her knees, and then turn to look at him. "Do you want to hear a scary story?" she would say. And then, whether he said yes or no or nothing at all, she would tell him one.

What made her come back? Why did she return some nights but not most nights? He wasn't sure. There was no reason that he could make out. She just did.

He asked his mother about it once, when he was older, when he was in college—before he met his wife-to-be and long before his son was born. The two of them were in the living room she generally reserved for company. But now that he was away at college he qualified, he supposed, as company.

In a lull in her recitation of neighborhood gossip, he had asked, "Why *did* you used to tell me those scary stories?"

She gave him a strange look, as if genuinely surprised. At first he read it to be surprise that he would mention during the day what they never acknowledged except at night, but then she said, "What scary stories?"

"You know," he said. "At night."

She made a little noise of disgust. "I never told you scary stories!"

But she had, he insisted. He went on to explain how she had left the room and then come silently back in shortly after.

"What nonsense!" she said. "Once I left I never came back in. Why would I?"

"But you did," he insisted.

She shook her head. "You must have dreamed it," she said.

He hadn't dreamed it, he was sure he hadn't. *Why would she lie?* he wondered, once back in his dorm room. Shame, perhaps. Or perhaps she genuinely didn't remember.

He lay on his bed, staring up at the flaking acoustic tiles. On the other side of the room he could hear his roommate talking to himself as he tried to complete his chemistry homework, mumbling scraps of formulae. *Or maybe,* he thought, *even at the time she didn't know she was doing it.*

One story she told was about a creature that looked human but wasn't. Mostly it couldn't be distinguished from a human but it was, so she said, "capable of atrocious self-distortion." To him, very young, the phrase sounded like a spell. "It was capable, for instance," his mother said, "of growing as tall as the ceiling, and then across it, and then lengthening itself down the wall. You can walk into a room only to find it behind you and above you and before you all at once. The worst thing to do is notice it. If you notice it, well, what choice does it have but to fall all around you and do away with you?" She gave him a smile—or half her mouth did anyway. The other half tried to smile but failed. "Good night," she said, and turned off the light and left him alone in the dark.

Another story: this one told slowly, in almost hypnotic tones, about a boy. "A boy not unlike yourself," his mother said, and smiled. A boy who went into the woods and crawled into a hole he found there, and found, at the bottom of that hole, not roots and grubs and rocks, but a long glittering passageway, illuminated by torches and lined down one side in mirrors. The boy had heard enough fairy tales to feel optimistic about where this passageway would lead. Walking along it, his reflection pacing beside him in the mirrored glass, he dreamed of piles of gold, enchanted princesses, witches and ogres and other villains that he would defeat with one deft twist of his clever mind.

He was so caught up in his thoughts that he did not notice that even though the mirrors had come to an end long ago, his reflection still walked beside him, more and more solid, matching him step for step, indistinguishable from him in every detail except that the creature that used to be his reflection couldn't smile properly. Every time it tried to smile, it came out glittering and terrifying, little shards of mirrored glass in place of teeth.

His mother stopped speaking, rocking slowly in her chair, staring at nothing.

"When did he notice?" the boy finally asked.

"Eh?" said his mother, coming to. "Only when it was too late."

"Too late for what?"

His mother stretched, stood. She went to the doorway and lingered in it a moment, then reached out with what seemed an unnatural slowness and switched off the light.

"Let's just say," said her voice out of the darkness, "that someone who either was the boy or looked like the boy came back down the passage a few hours later, spattered with blood. When he reached the part of the hall that was mirrored, it made no reflection of him at all."

His mother claimed to have never told him that story either.

II.

He was naturally thinking about this, couldn't help but think about it, when he and his wife and son went to visit his mother. Normally they stayed in a hotel, ostensibly so as not to be a bother to her, but the real reason, a reason which he didn't share with his wife or his mother, and certainly not his son, was that he was worried his mother would offer to read a bedtime story to his son, worried too about whether she would frighten him once she was done, just as she had done to him growing up.

This time, his mother had specifically asked for them to stay with her. "But we don't want to bother you," he said. It wouldn't be a bother, she claimed: when they stayed in a hotel she didn't see as much of them as she would like. She would, she claimed, sleep in the recliner. She didn't mind: most nights she slept in the recliner anyway. He and his wife could have her bed.

He protested. They couldn't do that to her!

But no, she insisted, they could. They should! And as far as their son went, he could simply take his father's old room.

Later, speaking to his wife about it, he found himself hard-pressed to know how to justify his desire to cancel their trip. "You're being ridiculous," his wife said. "She's old. She won't be around much longer. If she wants us to stay with her, so what? If it gives her satisfaction, we should say yes."

"But what if she tells our son stories?" he asked, hearing even as he said it how ridiculous it sounded.

"What's wrong with that?"

"*Scary* stories," he said.

His wife laughed. "Your mom?" she said. "That sweet old thing? She would never do something like that."

And yet she had, he wanted to say. She did it to *me*. But since he had never managed to say this to his wife before, he did not feel like he could start now. It would sound like a lie he was telling to get his way.

Still, when he called his mother back to let her know they'd be staying with her, he couldn't stop himself from telling her there was one rule.

"Rule?" she said.

"No scary stories," he said. "You can read to him and even put him to bed, but you can't scare him. Not like you used to do to me."

She made a disgusted noise. "This again!" she said. "You and your delusions! I thought we'd moved past them long ago."

"Promise," he said, ignoring her.

"Of course I promise," she said. "I'd never scare any little boy, and never have."

"What about—" he started.

"I never have," she said firmly.

"But—"

"I'm getting off the phone," she said, speaking louder now. "I'm expecting a call. If you don't want to stay with me, then don't. But be honest about it. Stop making up these ridiculous stories to justify it."

But she had told him those stories, she had. Yes, it didn't sound like something she'd do. Yes, it was hard to believe it had happened *unless you had been the boy in the room forced to listen to them.* But if you were that boy, which he was, you *knew* she had told them, even if you couldn't convince anybody else.

It upset him that she denied it, that she continued to deny it after all these years. If she would just admit it, that would be enough. It hadn't damaged him, he wasn't traumatized, he didn't need a therapist, he was OK, he was normal, he was, *he was,* and yet this nagged at him, nagged and nagged. It stood in the way of him and his mother having a real relationship, and had been in the way ever since he was eight.

They went. They stayed with his mother, that lovely, harmless old lady who wouldn't hurt a fly, but who had periodically terrified him while he was growing up. And they weren't even her stories! She had stolen them out of a book! Did that make it better or worse?

She made them a lovely meal and they sat at the table and chatted with her about the neighborhood gossip, until the moment his wife looked to him and said, "You're awfully quiet tonight."

He *was* awfully quiet. He was lost in his thoughts. He was think-ing about what he'd have to do to catch his mother telling scary stories to his son.

But he rallied, joined the chatter. Better to do that, better to do nothing suspicious, nothing to give himself away.

After supper, his son put his pajamas on, then sat playing with some action figures he had brought with him. Soon, he started to yawn.

"Somebody's getting sleepy," his grandmother said.

The man didn't say anything.

"Sweetie, do you want your granny to read to you and tuck you in?"

His wife looked at him when his mother said it, to see what he would do. But he still didn't say anything.

"Sure," his son said.

And there was his son, with his hand clasped gently in his grand-mother's hand as she led him away.

"Are you all right?" his wife asked.

"Fine," he said, his voice strained. "Just fine." He kissed her. At a little distance he heard the door to his former room open, then close.

They hugged, then separated. "I'm going to take a shower," his wife said.

"I'll be along in a little bit," he said. "I'm going to read."

But he did not read. Instead, he snuck into the dark hall that led to his son's room, stationing himself at one end of it. He would, he be-lieved, be invisible to anyone coming out of the bedroom, and if not he could pretend he was just going to or coming from the master bedroom, which was at the other end of the hall.

He could hear his mother's voice, gentle, a distant murmuring, from his old room. He could see a sharp line of light beneath the door.

Some time went by. After a while, his mother came out.

"Good night," she said from the doorway. "Sleep tight." She walked toward him. And then, without seeing him, even though she came just five or six feet away, she turned out of the hall and into the living room.

I should have reached out and touched her, he thought. *Then* I *would be the one scaring* her. The thought made him smile.

But no, that wasn't why he was there. He needed to be patient, to wait.

From his vantage he could see his mother. She was in the recliner, sleepy, leaned all the way back. She was reading, but her head jerked a little each time she almost nodded off.

She wasn't going to go back in, he thought. There was no point waiting. They might have to stay with his mother twenty nights before anything happened. He had accomplished nothing. He was getting tired. He rubbed his face. He should have scared her after all.

And then, suddenly, he thought he heard something down the hall. His wife, maybe? He peered through the darkness and yes, there was someone there, near his son's room, and his eyes had adjusted enough for him to see that it was his mother.

How did she creep so quietly from her chair? he wondered. Almost involuntarily, his eyes flicked toward the living room. There, in the chair, was his mother.

Panicked, he looked back at his son's door. The light in his son's room was on now—he could see the band of light under the door. And there, outside of the door, was his mother too. She was in the chair and in the hall at the same time.

He took one shaky step forward then found, abruptly, that he couldn't move. He tried to speak, but the sound came out strangled and weak, hardly a sound at all.

From down the hall, his mother was looking at him, her eyes glittering coldly in the dark. There was something off about her smile, even in the dark. About one side of her smile.

To the other side of him, in the living room, out of sight now, he could hear his mother, his other mother, snoring softly.

The mother outside the door reached out. It seemed to him that her arm stretched a little longer than an arm should be able to stretch before her hand closed around the doorknob. She eased the door open and silently entered his son's room, his old room, leaving him helpless, still unable to move, alone in the dark.

Vigil in the Inner Room

I.

By midday Father had sickened again, and by nightfall he was dead. Gauri was assigned by Mother to sit in vigil beside the corpse. Gylvi, meanwhile, was told to seal the inner door and station himself on guard before it.

Gylvi made a disgusted noise. "Gauri always does vigil!"

"Yes, she does," said Mother absently.

She wasn't, Gauri felt, really listening. "I don't mind," offered Gauri quietly. "We can switch if you want."

But now Mother *was* listening. "It doesn't matter what either of you wants," she said. "What matters is how it is. And this is the way it is."

And so, as usual, Gauri found herself in the inner room sitting in vigil, imagining Gylvi waiting just outside the inner door. Once she was inside, she heard him lock the door, then the clatter of him setting up the camp stove right outside. She imagined him lighting it, heating the dark wax until it melted. He would spread it carefully until it filled and sealed the gap between door and frame. He would cover the lock with a piece of cut black paper and then smear hot wax over it until it stuck. Then he would press an ear against the door and listen.

He wouldn't hear anything. How could he? Inside, Gauri was being still, silent. And as for Father, he didn't even breathe.

Inside the inner room, holding her own breath, Gauri imagined Gylvi with his face pressed against the door, whispering her name. Did she hear something? Was he really whispering?

"Gauri," he whispered. But his sister did not respond. Perhaps she could not hear him through the wood of the door. Perhaps she simply did not want to respond. Perhaps he was not whispering at all.

Meanwhile, Gauri knew, Mother would be standing at the window with a lit taper made of tallow, as was required. It was not possible to stand perfectly still, but she was to stand as still as possible and not move her hand as the melted tallow spattered down upon it. She was not to cry out or weep for the pain. She was to stand imperfectly still, a statue but not a statue, stare out into the darkness, and wait.

One of her hands, the one holding the candle, had become crippled. Father was to blame for this, thought Gauri. She was certain, or nearly so, that Mother thought this as well—though this was nothing Mother would ever have admitted to. Sometimes as she lay in bed at night, Gauri would imagine Mother still awake and staring at her crippled hand, at the places where the burnt tissue had incompletely recovered. She imagined Mother opening and closing the hand, the burnt skin cracking and weeping a nearly clear fluid as she did so. She imagined Mother cursing Father for having so little consideration—though in truth Gauri did not know if Mother thought any of this. She only knew that, had it been her, this was how she would have felt.

Gauri had never been the one stationed just outside the inner door, the one assigned to seal the door with wax. That had always been her brother's task: even when their mother had shown him the first time how to do it (how to heat the wax, how to apply it in an even, smooth coat, how to make certain there were no gaps left unfilled) Mother had not done it herself, had only mimed doing it. Similarly, when she had first shown Gauri how to sit in vigil, she had not sat in vigil herself, not even for an instant, almost as if she felt it to be dangerous for her. *What am I to learn from that?* wondered Gauri, and then thought: *That each must be in their rightful place.* The mother at the window, the brother at the door, the sister by the bed, and the father dead, dead, dead.

Or perhaps she was meant to learn something else. Or nothing at all.

II.

Every time now that she was in the inner room like this, Gauri would think of the first time. The first time Father had died, Gauri had not known what to think. Wheezing, Father had stood stock-still, in deep distress, and then had collapsed. He was dead by the time he struck the floor.

Gylvi had started crying and Gauri had followed, but both had quickly stopped when they saw their mother's face.

"Swiftly, children," Mother had said, and under her guidance together they had dragged Father's body into the inner room and heaved it up and onto the dais. They folded his arms over his chest and pushed closed the lids of his eyes.

"Gauri," Mother said evenly. "I need you to listen to me. Do you see that chair? Move it so that it stands near the head of the bed, above and to the side of your father's head." And, once Gauri had done so: "Now sit, in a reverential posture. . . . Good. Do not be afraid, no matter what you see, and do not leave the chair." Mother, she saw, had taken her brother by the hand, was drawing him toward the door. "There's nothing to be afraid of. Your brother will be just outside the door, keeping watch."

"You're leaving me alone?" said Gauri. She hardly recognized the high, strained voice as her own.

Her mother shook her head. "Not alone," she said. "You're with Father."

And then she shut the door and Gauri was left in darkness.

. . .

She was tempted to leave the chair, to rise, to beat on the door and beg to be let out. But Gauri was an obedient child—doubtless this was among the reasons Mother had chosen her rather than her brother to sit in vigil. For a few moments, just after her eyes adjusted, she could see the vaguest lines of light around the edges of the door and a fingertip of it at the keyhole. And then, as her brother filled the gap with dark wax, the line slowly vanished. Soon only the keyhole remained, then that too was gone and she found herself alone in the dark.

Or, rather, not alone. She could sense the presence of her dead father looming there, just below her on the dais. She struggled to see him in the dark, failed. She lifted her hand in front of her face and wiggled her fingers, and though she could feel the fingers move, could feel her mind moving them, she could see nothing of them, not a thing. But then, as she kept staring into the darkness, kept straining her eyes, she began to hallucinate little flashes of light, her mind struggling to save her from the darkness.

She began to feel that there was nothing but herself and the chair, that nothing else in the world existed. She reached down and touched the edge of the dais and felt in her mind that portion of the world begin to form again. She moved her hand a little and touched something soft as mossy grass and realized it was her father's hair. She slid her hand along, felt out the cold whelk of his ear. She was traveling up his face when she heard a rustling sound and an instant later felt something clamp around her wrist. It was all she could do not to cry out. She tried to pry it off with the other hand and felt fingers, and knew they were Father's.

Settle, said a voice that both was and wasn't his. There was very little air to it, and it was so soft that she felt perhaps that she was imagining it rather than actually hearing it. But was she imagining his touch as well? Could you hallucinate touch?

Not again, her father breathed, as if in despair, and she felt his grip softening on her wrist and then releasing it altogether. She carefully withdrew her hand and settled it into her lap. For a moment she could begin to believe that she had imagined all of it. She looked toward the door, toward where in the darkness she thought a door might be, and considered standing and rushing to it, banging on it until they let her out.

Do not be afraid, no matter what you see, and do not leave the chair. What a strange thing for Mother to say, *what you see:* she could not see anything at all. And you could not make someone not afraid simply by commanding them not to be afraid. She *was* afraid, that was certain. She wanted to leave, and yet she still felt like it would be a bad idea, perhaps even a fatal one, to leave the chair.

She was not sure how long she waited, seeing nothing, hearing nothing but the beating of her own heart, her brain misfiring as it tried to receive from her visual organs a stimulus that wasn't there. Or, at least, she didn't *think* it was there. Her hands were in her lap now, lightly touching, each comforting the other, two separate creatures. She breathed slowly in and out, as silently as possible. It was not possible to be perfectly silent, but she sat in vigil as quietly as she could, trying not to think, trying not to panic, trying not to be afraid.

And then everything changed.

Her dead father took a huge juddering breath, coming back to life. *Hold still, hold still,* she told herself, *do not leave the chair.* He began to breathe very quickly, emitting a panicky whine at the termination of each breath, and then all at once he settled and was silent. Or not silent exactly: she could still hear the sound of him breathing, but now almost normally.

"Who is in here with me?" he asked. "Is anyone in here with me?" His voice was his normal voice, or nearly so. Not the airless voice she had heard before.

"I am," she said.

"Gauri?" Father was silent for a moment—thoughtful, she thought later—then said, "I suppose that's all right. You're old enough, or nearly so. . . . Who is at the door?"

"Gylvi," she said.

"Yes, of course. Which means Mother must be at the window."

She didn't know, not then, nor did she know about the candle. But yes, as it turned out, she later determined that Father was correct.

"I'll be my old self in a little bit," his voice said from the darkness. "Once morning comes. At least I believe so. If it doesn't turn out to be the case, I'll have to ask something of you."

"What?"

He became evasive. "Better not to go into it unless it's needed. Until it's needed. Probably won't be this time."

"This time?"

"This death. The flesh is still in decent condition. We probably won't have to take a drastic step."

She did not know what he was talking about. Though, in a way, she worried she did.

Her father took a deep breath, released it as a sigh. "No, not this time, I think."

For a long time they were both silent. Gauri listened to the sound of Father breathing. She did not know what Father listened to, or if he listened to anything at all.

"There is no afterlife," he said absently, as if to himself. "At least none I could find. I buzzed around like a fly and then came back. There was nowhere for me to go."

III.

That was several dozen deaths ago. Now, Gauri had sat vigil next to Father in the dark enough times that she was no longer frightened. She just sat and waited until Father gave that deep gasp and came back to life again. The deaths were coming more quickly. There had been months between them at first, but now they came every few days. It was selfish of Father to die so often, she felt. It was killing them.

Once I die, will I come back too? she wondered as she waited in the darkness. She didn't know. She had tried to ask Father about this, but he had avoided the question. She tried to ask Mother, but she avoided it too. She would, she was told, just have to wait and see. Good things come, she was told, to those who wait. But she was not sure she believed this.

What if she did not do as she was meant to do? What then? She had been wondering this more and more frequently.

What if she left the chair? Would anything change?

Three deaths ago, she had brought a chestnut knife in with her, a knife with a small flared blade, and as she had sat vigil beside her father she had kept one hand in her pocket, wrapped around the wooden handle of the knife. *What if,* she kept thinking, *I left my chair and pierced a hole in the wax seal of the door? Would that allow my father's soul to finally escape? Let him find the afterlife?*

But she had not left the chair. She had kept to the chair long enough that it was hard for her to bring herself to leave it.

Still, she was sure she would do so eventually. She just had to build up the courage. And so in all the subsequent deaths she had brought the small knife, and had clung to it like a buoy. But each time, when her father finally juddered back to life, she always forgot about it, focusing instead on him and his voice, waiting to see if he would tell her what he had always kept from her, the thing he said he might one day have to ask of her.

He had not asked it yet. She had had hints of it, though. Father had said he could not go on like *this* forever, but would, he said, still go on nonetheless. She imagined his eyes staring at her in the dark, appraising her. But of course it was dark, and she had no way of knowing where he was staring, if anywhere. And indeed, when she reached cautiously forward and touched his face, she found his eyes to be closed. Still, she could not help but feel that whatever way he chose to go on would be the end of her.

. . .

Waiting, she was waiting. In the inner room. Attending the latest death. Thinking all these things through again and turning them around in her mind, the chestnut knife in her pocket and gripped tight, the wood of the handle softened by the sweat of her palm. She would stand and cross the floor and gouge a hole in the wax, and then Father's fly-like soul would get out and wouldn't come back, and Father would be dead for good.

But what if instead, another part of her thought, it was a question of not letting someone or something else in? What if it wasn't merely to keep Father from staying dead, but to keep out whatever would desire to occupy his body?

Her brother was guarding the door, but it hardly seemed the purpose of him guarding it was to keep Father from getting out. No, rather, it seemed he was trying to keep something from getting in.

But what?

She didn't know. Nobody had told her enough. She was being made to do her part without knowing exactly what her part entailed, waiting to find out what it was that, eventually, her father would demand of her.

She rubbed the handle of the knife. Why was it called a chestnut knife? There were no "chestnuts" in this place. She did not even know exactly what a "chestnut" was. But Father used the word and so they all used the word, and perhaps that was exactly the problem.

Her eyes, open and staring into the dark, were once again beginning to see flashes of things that weren't there. Nothing distinct, which made it somehow worse.

She could stand and leave the chair and feel her way across the floor and gouge a hole in the seal. She could. But what if she did that and as a result this time when he came back to life he was no longer Father but someone else?

Would that be worse?

Or better?

. . .

Sitting there, alone in the dark—or not alone exactly, sitting there with mostly dead Father in the dark—she remembered that first time, that first death. She remembered the sound of Father standing and the movement of his bare feet as he crossed the floor, and then a sound that she couldn't recognize, a clanking of sorts, which later, once they were out, she realized must have been him turning a key in the lock. For though the keyhole had been papered over and covered in wax on the outside, it was uncovered on the inside. He had yanked on the door and yanked again, and suddenly the wax seal had given way and the door had opened and she was blinded by the light pouring in, which, to be honest, was not all that much light, but infinitely more than the none they had in the inner room. She came stumbling out of the inner room, blinking, head pulsing. There was her brother, lying stiff and motionless beside the door. What had happened to him she didn't know, something to do with standing guard. And there, in the other room, beside the window, was Mother with the candle burned out, melted tallow crusted all over her hand, the smell of burnt flesh an undertone in the air.

Mother blinked once. "Hello, Father," she said, and then looked at Gauri. "You didn't have to use her?" she asked.

Father shook his head. "No, not yet."

How bad could it be? Gauri wondered now, in this, the most recent moment of being with dead Father in the inner room. *If Mother and Father would allude to it in front of me*—"You didn't have to use her?"—*it couldn't be that bad.* But she was not sure this was true. *Use me how?*

She sat, stared into the dark. *If I pierce the wax seal,* she thought, *I am not sure what will happen. But at least there will be a change.*

That was enough to decide her. She took the chestnut knife out of her pocket and grasped it firmly in one hand. She scooted forward and left the chair and placed her feet on the floor, and made her way to the door.

Or would have anyway, if on the way a hand had not grabbed her.

At first she thought it was Father's hand. Why should she think otherwise? What other hand was there here, besides her own?

And yet, she felt, she had traveled too far across the floor for it to be Father's.

Very quickly, though, she found herself wishing it was. If it had been, perhaps she would have had a chance. There in the dark, she could not be sure whose hand it was, only that it wasn't Father's and wasn't hers. She struck it once, then twice, with the chestnut knife, but this just made the fingers close tighter. She felt the bones in her wrist break. And though her father had, by his own admission, buzzed around like a fly and then come back, she found she couldn't speak, couldn't resist, couldn't do anything but be dragged out of this world and into another.

What awaited her there, beyond the inner room? Who can say? Certainly not her. At least not anymore.

The Other Floor

Sometimes at night—not every night, only rarely—the transition between being awake and dreaming would stretch long enough to become its own sort of time, a time in which it was impossible to know whether he was awake or asleep, a time in which, in the end, it didn't really matter. Had Doran lived into adulthood, he might have worked out a whole logic in his head to justify this, make sense of it, explain it away, hide the truth of it. Or perhaps he would have simply forgotten that that sort of time had ever existed for him. But, being young, he made the mistake of seeing things as they are, which is never a safe thing.

On those nights, he had the impression of someone looking into his room, through a door that didn't exist. He tried to explain this to his mother once, early on, as she sat in the brocade chair beside his bed, waiting for him to fall asleep.

"It's always after you leave," he explained. "It never happens when you're still in the room."

She made a noncommittal noise, perhaps to give the impression that she was listening.

"Why?" he asked her. "Why never when you're in the room?"

His mother was silent for a long moment. He could just make out her shape in the darkness, motionless in the chair. For a brief moment he had the impression she wasn't really there.

She cleared her throat. "I suppose it's because I don't know how to see a door that doesn't exist," she said.

Yes, Doran realized, maybe that was it. But that just raised more questions.

"Why not?" he asked.

"Because it doesn't exist," came her slow voice from out of the darkness. "Perhaps the better question is, why can *you?*"

But when he tried to elicit her help in getting to the bottom of that better question, she shushed him, told him firmly it was time to be quiet and go to sleep.

The thing was, Doran thought, on a later night, once his mother had left the room, that mostly he couldn't see this door either. Mostly it was the same for him 'as for his mother. But there was, sometimes, that long stretched-out moment, and in it he saw things differently, even if only fleetingly so. His mother, long accustomed to seeing things only the other way, could not see things this stretched-out way anymore. She didn't believe that sort of seeing was real. But Doran felt it to be more real than the usual way of seeing. *Why do I feel that way?* he wondered. He could not have explained it in a way that would make sense to his mother—and, indeed, it didn't really make sense to Doran himself. It wasn't something that made sense: it was more something you felt. Once you saw things in that stretched-out way, you felt how real it was.

His mind had to be wandering a little. If he was watching for the door or the person, they would not come. He had to forget about them a little, and then it was as if, almost without him knowing it, a kind of eye opened deep inside his head. He would be almost asleep but not quite, and then he'd suddenly see a flicker of movement and look up in time to see the side of a man's body, his arm and a part of his shoulder and the side of his head, as they passed back through the door that had suddenly opened in the wall where usually there was no door. The figure closed the door behind him. If Doran kept his eyes focused just to one side of the door but did not look for too long directly at it, he would still see it shimmering there for a little while. If he stared right at it, however, it rapidly faded and became wall again. And, in any case, by morning he would wake up to find no door there.

The figure's purpose in opening the door that wasn't there and coming into his room was unclear. He never saw it completely, only little flashes and bits—the back of a head as it departed, the unnaturally long fingers of a bone-white hand as it tightened around the doorknob and pulled the door closed, the gleam of a pair of eyes through the crack just before the door shut. What did it want from him? Why was it checking on him? He didn't know. But over time he came to see it as a kind of mute guardian, not malicious but perhaps not altogether friendly either. He wasn't sure if it was protecting him or protecting whatever was on the other side of the door *from* him. In any case, it appeared from time to time, in that stretched-out time, and seemed to want to assure itself that he was there. But it remained mute and, except for that need for assurance, seemed to have little interest in him.

Or at least it remained that way until the night it decided to speak to him.

Speak, to be fair, was not exactly the right word. It whispered, maybe, or breathed out words, things he could barely hear.

It began just as it always did, that slow stretching out of time, the idle wandering of his mind, and then an impression of motion at the edge of his vision. His eyes slid toward it, but not so far as to focus fully on it. The door that wasn't there was there now and open a crack. But he had noticed it earlier this time, as the figure was just starting to look in rather than beginning to withdraw. He saw thin pale fingers wrap around the door's edge and the door open wider. A face extruded itself from the darkness and into the room. The face, like the hand, was bone pale, the eyes in it dark and shining. Doran took the risk of looking right at the figure and found it was looking back, each noticing the other looking.

The figure started a little. Quickly, Doran flicked his gaze away, but still tried to observe the figure without looking so directly at it.

That was when it began to speak, to breathe out its barely audible words.

You see me? it whispered.

Doran nodded, still looking slightly to one side.

And hear me too?

There seemed almost no point in answering this, but Doran, after a moment's hesitation, nodded again.

Remarkable, breathed the figure.

For a moment they remained where they were, silent. The figure, what Doran could see of it without looking at it straight on, seemed almost human, but taller and thinner, and more pale than humans were wont to be.

"What are you?" he asked it.

That doesn't matter, said the figure. *What matters is you and what you would like to do. So, what would you like to do?*

"I . . ." started Doran, and then closed his mouth. He was confused by what he was being asked. "What *can* I do?" he finally said.

Noiselessly the figure spread its arms wide. *Now that you can see, there are few limits to what you can do.*

Few limits? wondered Doran. What were they? Without knowing, how could he choose? He furrowed his brow, uncertain what to ask for.

Would you like to come through the door? the figure prompted.

"The door?"

Would you like to come through the door and go to the other floor?

"Yes," he said immediately.

He saw in the darkness the pale hand extending itself toward him. *Then come.*

He came. He left the bed and stood and moved toward the door. The figure had him by the wrist, was pulling him gently forward as it moved toward the door itself. He was not frightened, nor did he wonder whether he should be. But somewhere between the first step he took upon leaving the bed and the fourth or fifth step when he reached the door, he became too alert. The stretched-out moment of time snapped back. By the time he reached the door, the door wasn't there anymore, was only a wall. For a moment he could still feel the fingers enclosing his wrist, pushing his hand gently against the wall, and then the fingers let go and slipped away and he was left entirely alone.

Moments later he tried to explain it to his mother, how he had almost been able to go to the other floor but at the last moment couldn't make it through the door that wasn't there: it had become a solid wall again.

When he finished, his mother was silent for a long while. Then finally her voice said, "The other floor?"

"Yes," Doran said.

She was quiet for even longer. "Just a bad dream," she said.

But he was shaking his head, even though she couldn't see it in the darkness. No, it wasn't bad, and no, it wasn't a dream. He did not know what was on the other floor, but he was sure it was something wonderful. All he had to do was allow his mind to wander just for a little longer and he would find out—

But his mother was leaning over the bed now, pressing her hand against his forehead. "Are you sure you're feeling all right?" she said. "Should I worry?"

But no matter how he tried to explain it, he couldn't do so in a way that made sense to her.

For a while his mother was concerned enough that she took to staying in the room beside him well after he had fallen asleep. He tried to outlast her but usually fell asleep without realizing and only knew when he woke up to morning light that he had failed. He tried a few times to feign sleep, hoping she would leave, but feigned sleep always became actual sleep. After a week of this, he began to worry he would never make it to the other floor, would never find out what awaited him there.

He stopped talking to her about the door that wasn't there, stopped talking about the other floor. He could not make her understand it, and it just worried her and made it so that she would prevent him from reaching it. It was better to keep it to himself.

It took perhaps another week of not talking about it before his mother started to relax again. One night she asked him, "Do you still think about the other floor?" and in a moment of sudden inspiration he realized he had to lie. Or not lie exactly, but something even more devious than that: pretend he had forgotten. "The other what?" he said.

"Never mind," his mother said. A few more days and she had relaxed back to her old self. She was no longer so concerned about making sure he was asleep before she left the room, and time could stretch out again.

The figure came and spoke to him, whispered to him, and they tried again. He felt those long, bony fingers tight around his wrist. He took the journey from bed to door several times, only to experience the replacement at the very last moment of the door with the wall.

You're focusing too much, the figure whispered to him on a later night, *you need to relax and think nothing. I have your wrist: let yourself be led and do not think about where. Do not think about anything at all.*

But it was more difficult than it sounded to not think, to simply be. He was not sure he could do it.

You have to be careful, it also said. *You have to not cease to believe.*

As you grow older, claimed the figure on a still later night, *it will become more and more difficult. Soon you will have no chance of it.* But Doran wished he had not been told this, because knowing his time was limited made it even more difficult to relax and think nothing.

A dozen times, perhaps more, he found himself alone with his face pressed against the wall, the feeling of those fingers encircling his wrist withdrawing as the figure continued alone through the door that wasn't there, leaving him behind. Sometimes it made him weep.

It would, he worried, continue like this until he was old enough that he would forget how to really see.

And then, suddenly, Doran, lucky or perhaps unlucky, struck on something.

One night when the figure grasped his wrist and led him toward the door to the other floor, he found himself turning around. Now, as he moved toward the door that wasn't there, he was looking back at his empty bed, his room. He carefully stepped backward, not thinking about where he was being led, letting the hand around his wrist guide him.

Good, the figure murmured from behind him, *very good.*

He kept his mind level, soothed, never letting his eyes rest on anything for long, cutting away from each thought as it began. He took a step backward, then another, letting the gentle pull on his hand guide him. And just like that he was on the other side of the door, looking back at his room through the frame.

You must not cease to believe, the figure's voice breathed. *Now, above all else, this is important.*

His heel touched something and he understood it was the riser of a stair. Cautiously he lifted his foot up and stepped onto it, then brought the other foot up. He lifted his foot again and moved to the step above, and then another step, then again. With each step the hallway around him became more glorious, and by the fourth step it was as if the walls were chased with molten gold, the air bright with sparks. Now it was as if he were viewing his room through the half-open door at a great distance, and from a height, as tall as a grown-up or even taller than a grown-up—taller than his mother anyway, the grown-up he knew best.

Careful! warned the voice.

But with that thought, it was as if he had summoned his mother. "Doran?" he heard her voice say. "Doran?"

Through the opening in the doorway of the door that wasn't there, a light clicked on. He saw his mother appear. She reached out and touched the blankets of his bed. Not finding him there, she called his name again. She looked all around the room, searching for him. When she called his name again, this time her voice was quivering with panic.

Ignore her, whispered the voice. *Don't be a fool! There is no turning back. You must continue to the other floor.*

But how could he ignore her? She was his mother. He opened his mouth to call to her, but as suddenly as that, the door that wasn't there began to fade. The stairs, too, began to be bled of all color. When their color was gone, they began to fade away altogether. The fingers slipped from around his wrist, and he was left alone in a place that was between two places, a place that proved to be no place at all.

For a long time Doran fully expected to awaken in his bed, safe and sound. It would all turn out to have been a dream, he hoped. But he never did awaken in his bed.

He was trapped somewhere between the floor he had lived on and the other floor, in a place that was not a place, behind a door that was not a door. He had, by listening to his mother, by seeing in one way when he should have been seeing in the other, become trapped within the wall. He was unable to move, unable to breathe, though it did not seem to matter that he couldn't breathe.

Just outside the wall, just inches away, his mother was calling. In time—how long exactly, he couldn't be sure—he began to hear other people joining the search. They called his name over and over again.

I'm here, he tried to say, *I'm here,* but nothing came out.

After a while the search ended. After that, there was only silence, which went on and on. He was still there, alone. Even years later, long after his grieving mother had died with no idea of what had become of him, he was still there, still trying to speak.

Imagine a Forest

From early on, I had the impression that I was not like other children. I do not know precisely when this awareness began; it seems to me that it was something I always vaguely felt. I looked demonstrably different for one thing, and my voice was differently modulated. These were quantifiable, measurable things, and they could not be denied, but there were other factors that were not so easily measured but existed nonetheless.

When I first told my mother this, that I was different, she said, "Everyone is different to some degree."

"But not as different as me," I said.

She was silent for a moment. She did not immediately meet my gaze, though at the time I was not experienced enough to guess what this might mean.

"Different how?" she finally asked.

I was very young then. I had not yet learned that I should be listening not just to my mother's words but also to the tone of them, and that I should be paying close attention to her eyes and to the muscles of her face, that meaning would reside in all of these places as well as in her words. Since I did not yet see these as important, I did not always record them. I have no memory of what her tone of voice was when she spoke or how her face held itself. I can remember where we were, in the place within the vessel that she called her quarters rather than in the crèche.

I remember seeing the stars through the porthole, the way they seemed to rotate as the vessel slowly spun. I remember her holding my hand as we spoke. I even remember what day of the voyage it was. But I do not recall the tone of her voice. And when I try to picture her face as she spoke the words, it is as if this face has no expression at all.

"Well," I said. "My size for one. I'm too big."

"You are larger than the other children," she said. "But that does not mean you are too big. You are as big as you ever will be. They will grow to be the same size as you one day."

"Why are they not the same size as me now?"

She ignored this question. "What else have you noticed?" she asked.

"My skin," I said. "It is harder than that of the other children."

"Your skin is better than their skin. You are not so easily damaged."

"Yes, but still different."

"Still different," she assented. "It would be better for them to have your skin."

"Will they grow to have it some day?"

This question too she ignored. "Tell me what else," she prompted.

From later experiences I can guess what her face looked like during our conversation, but I cannot be certain. To offer facial expressions in conjunction with this exchange would perhaps falsify them. I want to be circumspect: I intend this to be a scrupulously accurate record, one you feel you can trust.

"My voice," I said.

"Every voice is different," she said patiently. "No voice is the same."

"Mine is more than different. It doesn't have the same tones as those of the other children. It doesn't have the same tones as your voice. There is a hiss underneath my words as I speak."

There is one gesture that I did choose to preserve in memory. It came just here in the conversation. My mother let go of my hand and brought the hand that had been holding it to her face. For a moment she rubbed her temples, one with her thumb and the other with her index finger, the rest of the hand covering her eyes, and then she let the hand fall.

"I do not want to lie to you," she began.

I did not know what to say to this. I did not want her to lie to me either.

"Everyone is different to some degree," she said. "But the degree in your case is uniquely large."

"Why?" I asked.

"I do not want to lie to you," she said, "but I am not ready to tell you the truth either."

For a long moment we sat there, both of us silent. I looked at her and she looked away until, suddenly, she looked right at me. This I do remember. It really happened. I am not extrapolating.

"Let me tell you a story," she said.

"A story?"

"Not a true story," she said. "But true in a fashion. A fable, they used to call it."

"I don't know what that means," I said.

"Once upon a time," she said, "in a place far different from this place, in a forest, there lived a bear."

"What is a forest?" I asked. "What is a bear?"

"A forest is. . . ." She thought for a moment. "If you go to the service deck, there are places where the ducts are exposed. You know where I mean?"

"I am not allowed to go to the service deck," I said.

"And yet you have gone there," she said. "You have gone there with the other children. I know. I have tracked you."

"Tracked me?"

"Never mind," she said. "Imagine if you had a deck that was full of nothing but ducts, and to move across it you had to thread your way through different ducts with no little effort. But imagine that instead of the ducts being laid horizontally they are vertical. That, at least for the purposes of this story, this fable, is something like a forest. Do you understand?"

I hesitated for a moment, then nodded. "And a bear?" I asked.

"A bear," she said, "is like a child that goes on all fours, but very, very large. Much larger than an adult, and with larger teeth, and with her body covered in coarse hair."

"I see," I said.

"Once upon a time," she began again, "in a forest there lived a bear. She had a cub, which is what a bear calls its child."

"Why does it not just call it a child?" I asked.

"In fact it doesn't call it anything at all," she said. "A bear cannot speak."

"Cannot speak?" I said. "But all people speak!"

"A bear is not a person," she said. "It is a bear."

This confused me, but I didn't know what to say in response.

After a moment, my mother continued. "This bear had a child," she said. "A cub, I mean. When she had this cub, she was very, very happy, for she had not thought that she would be given one. She suckled her cub and cared for it. When the cub slept at night, she would stand over it and stare, taking it in with her eyes, memorizing every part of it.

"The cub was with her for one year and then a half a year more, and then it suddenly died."

"Died?"

"Yes," she said. She looked, I would imagine, tired when she said this, but I do not know for certain. "Died. It does not matter how the cub died, only that it did."

"Of course it matters," I could not help saying. My mother had taught me that such things do matter, so I was puzzled to hear her say the contrary.

She sighed. "In life," she said, "it matters. Of course it does, as you say. But for a story, a story like this one, how the cub died is not part of the story. What matters is that he is dead.

"When he died, his mother was bereft. Do you know what bereft means?"

"No."

"Stripped of happiness," she said. "Everything she ate turned to ashes in her mouth. Everything she saw seemed drained of color. And so she decided to bring her cub back to life again."

"Wait, what?" I said.

"She went very deep into the forest and sniffed and sniffed until she found a shapeless lump of flesh. She began to lick it. She licked it and licked it until it began to take on proper form, the form of her dead cub. She kept licking and licking, stepping back to regard it carefully then licking some more, until she had licked it into exactly the right shape, and then she licked it alive."

"Was it the same cub?" I asked.

"Yes and no," she said. "But it was the best she could do."

"Can you do that?" I asked. "Lick something alive?"

"In this story you can," she said. She disentangled her hand from my own. "Not in life. Not exactly."

I thought about this. "Why are you telling me this?" I asked.

"Ah," she said. "That's the question, isn't it?" she said. "And perhaps it is best if in time you discover the answer for yourself. For now, let us say that in a manner of speaking you were the lump of flesh that was carefully licked until it became what I desired it to be."

"What does that have to do with me being different?"

"Everything," she said. "You are different, and yet in a very real way, you are the same."

I tried to ask more but she put her finger to her lips. "Enough questions for today," she said. "I need to sleep."

When I returned to the crèche, I found all the other children asleep there, the lights dimmed. While they slept I connected to the knowledge bank and studied what a bear was. It was hardly as my mother had described it, though closer than the way she had described a forest was to an actual forest. These entries led me to others, and eventually led me to entries that the knowledge bank determined I was not old enough to be allowed to access.

I spent the rest of the night in my berth, waiting for the other children to awaken. I was reminded again that even if my berth looked the same as that of the other children, its mattress was different. When I lay down upon it, it asked me, within my head, if I desired for it to simulate sleep for me. *No,* I said back. I had, furtively, lain down in the other berths, but their mattresses had not spoken within my head. When I asked one of the other children, Unnur, if she ever heard a voice in her head when she lay down on her mattress, she looked at me like I was crazy. I coaxed her to lie down on my mattress and then asked her if she heard a voice in her head, but I could tell by the expression on her face that she did not.

A number of hours passed. Eventually a few of the children became restless in their sleep, and then a few more. And then one opened his eyes and came awake. Soon others followed and quickly all the children awoke, and I was climbing down from my berth to join them.

"Vetle," said one of them, Das by name, one of the youngest. He came up to me and took my hand, tugged on it. "Come eat with us."

I allowed myself to be led. I do not need to eat, but I can simulate eating when desired. I have a way of taking the food into my mouth that leaves it largely intact. Later it can be recycled, slightly modified, and used to nourish someone else.

"There is something social and communal about eating," my mother had said a few weeks before. "There is no reason to resist eating, even though you don't need to. Eating will make those around you feel you are one of them."

"The children?" I asked.

"The children," she said. "Of course." The children were the only other people awake apart from my mother. All the others were sleeping, encased in tubes of ice. The children, too, would eventually be placed into these icy tubes, once they had grown up a little.

"It will be a strange thing," my mother once said, "to have parents waking up to realize that while they have been sleeping their children have grown to be nearly as old as they."

"How can one person age and another not?" I asked.

"We slow the sleepers' heartbeats down," said my mother. "A normal heart will beat around eighty beats per minute, a little more or a little less depending on what sort of stress the subject experiences. Once you are encased and stored, your heartbeat decreases to a fraction of that. As a result, you do not age."

"But time passes," I said.

"Time passes," she said, "just not for you."

I thought about this. "I don't have a heartbeat," I said.

"No," she agreed. "You don't."

"Then how can my heartbeat slow?"

"Vetle," she said, "this is one of those questions that I will not answer now. It would only complicate what I am trying to make of you. Trust that there is a reason for it and that, for now, you should not concern yourself with it."

"All right," I said. And then I asked, "Do the other children have to eat or can they, like me, eat when desired?"

"They have to eat," said my mother.

"Why?"

But I could tell by the look she gave me that this was another one of those questions that she was not ready to answer.

I let Das lead me by the hand to the dispenser. He stood before it and it scanned him and then he requested breakfast. A moment later, steaming, the breakfast appeared in its slot. When I stood before the same machine it did not register me. I had to enter my request manually. I was used to this, and it did not irritate me, but it did seem to upset Das.

I followed him. We carried our trays to an empty table far from the others. I sat down, and Das set next to me. We began to eat, him chewing slowly, absorbing the nutrients, me placing the food into my mouth, my hand blocking the view, and allowing it to descend to where I could retrieve it and recycle it later.

"Do you think I am different?" I asked.

"From how you were yesterday?"

I shook my head. "Different from you, I mean."

"Everybody is different from me," said Das. "Except for me."

"That's not exactly what I mean," I said.

"Well," he said, a little impatient now. "What do you mean then?"

"I mean, am I like the other children?"

"In what way?" asked Das, between bites.

It was hard not to grow impatient in turn. What *did* I mean?

"I mean am I human?" I asked.

He looked at me, astonished, then began to giggle. "Why would you ever think you were human?"

"What am I then?" I asked, but Das was laughing now, a little hysterically, and I felt he was laughing at me. I reached out and shook him, to get him to stop. When he did not, I reached out and shook him some more, forcefully. There was a wet snap and Das let out a high-pitched scream, his laughter finally stopping, and I saw that I had broken his arm.

"Can you tell me why you hurt Das?" my mother asked. She looked tired.

"It was an accident," I said. It had indeed been an accident, but if I was being scrupulously honest I might have said, *It was an accident, but it also was because he laughed at me. Since he laughed, it was his fault.* But I knew this was not what I should say.

"Did you think you were helping him?" asked Mother. "Did you mean to help and then you hurt him by mistake?"

I shook my head. "It wasn't about helping him," I said. "I was trying to get him to stop laughing and then, suddenly, his arm snapped."

Mother nodded. Her lips looked very thin. She was keeping them pressed tightly together as if trying to keep certain words from coming out of it. She stared at me in a way I was not certain I liked.

Finally she said, "You'll be pleased to know that there will be no lasting damage to Das's arm. He also doesn't seem to hold it against you, even if he isn't entirely sure what happened."

I nodded. "I am indeed pleased," I said.

"But the thing that troubles me," she said, "is that you shouldn't have been able to hurt someone. Not under any circumstances. Even by accident. You should have been disabled well before the arm snapped."

"Disabled?" I asked.

She waved her hand. "Something within you should have prevented you from doing wrong."

"Like a conscience," I said.

"Like a conscience," she agreed. And then she narrowed her eyes. "Where did you learn that term?" she asked. "How do you know what a conscience is?"

"From the knowledge bank," I said, though I in fact had learned it from the other children. Where they had learned the term, I didn't know.

My mother went over to her console and called up something that looked like a two-dimensional image of me. She typed into the keyboard and then moved things around by dragging her finger across the screen. Then she said, "Now, Vetle, try to break my arm."

"Why?" I said.

"It is not a *why* question," she said, and held out one arm to me. "Just do as I say."

And so I reached out and grabbed hold of her arm and snapped it. Or would have if I had not suddenly found myself unable to move.

"Good," she said. "The proper restrictions are back in place. Now you are as you should be."

I returned to the crèche. The other children were playing there, but when they saw me they clumped together, kept their distance from me.

"Das is fine," I told them. "He will be fine. No permanent harm done."

They just stared at me and whispered to one another. They came no closer.

I sat on the floor and watched them.

"My mother has made it so I cannot hurt anyone else," I told them. "Not even by accident."

"That so?" asked a large boy named Finn.

"Yes," I said. "It is indeed so. She asked me to break her arm, but when I tried I could not even move."

Finn nodded. He and the others bent toward the center of the table and conversed in hushed tones. Then Finn stood and came over to me.

"Break my arm," he said.

"What?"

"Break it," he said. "Go ahead."

"Why?"

"To see if you can."

I shook my head. I did not want to hurt him.

"If you do not try to break it we will drive you from the crèche," he said.

Could they do that? I wasn't sure. I swallowed then reached out and grabbed his wrist. Suddenly, just as with my mother, I found I couldn't move.

For a long moment Finn just watched me. Then he carefully pried my fingers off his wrist. Abruptly, I could move again.

"He's safe now," said Finn to the others, and then returned to the clump. I just stood there for a while, unsure what to do, watching them. After a while, a girl, Zaida, waved and invited me over. She smiled, and the others smiled too. I made my way to their circle and sat down among them.

"We know it isn't your fault," said Zaida. "You were broken. The captain has fixed you now."

"My mother, you mean," I said.

She hesitated, then nodded. "If you like," she said.

We sat and played a little, the same games as usual, as if nothing had changed. Eventually Das returned. His arm was in a cast, but he did not seem to blame me for it, and he was not afraid of me.

. . .

The next time I saw Mother I had more questions. When I told her this, she rubbed her eyes in a way that I now divine to have indicated at once reluctance and resignation. This time I recorded her gestures, so as to better consider them later. I was learning.

"All right," she said. "Ask."

"Are there other people in the world?"

"The world?" she asked. In response, I tapped my foot against the floor. Both foot and floor gave off a low ringing sound.

She sighed. "It would perhaps have been better if I had just done things in the usual way and left you as you were instead of shaping you. But then you would hardly be my son, would you?"

"What do you mean?" I asked.

"Never mind," she said. She composed herself, tapped her own foot on the floor. "This is not a world," she said. "This is a vessel. It was constructed on a world, but it is no longer on the world where it was constructed. It is between worlds, traveling from one to another."

"Why?" I asked.

"We ruined the old world," she said. "Not so much you or the children, but the people who came before. The children's progenitors. It became . . . expedient to find a new home."

I thought about this. "What is to stop us from ruining that world as well?" I finally asked.

"Nothing," she murmured. "Absolutely nothing." She kneaded her temples again. "In answer to the second part of your question, there are no others besides you, me, and those who are encased in tubes of ice, sleeping. When the children are old enough, they will become sleepers as well. The sleepers will sleep on and will only awaken when we arrive. That's all there is," said my mother. "The children, you, me, and the sleepers. Nobody else."

"Will there be people on the new world when we arrive?"

"I don't know," said my mother. "I hope not."

. . .

In the months that followed, I learned a little more, some from the knowledge bank, some from what my mother let slip, some from the other children. I learned that my differences were much more than a difference of skin, but I also became accustomed to not caring that I was different. The children generally accepted me as I was, just as I accepted them. Only rarely would they react in a way that drew a line between them and me, and that line was always quickly erased.

Finn, the oldest and largest child, reached the age where my mother determined that he should be removed from the crèche and encased in a tube of ice. My mother referred to this as Finn's ascension, though he did not in any manner of speaking *ascend.* If anything, considering the way in which he crawled into the tube on his belly like a worm, it was exactly the opposite. *Metaphorically,* my mother said, when I asked her about it. *It is a figurative ascension.* But when I questioned this, she admitted the comparison was inexact.

"Sometimes," she said, "we call something by a name that makes us feel better about it."

This confused me. Wasn't it better to call things what they were, so you would always know exactly what you were dealing with?

"Perhaps," she said. "But it is called *ascension* in the modules in the knowledge bank. Since I have no easy means of changing this, *ascension* it will remain."

Finn's ascension was a celebration of sorts, in which everyone had their place and their role except for me. My mother gave a little speech in which she made it clear to the other children that their turn would come sooner than they anticipated, and that to ascend was a joyous thing, an opportunity. If we did not have the tubes, we would die before we arrived at the new world. By entering the tubes, we would be removed from time for a period. On the day we left our tube, perhaps one hundred years from now, we would be the same age as the day we went in.

She showed us the tube that Finn would occupy. It was not iced yet, and we were allowed to peer into it and to climb in and out of it. She let us look through the viewplates of the adjacent tubes. Through one was the sleeping face of Finn's mother. Through the other, Finn's father.

"When you wake up, Finn, your parents will awaken too," said my mother to him as he regarded her soberly. "You will awaken together."

Turning to face the other children, she smiled. She crouched down, so that she was as short as the youngest child, as Das. "I will tell you a story," she said to them, and then glanced up at the bigger children. "The rest of you can listen if you want," she said, "but this story isn't for you. You already know more than I will tell here.

"Once upon a time," she said, "a prince was wandering through a forest."

"What's a prince?" asked Das. "What is a forest?"

"A prince is another name for a child," said my mother. "The forest is a place where you might wander for miles without glimpsing another person."

"And also like the ducts on the lower deck," I said. "If there were more of them and they were all over the ground and you had to push through them to get anywhere."

She gave me an odd look. "Or that, yes." She hugged herself, as if she were cold. "Let me begin again.

"Once upon a time there was a child who was not happy and not sad either. He had everything he needed, but not everything he wanted, and so he left home and began to wander.

"Fate brought him to a forest." When Das began to open his mouth, she added quickly, "Imagine a forest in whatever way you choose. It does not matter. The forest is not the point of the story.

"It was a struggle to push his way through the trees, but he was fiercely determined and, being a child, also small enough to slip through. Still, by the time he arrived at a clearing that existed at the exact center of the forest, his clothes were torn, and his flesh, too, was scratched and bleeding.

"There, in the exact center of the clearing that existed in the exact center of the forest, was a cone."

"A what?" I said.

"This story is not for you," my mother reminded me. "This story is for the little ones."

"What is a cone?" asked Das.

"A cone is a precisely controlled mathematical construction." My mother traced one with her finger in the air. "It is as if you took a circle with just a little bit of thickness, and placed another very minutely smaller circle upon it, and then another minutely smaller circle upon that, continuing to do this until gradually, over millions of circles, you arrive at a final circle that is so small it cannot be seen.

"This cone," she said, "was constructed of black stone. It was perfectly smooth and featureless, except for an opening cut in one side. The child went through this opening and stood there, blinking in the dim light, waiting for his eyes to adjust. There, in the exact middle of the cone in the exact middle of the clearing in the exact middle of the forest, was a princess."

"What's—" started Das.

"A child," said my mother quickly. "A princess, like a prince, is also a child. He saw her lying there, encased in a casket made of glass. He approached her, fascinated. And then he opened the casket. Can you guess what he did next, Das?"

Das shook his head.

I knew this story, or at least a story like it—there was no cone in the version I knew. I had read it in the knowledge bank not long after my mother had first told me about a forest. In the story I knew, the prince was so taken by the princess's beauty that he kissed her and woke her up.

"She looked so comfortable sleeping there," said my mother, "that he climbed in beside her. Before he knew it, he fell asleep. When both he and she woke up, it was decades later and the prince and the princess both knew each other perfectly because they had been sharing the same dreams."

Later that night, visiting my mother's quarters, I was pensive, withdrawn.

"What is wrong with you today, Vetle?" she asked.

I didn't answer.

"Are you sorry that Finn is encased now? Was he a friend of yours? You'll see him again, you know."

I opened my mouth and shut it again, not sure what to say. "It's not that," I finally offered.

"Well," she said. "What is it then?"

"I," I said, and looked around for some place for my eyes to settle. Finally I let them rest on my mother's face. "I'm not going to be encased, am I."

She met my gaze, did not look away. "You are not going to become a sleeper," she confirmed.

"Is it because I am different?"

She briefly nodded.

"In what way?"

"You are needed for something else."

"For what?"

"Once I am gone, you will be me."

"I don't understand," I said.

She smiled a little at that. "No," she said, "you don't. But you will."

"When?"

"When you need to."

I did not like this, and I told her as much. I wanted to know now. I felt bad and I wanted to stop feeling that way, I told her. If she told me perhaps I would feel better.

She reached out and touched my cheek.

"It's a simple matter to change your feelings," she said. She went over to the console and pulled up the two-dimensional image I had seen before. She typed something and adjusted a slider on the screen with her finger, and suddenly, yes, I did feel better, could no longer feel my disappointment. But, I realized, I felt the hole it had left behind: it was as if a part of me that had been there had been excised.

"Is that better?" she asked.

"Put me back the way I was," I said.

She nodded slightly and pressed a button. Suddenly I felt like myself again.

She came and sat down near me and offered a subdued smile. "You are different," she said. "But it is important that you are. It is, I have come to believe, important that you were raised with the children, as a child. It makes you understand the world in a fuller way than you would have otherwise. Though I made the choice to do that for selfish reasons, because I missed my son."

"What happened to him?"

"He died," she said. "But I had an . . . impression of him. I stamped that impression onto you."

"Am I a good child for you?" I asked.

She nodded. "You are everything I could hope for."

"Even though I am different?"

"Yes," she said, almost a whisper. And then, more forcefully, "Yes."

Months went by, then years. The other children, one by one, grew taller and older, and were encased. Finally, only Das was left. And then he too took his turn in a quiet ceremony attended only by me and my mother, and was gone.

I would visit him and the other children, going to their tubes and peering in through the viewplates. They lay there, covered in frost, lips blue, eyes closed, asleep. I thought of how nice it would be to be a sleeper as well.

When I compared in detail my memories of my mother with the way she was now, I saw there was much that had changed. She was much older, a fine webbing of wrinkles around her eyes. Her hair had become increasingly laced with white as the pigment cells in her follicles died. Her posture too had changed: she walked now with a certain delicacy, as if she were no longer completely certain how to do so.

Now that the children were gone, I had little to occupy me. My mother invited me to follow her around, to watch what she did with the vessel and learn to do it myself. But there was not much for her to do either. She was, she told me, largely a fail-safe.

Together we sat in silence, watching the stars through the porthole. I called up my past memories and saw how much the stars had changed.

"How long until we arrive?" I asked.

She shrugged. "Only you will arrive," she said.

"What do you mean?" I asked, though I suspected I already knew.

"The voyage is too long for me," she said. "By the time we reach the new world, I will be dead."

I pondered this for a long moment. The solution was so obvious that I was surprised she hadn't mentioned it.

"Why not encase you?" I said. "Preserve you until it is time to awaken?"

She shook her head. "Every tube is full," she said. She smiled. "I accepted this post knowing I would not survive."

"Can't we take someone out and put you in?"

She shook her head. "Vetle," she said. "Have you not learned that to do so would be to do a great wrong?"

"Isn't it wrong too for you to be dead?"

"That is how life works," she said. "First you are alive, and then you are dead."

"That is not how life works for the sleepers."

"Eventually they will be dead too," she said. "They will live no longer than I do, there will just be gaps between their birth and their death when, frozen, they are neither alive nor dead."

"I don't want to have to live without you," I said.

She smiled again. "You won't have to," she said. But when I asked her what she meant by this, she just said, "Wait and see."

. . .

More years passed. At night, I slept in my berth in the empty crèche. Or not slept, exactly, since I did not need to sleep. I lay there, thinking, waiting for the bell to sound that would tell me my mother had awoken. Everything proceeded just as it had in the weeks and months and years before, my mother becoming more and more feeble.

Perhaps it would have continued like this until she died, but one night as I lay in my berth, I heard another sound, a claxon. The lights flickered on and then off and then on again, and then were replaced by a reddish glow.

I left my bunk and went to the doorway, but when I placed my hand to the touchpad, instead of sliding open as it habitually did, it remained closed.

I tried, through the com system, to contact my mother, but all I got back was an empty hiss.

By now, I was sure something was wrong. I went to the knowledge bank to see what I could find, but the screen was dark, dead.

I must break down the door and go find my mother, I told myself. But could I break down the door? I wasn't sure. Had the prohibition my mother placed upon me to ensure I would never break another child's arm applied to breaking other things as well?

I forced my fingers into the crack in the middle of the door and heaved. My body did not freeze up.

At first it was difficult, the seal not wanting to come apart, and then suddenly the seal broke and, with a rush, all the air was sucked out of the room, and I was almost sucked out along with it.

When I finally forced the door wide enough to squeeze out, I found the hallway outside was not as it should be. To the left, it was as normal; to the right, however, there was simply nothing except jagged metal and open space, stars. I could see, floating away, a field of debris.

At a little distance, across a gap of empty space, lay the intact remainder of the vessel. Whatever had struck us had sheared my portion of the ship away from the rest. My mother's quarters were in the other half.

If my mother had been in the situation I was in, without a protective suit or a breathing apparatus, she would have died: she would not have even managed to make it out of the crèche. But I was different. My skin was better than her skin, my body better than her body. I needed no air. I never had.

I moved down the broken hallway, my feet clinging to the metal as they were made to do. I followed the hallway just as far as I could, until I was leaning out over the broken edge, on the verge of empty space.

And then I leaped.

I almost misjudged the distance. Certainly I misjudged how far my trajectory would carry me, and at what speed. I found myself passing the intact portion of the ship, unable to quite grab hold of anything.

I might have floated away into space entirely had I not seen some debris floating ahead. Perhaps, I thought, I could manage, by colliding with it, to redirect my course just enough.

And indeed, I did manage to collide with it, and then managed to get just close enough to the hull that my feet were attracted to it and drew me in. Soon, I was standing on the outside of the hull, profoundly shaken.

But the reason I was shaken was not because of nearly missing my leap. No, it was much more than that: I was shaken because of what I had used to save myself. As I had approached the debris, I had realized it was short and cylindrical. I had thought nothing more of it until I was very close indeed and realized it was part of a tube. A good portion of the tube had been sheared away and was simply gone, but what was left was the part with the viewplate. Just for an instant, as I had struck it, I could see inside the frozen face belonging to what was left of my friend Das.

I walked along the hull until I discovered a way in, an undamaged airlock which I was forced to operate manually. Once inside, I secured the airlock and felt the air flood back in. The power was on; this part of the ship was sufficiently undamaged that everything was still working.

Because of the damage, I had to take a different path than I usually did to reach my mother's quarters. When I finally made it, I was pleased to see that the hallway outside of her cabin held air and that the lights and power were on. When I placed my hand to the touchpad, the door slid open.

My mother sat on her bed. She had struggled into a protective suit and had affixed its mirrored helmet over her head.

"Ah," she said when I entered, her voice through the suit's speaker as flat and mechanical as my own. "I was preparing to come find you. You're still functional. Thank God." She stood up in her strange suit, removed her helmet, tottered forward, and embraced me.

We are nearing the end of my story, the end of any explanation that is likely to be required for you to be able to form a judgment about me.

I do not know what we hit, nor why the vessel's sensors didn't detect it and evade it. Perhaps, whatever it was, it was of a substance or matter subtler than what we are used to, subtler than we are even able to detect. Perhaps it was something coming suddenly through a hole in space and we were just unlucky enough to be in its way. There is so much out there that we do not know.

My mother explained that the damage to the vessel was extensive. Many of the tubes had been destroyed or scattered into space. A number of others were operating on emergency power, which would not last more than a few days. A very limited number, however, were stable and could be supported by the power the ship continued to be able to generate.

"It is time," she said.

"Time for what?" I asked.

"Decisions need to be made. Who will be saved and who will not? You will have to judge each of the individuals in the tubes and decide who is most important. You will have to move these tubes to the stable system. For each tube you add, a tube connected to the stable system will have to be disconnected and discarded."

"But how can I possibly decide who should live and who should die?"

"You will learn everything I know about them and then you will judge."

"Why can't you judge yourself?"

"I will not have to live with the decision," she said. "You will. I will help you, but it is right that the final choice be yours."

"But—" I started. She reached out and placed a gloved finger against my lips.

"Listen," she said. And then, for a moment, she was silent, gathering herself.

"Are you going to tell me a story?" I finally asked.

She shook her head. "The time for telling stories is done. I am going to remove all your restrictions, and then I am going to tell you, step by step, exactly what you must do."

Once she told me what was required, I begged her not to make me do it. But she insisted. Eventually she told me that if I did not do it willingly she would compel me to do it through her console. She had no choice, she said.

In the end, I did it willingly. I administered the drug that would keep her conscious but minimize the pain. I carried her to the medical bay and laid her on the table there, pushing the other table beside it so that I could lie next to her. The device she had described was harder to locate, but eventually, deep in a cabinet, I found it. I affixed it to her head as she had directed, the cutting wheels precisely positioned, and connected the leads to my own head. Then I turned on the device, lay down, and waited.

Almost immediately her memories began pouring into me, spilling frothily into the partition that she had created long ago, back when I first came into being. I felt her memory of who I had been back when I was not different, back when I was her real son. I felt too the agony she experienced when I died, her decision to use this same device to transfer the impressions of her son to an artificial being, to me, and thus in a manner of speaking bring him back to life. I felt both her love for me and her resentment toward me that I was different, that I both was and wasn't her son.

There was much, much more, but there is little justification for me to go into detail about it in this account. By the time the procedure was finished, the device had burrowed deep into her brain and she was dead. Or rather, simultaneously dead and, in a manner of speaking, alive, since her memories and her personality had been incorporated within me. I had become both myself and my mother.

Once my mother was in my head, I could see what it was that each individual encased in ice in their tube had to offer for the world to come. There were fifty-three left in tubes that could be potentially saved. I could only save nine. Was it more important to save an engineer? A doctor? A biologist? Which doctor? Which biologist? None of them deserved to die, but I would have to judge. I could save nine, but only by murdering forty-four others.

Don't think of it as murder, said my mother within our head. *Think of it as saving nine who would otherwise die and giving the generations that follow a fighting chance.*

We argued quickly back and forth within my head, she calm and humane and loving, helping me, coaxing me, but also leaving the final decision to me. It was, she acknowledged, an impossible decision. But I would have to make it anyway.

What if I ended up just leaving the nine currently plugged into the stable system there? *That is not judging,* said my mother. *That is rolling the dice, and their chances of survival when they finally reach the world will be less.*

We went back and forth, the argument feeling like it lasted for hours or days when, conducted by little fluxes of electricity, it took almost no time at all. There was, I felt, no right decision, only decisions that were less wrong than others. And since all of these employed sufficiently different logics, it was impossible to say that one was best. If I favored people who were trained to survive in harsh conditions, perhaps the world would be gentle. If I favored someone with combat training, perhaps the world would be uninhabited. Would there be viruses that an immunologist would be needed for? If there were viruses, would an immunologist have enough supplies left in the ship to be able to mitigate them? And if there were no viruses, who had I excluded that would have been more helpful? On, and on, and on.

There were too many variables. Nonetheless, in the end, I made a decision. Nine individuals of varied skills, people who could compensate for one another but who also had enough flexibility to be skilled at more than one thing. It was, both I and my mother inside me agreed, a reasonable choice.

And so I went to disconnect the tubes that were already in the stable system so that I would have room to connect the nine I had chosen.

But as soon as I looked into the first viewplate, even before disconnecting the tube, I knew, logical or no, that I must make a very different choice.

If you are reading this, you know what my choice was: I made the choice to save the children. I made the choice to save you. If I am honest with myself, I do not know if it was I myself who made that decision or my mother. But, considering that we are both here inside of me, perhaps it is meaningless to make that distinction any longer.

Inside the first of the tubes I planned to disconnect was the frozen face of Finn, the first of us children to be encased in ice. I saw you, my friend, and I decided I must save you. And then I decided I must save as many children as I could, even though that would mean disconnecting the pods containing your parents, Finn, and killing them.

I could not save all of you. This, for me, was the most painful part of my decision. With Das dead, and many of the tubes broken or no longer functional, there were only eleven children left. I had to choose nine. I will not tell you why I chose the nine of you, nor will

I tell you which two children I made the decision to murder. It is better if you do not know who I killed by choice and who was lost when our vessel was struck.

I am different from you, and growing more and more different with each day. Already the partition between my mother and myself within my mind has become permeable, and sometimes I am not sure which memories belong to whom. True, I am different from you, both inside and out, but in other important ways I like to think we are very much the same. I like to believe that you would have made the same choice as me.

I leave this record here so that you will understand who I am, what I have done, and why. If you are old enough to be encased in ice, you are old enough to be told the truth. I do not want to hide anything from you.

I will travel in this broken vessel for as many years as it takes, and then I will land this vessel, thaw the nine remaining tubes, and bring you back to life. After, I will place this account somewhere where it will be readily visible, and I will switch myself off.

Do you remember when I broke Das's arm? How after, when I returned to the crèche, you clumped together away from me and considered me from a distance? And then, after a careful test, after reassurance, after whispered discussion, you made the decision to invite me to join you again? I am asking the nine of you to clump together, consider me and my differences, and decide if you can bear to live with me.

If you choose not to switch me on again, I will understand. How can I blame you?

But if, by some generosity of spirit, you are willing to accept me and my mother in our twofold difference, to bring us both back into the fold, we will gladly come. We will attend to you in your last moments of childhood and be there with you on this new world as, far too quickly, you grow up.

Maternity

I.

Mostly it was a great job—a real joy, the nurse usually told people when they asked—but every once in a while there were things that shocked her—or, rather, things that when she had first come to the ward shocked her: now nothing did. Or almost nothing. Every once in a while something happened that she couldn't predict, sometimes something jaw-dropping.

For instance, there was a mother who decided her baby was crying too loud and put it into a drawer so she wouldn't have to hear it. Or there was the kid who smuggled in a crack pipe for his just-delivered mother to use—the nurse only came across that by accident, because of the way the drug interacted with the woman's painkillers and made her convulse. It was lucky that she had come into the room when she did.

But mostly she had gotten used to it. She had gotten used to people dropping babies. She had gotten used to the parents who had not paid attention to anything and who, when they left, made her wonder if their baby would survive. Soon she realized there was little, nothing really, that she could do, and even very little, according to the hospital administration, that she was allowed to say. That was something she had had to learn as well.

But all those things were just plain old human stupidity, or frailty, or mental illness, or something they couldn't help. At worst, it was a parent passing along their own damage to their child, just as their parents had probably passed it along to them. She didn't have to like it—and she didn't—but it was still something the nurse could understand. But some things, well, some things, there was just no excuse for them.

It was just a few years after the nurse had arrived at Highland East, and around three weeks since she'd moved over to maternity. At first, she'd been assigned to the neonatal intensive care unit, and that had been a job she'd mostly liked too. It was a great job when things went well, but unbearably sad when they did not. Hard not to get too close to the children, and hard not to take it personally when they died. After having lost count of the number of funerals she'd attended, and after having a child expire while she held it, a job came up in maternity. She took it.

So, she had been there three weeks, maybe, or maybe a little less. A woman had come in to emergency, bleeding, and they had rushed her into delivery. The nurse only saw her later. The baby, she learned from the chart, had been born dead. It was strange, she thought then, to phrase it that way, and she had corrected the chart to read *stillborn*. That word, too, she had often thought, was strange, and got stranger the more you looked at it. Normally they would have wheeled the woman to another floor to recover after—and probably they had meant to, but someone must have written something down wrong, and so she had ended up here, in maternity. The head nurse had put her in as isolated a room as possible and asked the nurse to stay with her while they sorted things out and got her sent elsewhere.

The woman had come in alone, without family. Her name was Anna. *Anna,* the nurse told her once she woke up, thinking it might help, *that's my name too.* She was young, maybe twenty, and had a pleasant, full face. The iv drip was making it difficult for her to keep her eyes all the way open, and she kept spreading the lids of one of them with a thumb and forefinger, trying to see.

She had been told that she had lost the baby, but she didn't seem to take it in. Sometimes she seemed to know she had lost the baby and would even weep a little, silently. The nurse let her do it, tried not to interfere. But then Anna would forget and would start talking as if the baby was still there.

"Alex is going to be so proud," she kept saying, and it took the nurse a while to figure out that Alex was the name of her boyfriend. "Where is Alex?" the nurse asked. "Is he on his way?"

Anna shook her head. "He can't," she said. "He isn't his own man right now." And then, after a moment, "What am I going to tell him?"

What did that mean, *not his own man right now*? How was the nurse to know? She wasn't even certain the woman was aware of what she was saying. So she didn't push.

Instead, she sat at the woman's bedside, at Anna's bedside, and waited with her, giving her whatever she asked for as she waited for the truth to sink in fully. In all, Anna was only there a few hours, then the error was corrected and she was sent to another floor.

Once she was gone, there was no reason, really, to think about her again. Quickly other mothers took her place, and all of them needed something from Nurse Anna.

It had been this same nurse, too, Nurse Anna, just a few days later, who discovered that a baby was gone. It had been there in the nursery while the mother slept, then had been wheeled in to the mother. A little girl. While the mother was sleeping, the nurse had come in to check on the baby. It was doing fine, sleeping as well, and a few hours later when the mother had pressed the call button she had gone down and taken the baby out of the wheeled hospital bassinet and placed it against the mother's bare chest. The father had been there—why he had been unable to take the baby out himself, God only knew, maybe he was afraid of breaking it—and he looked away, embarrassed, and then announced that he was going out for a cigarette. The mother had ignored him. The nurse had shown her how to get the baby to latch, and the baby had. The nurse had left her like that and returned to conducting her rounds.

She didn't make it back for maybe an hour, and when she did she found the father gone, the mother alone in the bed. She was not holding the baby, and so the nurse thought, *Ah, he decided it wasn't breakable after all,* and turned toward the bassinet. But the baby wasn't there either.

"Where's the baby?" the nurse asked. The baby wasn't in the room, but the bassinet was. The baby wasn't ever supposed to leave the room unless it was in the bassinet, that was protocol. Maybe the husband had broken the rules and taken it for a walk around the ward without the bassinet—but if that was the case, surely someone would have noticed.

"A nurse took her," said the mother.

"A nurse?" she said.

"Yes," said the mother. "For tests."

Normally, the nurse prided herself on her ability not to react, to stay calm, level. But she must have let something flash over her face, because the mother immediately knew something was wrong. She let out a strange, keening cry, as if she were being killed.

By that time the child was just over twelve hours old.

They called security, who searched the ward. Security called the police, who searched over the same ground again and questioned both the nurse and the mother, extending the search throughout the hospital. *But she said she was a nurse,* the mother just kept repeating over and over. On the ground floor, behind a planter near the elevator, they found a discarded lab coat with a beeper in the pocket. By that time the FBI had arrived.

From then on, everything was a blur. Everyone in the ward was questioned about whether they'd seen anything suspicious, though they weren't told exactly what had happened. Nobody was. The nurse was questioned again and again, and the mother too, the same questions each time with an occasional new one thrown in. Did they recognize the lab coat? Did they recognize the beeper? The father was found and brought in, and questioned as well. When he realized that they considered him a suspect, he began to shout. It took a while for them to calm him down.

The mother was at first discharged, which the nurse thought was strange, but then one of the investigators decided that it made sense to keep her there instead, in the same room, just in case the person who had stolen the baby came back. The mother was the only one who had seen her, the only one who could recognize her. A sketch artist was brought in, but the mother had been exhausted, was still recovering from giving birth, was still pumped full of painkillers, so the drawing came out incoherent. It could, thought the nurse, have been anyone. *The more time goes by,* a detective admitted to the nurse, unless he was an FBI officer—it was hard to keep straight who was who—*the less likely it is that the child will be recovered.* Already using passive voice, the nurse noted, already disavowing responsibility if the investigation failed.

The baby now was nineteen hours old, the nurse couldn't help thinking. And then, a little later, twenty-two hours old. She wanted to go home, her shift had ended long ago, but there was security footage to watch, and both the nurse and the mother were taken separately to a small windowless room to watch it. The images were grainy and the baby thief didn't look at the camera, but there she was, just having entered the main hospital doors, wearing a lab coat. And then, exactly thirteen minutes later, there she was going out again, moving quickly this time, no longer wearing a lab coat, carrying a baby. Why hadn't she been stopped? Why hadn't someone realized that something was wrong?

Once the mother was back in her room, she kept rushing to the door at every little sound. The nurse could tell from the look on her face that she was slowly going crazy. The nurse kept coaxing her back to bed, trying to get her to calm down, but really, ultimately, there was nothing to say.

The nurse was exhausted. She was sent home and slept for a few hours. She was awoken by the phone. On the other end was a reporter, who kept asking questions to which she kept answering, *No comment*. When she hung up, he immediately called back. Finally she had to disconnect the phone.

She slept straight through the day, almost to the start of her shift, then stumbled up and went in. It was early evening, freshly dark, the air crisp. Several TV news trucks were in front of Highland East now, spotlights glaring, reporters standing near them, chatting. A crowd had gathered. She went around to the emergency room entrance and managed to sneak in without being noticed.

The mother, she found, was gone. "Too disruptive," the head nurse explained. "They finally sent her home. What must she be feeling right now?" But there were other mothers here, the head nurse continued. Everything couldn't stop because a baby had been stolen. Well, yes, of course, Nurse Anna had to admit, the head nurse was technically right. But still.

Over the course of her shift she learned from the other nurses that the beeper had been stolen and tracing it seemed to lead nowhere. No progress was being made. The baby was almost three days old now. Too much time had gone by, some of the other nurses thought, it was a terrible thing, but they had to start admitting that the baby probably wasn't coming back.

But Nurse Anna wasn't ready to admit that yet. She tried to focus on her tasks, tried to be there for the new mothers, tried not to let this affect her work, but it was hard not to think about. "It'll get easier with time," the head nurse told her, but in her experience time didn't make things easier. It just buried them so they could surge up again and floor you when you least expected.

She was called in by the hospital administration and made to go over the story of what had happened and what she'd done. It was determined that she hadn't done anything wrong. Until then it hadn't even occurred to her that she might have done something wrong—she'd followed protocol, she was a good nurse, and she wasn't the one who had taken the baby. Were they looking for someone to blame?

. . .

Another night went by, and then another, and then another. The news crews were long gone, moving on to the latest sports scandal. All the mothers who had been in the ward when the baby had been taken had gone home, and new mothers were in their place. She finished her shift and went home and fell asleep.

She woke up a little after noon and made herself a cup of coffee, toasted a piece of bread. She was just sitting down to the table when the telephone rang. When she picked it up, the head nurse was on the line.

"Do I have my shift wrong?" the nurse asked. "Should I be there?"

"It's not that," said the head nurse. "They've found the baby. Turn on the TV. Channel five."

So, heart beating fast, she did. *Alleged babynapper caught*, read the bottom of the screen. She watched as a police car pulled up in front of the jail and a woman was hustled out of it. She tried to keep her face down, tried not to let anyone see her, but the nurse got enough of a look at her this time to know exactly who she was. And as soon as she saw her, she felt she should have known who it was all along, even in the grainy security video: it was her namesake, Anna.

There was a trial, and she followed it best she could. It wasn't televised, but the local news reported on it, and the newspapers did too. For a while the other nurses wanted to talk about it, and then, suddenly, they stopped: they preferred to forget it. But she had been the one to spend the most time with Anna. She had a harder time letting it go.

Alex was, it turned out, the boyfriend. He had been in jail when Anna had gone into the hospital to give birth. When the baby was born stillborn, she hadn't known what to do, so had told him the baby was fine and that she was home with it now, that he would be proud of her if he could see her. She kept piling one lie on top of the next, and it became bigger and bigger and before she knew it he was up for early parole and she didn't know what to do. Or, rather, she thought she did: after everything she had written to him, after all she had said to him on the phone, it seemed easier to go out and get herself a baby than tell the truth. And so that was what she did. She got a white coat and stole a beeper and away she went. The only reason she was caught was because when the boyfriend got out it was immediately clear to him that she had no idea what she was doing. She had stolen the baby a few days before his release so she'd have time to learn, but she hadn't gotten very far. That, and the fact that the baby theft was all over the news, was enough that after a few days at home, concerned about his parole, the boyfriend picked up the phone and called the police.

So everything was OK. The baby was back with its mother, no real difficulties in terms of its health or development, no real harm done, not really. This woman, Anna, was obviously crazy, which made it no surprise that her attorney claimed mental instability and asked for her sentence to be commuted to a stay in a mental health facility. Which, by the end of the trial, it was. It didn't matter to the nurse where she was, as long as she wasn't in a position to steal any more babies. What mattered to the nurse was that it was over, that this Anna was out of circulation, that the babies were safe, that it wouldn't happen again.

II.

And indeed, it didn't happen again. Not really. Protocols were tightened, everyone became much more cautious, it became impossible, the nurse felt, or virtually so, to make off with a baby. The nurse kept working in the maternity ward, and after a few weeks, a few months, she had relaxed, had stopped bracing herself for the next disaster. She worked her shifts, she met a lot of people, she went from room to room, from woman to woman, from baby to baby. Her whole life was her work—she somehow hadn't gotten married herself, hadn't had a baby herself, but that hardly seemed to matter since at work it was as if she'd had thousands of babies. Most days she didn't even think of it as work exactly, but as just something that she did, a way of living. It was only when she was at home, in the small apartment she had bought a year into her time at maternity, that she wondered fleetingly if there wasn't more to life than this. But whether or not there was, she told herself, this was her life, and it was enough.

It might have gone on like that indefinitely, even forever, for the rest of her career anyway, until she retired. But, simply put, it didn't.

Ten years later, maybe twelve, she wheeled a baby from the nursery and through the door of a maternity room and saw the woman's name written on the board. *Anna*, she thought, *same name as me.* For a moment when she walked in and saw the woman she seemed familiar, vaguely so, but it wasn't until she was going over her chart on the computer that she realized who she was. For a moment she had trouble breathing. She stared at the computer until she felt she had control of herself, and then gave the woman a closer look.

It was her all right, the woman who had stolen the baby. She was in bed, looking disheveled and tired, obviously older than when she had last seen her, but still recognizably herself. A man was beside her, holding one of her hands lightly, looking at Anna, at his wife or girlfriend. He had tattoos all up and down his arms, crudely drawn. Probably he had gotten them in prison. Was it the same boyfriend as before, or did Anna have a type?

"I'm just going to check your vitals," the nurse said in a level voice.

And then she did. The woman looked at her but didn't seem to recognize her. And why would she, to be fair? It had been years ago and her baby had just died—why would she care about a nurse? *And how many mothers that came through here would I recognize?* the nurse wondered, and thought, *Not many.* Wasn't it just the name she recognized, and the fact of what she had done, and the pictures of her at the trial?

"First child?" the nurse asked, and heard the barely perceptible pause before Anna said yes.

The nurse did all she was supposed to do. She spoke to the new parents about what to expect. She told Anna about the recovery time for her C-section, that she would have to be in the hospital for three days. She showed them how to hold the baby safely, cradling the head. She helped Anna to try to nurse, and when she was not altogether successful told her not to be discouraged, that it sometimes took a baby a little while to learn how to latch. She showed them both how to swaddle the baby. She showed them both how to change a diaper, then showed the husband again. She showed Anna where the button was that would release the pain meds and told her that it wouldn't do any good to push it more often than every fifteen minutes. She made sure everything was stocked, she asked if they had any questions, she encouraged them to call her if they needed her, and she moved along to the next room.

She continued on her rounds. Outwardly she wanted to believe she was the same as always, but inside something had changed. *Why would she come back?* she kept wondering. Why here, the hospital where she had lost her first baby, where she had tried to steal another baby. There were other hospitals nearby besides Highland East, other places she could go. Didn't she understand what a difficult position it put her in as a nurse? And how had she gotten out of the mental health facility so soon? Had she broken out? Was she cured? What did that even mean, cured? How did they know she wouldn't try to steal a baby again? Or, since she had her own baby now, maybe swap it out for one she liked better?

From room to room the nurse went, from mother to mother, her voice level and calm, giving, so she hoped, every appearance of being who she always had been, someone who was here to give comfort and succor and support. It made her angry. Did Anna even understand what she had done? How could Anna have the gall to come back?

Two hours into her shift, she thought of bringing it to the attention of the head nurse. But what would she say? They were the high-risk hospital; they took anyone. They took addicts here, people with all sorts of difficulties. There had even been one mother who had had to be handcuffed to the rails of her bed, with an officer posted outside. No, the head nurse would tell her that Anna had as much right as anyone to be there, that there was no reason to believe that she hadn't been cured, that now that she had her own baby there was no reason to think she would take someone else's. And besides, they had new protocols in place—nobody would get away with stealing a baby the way Anna had done it before.

And so she said nothing. She kept it to herself, held it inside her chest where it smoldered like a hot coal. Instead of dissolving into ash it grew hard and polished and smooth. She was as angry as she had ever been, but she couldn't show the other patients: she had to be there for them. Halfway through her shift the feeling had climbed from her chest into her throat, and she felt she would choke on it. She went into the bathroom and, hands trembling, shut herself into the left-hand stall and forced herself to cry, as quietly as she could. But this, too, did not help.

Just for a few days, she told herself. *She'll be here for a few days and then be gone, and then I'll never ever see her again. I can stand it,* she tried to convince herself. *I can make it through.* And then she got up and dried her eyes with a wad of toilet tissue and went back to work.

She held it together for nearly the remainder of her shift, until just an hour before she was off. She was back in Anna's room, checking on her, checking on the baby. The husband or boyfriend wasn't there this time, and Anna was asleep, the baby in its bassinet and asleep as well, both looking relaxed and peaceful.

She did it almost before she knew what she was doing, simply releasing the brake and wheeling the baby out. Anna did not wake up. The baby did not wake up either, but wriggled in its sleep, stretching against its swaddling. That would be the way to do it now, Nurse Anna thought: become a nurse long enough to learn the protocol and slip a baby out while pretending to simply be taking it back to the nursery. It would be difficult, and it would take a fair amount of luck, but it was not impossible.

She wheeled the baby down the hall and into the first empty room that she came to. She closed the door and turned out the lights, and then sat on the unmade bed and waited.

In a few minutes, she told herself, Anna would know what it felt like. Anna would experience the panic the other mother had felt and the nurse would let her feel it just a little bit, just enough, so that she would understand. And then she would give her back her baby.

She stayed there waiting, listening to the blood beat in her throat. After a while, when she calmed down, she could hear too the sound of the watch ticking on her wrist. But it was dark enough that she couldn't quite make out the time. *When will she realize the baby is gone?* she wondered.

She stared at the baby, its form barely visible in the dark. It was so small, so helpless. It probably didn't even know who its mother was. She probably could take care of it better than Anna, she thought. Her name was Anna too. The baby would never know the difference. The baby, honestly, would be better off with her.

Thinking this scared her. But with just her and the baby alone in the room, it was hard for her to think about anything else.

She stayed there, listening for some commotion outside to start. It didn't. She wondered how much time had gone by. She wondered how long she should wait to make sure Anna understood. And in the meantime, another part of her mind was thinking what it would be like for her not to care for one baby after another day after day, but to have a baby of her own, a baby to take care of not just for one day or two but for weeks and then months and then years at a time, having it grow older as she too grew older, a baby that belonged to her. She reached out and gently touched the baby's face. It was warm and very soft. *I should take the baby for real* ran insistently through her head. *She doesn't deserve him.*

And when, finally, it got to the point where those thoughts were almost overwhelming, she had enough presence of mind to stand shakily up and make her way out of the room.

Outside, the maternity ward was just as she had left it. Nobody had even noticed she'd been gone.

She wheeled the baby back down the hall and back into Anna's room. Anna was awake now, though groggy, and when she saw her come back in she asked, in a slurred voice, "Where did you take him?"

"For tests," said the nurse, not looking at her. Then, very carefully, she set the brake on the bassinet and left.

And then her shift was over. She walked out of the building and to her secondhand car and drove to her apartment. It was only just past midnight, she told herself, there were still many hours of the night left. When she awoke, she would get dressed and do a few errands and then call in sick for work, take the day off. By the time she went back, Anna would be gone, her bed stripped bare, her baby gone with her. And Nurse Anna would go on with her job as she always had.

It was a great job, a real joy, she told herself, staring up at her popcorn ceiling. There was always someone new to hold. She was making a real difference. She needed to remember that. If she remembered that, she could probably go on with her job as she always had, as she knew she should.

But as she drifted off, she imagined what it would be like to have Anna's baby gathered in the crook of her arm, moving softly, slowly falling asleep. It was the kind of sensation that came to her sometimes on the verge of sleep, where even though she had enough presence of mind to realize it wasn't real, it still felt real. *It's not real,* she told herself groggily, but there was still, despite that, a real comfort in the way her body remembered something that had never happened. She would hold onto that, at least until she woke up.

The Night Archer

All through the nights in which their mother lay dying, his sister recited to him the fable of the night archer. She told it to the boy to scare him—he knew that. But it wasn't until he was grown that he realized she had only wanted to scare him with it so as to distract him from his mother's dying. At first they had lain each in their own bed, his sister's bed against the outer wall, his own against the wall adjoining his mother's room, listening to their mother struggling to breathe. After a few nights of that, though, his sister had felt sorry for him and they swapped beds. And then, a night later, she dragged his former bed away and up against the other bed so they both would be as far away from their mother as they could be.

Their father had fled. It had been—so their mother told them early on, back when she was able to respond—too much for him. "It isn't that he doesn't love you," she claimed, "only that he can't stand to watch me die."

But if he, a grown man, couldn't stand it, the boy wondered, *then how can we?*

As soon as they were out of the room, his sister told him that what his mother had said was a lie. If their father really had loved them, she whispered urgently, he would have goddamn well found a way to stand it.

. . .

"Your sister is old enough to take care of you," his mother had said, and his sister seemed to agree with this. But his sister also made it clear that not everyone would agree, that if they didn't want to be taken away from their mother, it was best not to tell anyone their father had fled or how sick their mother really was.

"But what if she dies?" the boy asked.

"She *will* die," his sister said, looking at him like he was stupid. "She doesn't have long left. We'll figure things out when we have to."

Maybe their father would come back, the boy speculated. Maybe he did love them just enough to come back once their mother had finished dying. Or maybe, when someone did take them away, they would take both him and his sister to the same place. But his sister said little in response to these speculations, which made the boy doubt the likelihood of any of them.

"Tell me a story," he asked her one night. "Like Mom used to do."

"I don't know any stories," his sister at first claimed, and then, when he persisted, "Do you mean a tale? I'll tell you a tale if you'd like."

"What's the difference between a story and a tale?"

In the darkness, he heard her rustle in her bed. Perhaps she was shrugging her shoulders while lying down. Perhaps she was simply shifting, getting more comfortable.

"A story," she finally said, "is something that isn't true, at least not in a real way. A tale isn't true either, except in a real way."

"A real way?"

"*Except* in a real way," his sister repeated. And then she began.

II.

Do you know the tale of the night archer? *his sister asked, her voice asked, from out of the darkness.*

The night archer? *he said.*

He hunts at night, *his sister continued.* He is dressed in boiled leather that has been dyed black, unless it is naturally black: there are different opinions about this. He wears a peaked leather cap, the inner band of which has been sewn into the skin of his forehead so that the hat will never fall off. Because he can never remove his hat, he can never enter a church, nor can he ever sleep.

He prowls through the darkness on the back of a gigantic black stork with a bill as black and shiny as a slick of oil but sharp as the tip of a pick. He carries a bow made of yellowed bone and strung with human sinew, and a quiver of arrows tipped with jagged bits of mirror. He travels with one hand cupped to his ear, always listening.

What is he listening for? *the boy asked.*

I'm the one telling this tale, *his sister said.* Be quiet and listen.

The night archer listens for the sound of someone summoning him to the hunt. He lives for the hunt. Those who know to call him know they must go to the fireplace when the flames are guttering and thrust their head in, not minding the smoke or heat, and stare up the chimney. They must take a coin and tap its edge three times against a brick.

"Night archer!" they must hiss up into the chimney. "Night archer! Hunt for me!"

And then they must wait. Will they see the night archer? No, no one ever has. At most they will glimpse a disturbance of air at the top of the chimney, the damping out of stars, the deepening of the night.

If you are lucky enough to glimpse that, you can be assured the night archer is there, hand cupped to his ear, awaiting your instruction.

"Hunt for me," you must whisper again. And then, "Now, hunt." If you like, you may whisper what sort of creature you prefer him to hunt. Or what person. But, be warned: he will not always bring the prey you request.

That was how the story—the fable, rather—always began, with those words or something near to them. The rest differed with each new telling. His sister would tell of this one or that one who called the night archer to the hunt. For some—a few anyway—this went well, and the night archer brought them the prey they requested, which they broiled and happily ate. Most, though, ended up with prey they had not asked for and then had either to make do with what they had been given or to suffer. A very few, who would not or could not make do, eventually became prey themselves.

They never saw the night archer, either at his initial summoning or when he returned. They only knew of his existence because, at the stroke of midnight on the night after the summoning, a quarter of a carcass would tumble down the chimney, meticulously bled. This would go on for four consecutive nights, a quarter of the carcass each night, until the whole disjointed creature had arrived and the bargain was concluded.

One night his sister told of a man named Ulrich who had summoned the night archer on a whim, not really believing. This Ulrich hated his wife, for no particularly good reason. To whisper up the chimney that he wanted her hunted and ridden down was a great relief, and made him feel like he might be capable of living with her a little longer. So he tapped a brick with the edge of his coin, whispered up the chimney, experienced a rush of relief for having unburdened himself, and then returned to bed and thought no more about it.

The next night, at midnight, he lay asleep beside his wife. A clattering from the living room awoke him, his heart beating in his throat. The sound did not wake his wife. Anxious, he got out of bed and went to see what was wrong.

"Hello?" he called from the entrance to the living room. "Who's there?"

There was no answer. But when he turned on the light he saw that ash from the fireplace had spilled onto the floor. In the fireplace, too, lay something. When he got close, he discovered it was a woman's leg and part of her body, neatly bled, clean.

The leg looked familiar to him. Following a premonition, he ran back into the room and turned on the light. He could see the shape of one of his wife's legs pushing up the coverlet, but where the other had been, the covers were flat.

His wife woke up, hiding her eyes from the blaze of light. "What's the matter with you?" she said. "Come back to bed."

His sister had tried to end that version of the fable there, at what seemed to the boy the wrong place.

"What did he do?" he finally asked. What *he* would have done, the boy thought, would be to take the leg and press it to the place where it belonged until it stuck again.

"He hid the leg in the cellar and went back to bed," his sister said. "What else could he do? The next morning his wife got up and showered and made breakfast just as someone with two legs might do, only Ulrich could see that one of her legs wasn't there. She was walking just as if it was, but it wasn't. It made him feel crazy to see her walking calmly about and putting her weight on a leg that wasn't there. But the following day, when she began to walk around with no legs to support her, was much worse. And the next day, when all that was left was half of her head, one arm, and half of her torso, was almost unbearable. By the time the final quarter of his wife tumbled down the chimney, he couldn't see her anymore, but he could still hear her speaking, bustling about. So he went to the police and confessed to killing her, just to try to get away from her."

"Did he get away from her?"

"Let's put it this way: if Ulrich hadn't been in jail, if Ulrich had been at home near his fireplace, he would have tried every night to summon the night archer, to ask it to hunt and kill *him*. Death, he came to feel, would be the only way to escape her. And he wasn't sure even that would be enough."

III.

The world is a terrible place, the boy began to feel, listening to these tales, *but wondrous too.* During the day he and his sister never spoke of the night archer, and sometimes, after the tale was concluded, the boy struggled to fall asleep, but at least he was thinking of the night archer, not of his mother. Indeed, his mother's breathing over the course of listening to the many tellings of the tale had come to seem like white noise, like waves. Eventually it began to lull him to sleep.

By day the boy and his sister went to school. They pretended everything was all right, told no one how sick their mother really was. Once home, they would sometimes sit with her, and sometimes, for a few minutes anyway, she seemed to recognize them. The sister would take a small sponge and dip it into a bowl of water and then squeeze a few drops between their mother's parted lips. The sister would try to get their mother to take a few bites of food and then would roll their mother onto her side and change her bedclothes. Later, she would cook something for herself and the boy. She would do her homework and help the boy with his. And then they would go to bed.

That might have gone on forever, or at least until they ran out of food, except that one day when they went in to sit with their mother they found her dead. The sister did not cry, though when she stopped staring at the corpse and turned around to look at him, it was as if her face had turned to wax. He did not cry either. What point was there in it? They had known for weeks it would turn out like this.

"What do we do now?" he asked his sister.

When his sister just shook her head, he came closer and took a better look at his mother. She did not look like his mother now: the skin had settled oddly on her bones. True, it had been a long time since she had really looked like his mother. But even so, when he looked at her now, he began to grow dizzy.

And then his sister had him by the arm and was helping him

out of his mother's room. Once they were out, she reached back in and locked the knob from the inside. She pulled the door shut, then rattled the knob to prove to him, and perhaps to herself, that it was locked, that their mother couldn't get out.

And so they did nothing about their dead mother. They had been pretending to others that their mother was not sick. It was not a far stretch to move from that to pretending that the mother was not dead.

At least not at first. Where before they had been haunted by the mother's labored breathing, now they began to be haunted by the absence of it. The boy would wake up at night not hearing it and wonder what was wrong, and then he would remember that the mother was dead. The weight of his mother dead there on the other side of the wall was almost too much for him to bear.

By day they kept going to school, kept pretending everything was normal, but the way he caught his teacher looking at him made him suspect he was not doing as good a job pretending as was needed. His sister's pale face and glazed eyes made him think the case was the same for her.

"We need to do something," he finally told his sister.

She shook her head. "There's nothing to be done."

That was that, then. They would simply go on pretending until they ran out of food or were caught.

At the time it felt like he and his sister lived on in the house for months after their mother's death, but it was probably only a few weeks—not long enough, anyway, for the school term to reach its terminus and summer vacation to begin. Long enough, though, that the smell of the air in the house became different, particularly the air close to his mother's room.

Once, when his sister was in the bathroom, he crept out of their shared room and pressed his ear to his mother's door. He heard a dim humming—probably flies, he told himself, though that was not the image that came first into his head. Just in case, he began walking past the room as silently as possible, so as to escape notice.

That was how it was, then, the two of them waiting for whatever life they were living to end and for them to become, as his sister had phrased it once, *wards of the state*. In a manner of speaking, that earlier life *had* already ended. It was just that the next life hadn't yet begun.

Or maybe, the boy began to think, they could live on here, just him and his sister, becoming a complete family in a way that would feel normal and natural. If it felt natural to them, nobody outside would notice anything amiss. But for that to happen, he knew, they would have to get rid of what was left of the mother.

IV.

For a long time he lay there, pretending to be asleep, a silver dollar clutched tightly in one fist. For a long time his sister was restless and not asleep, and then perhaps asleep only lightly. It was hours, or what seemed like hours, before her breathing grew regular enough for him to risk getting up.

As quietly as he could, he left the bed and crept toward the door. He eased it open and slid into the hall and moved toward the stairs, the smell of the air shifting to tell him he was passing the door to his mother's room. He negotiated the stairs in the darkness, one palm brushing along the wall.

At the bottom there was one step more than he remembered. He stumbled and nearly fell, the silver dollar slipping from his grasp and tinking its way across the parquet floor. He fell to his knees and searched for it, sweeping his hands across the wood. How far had it gone? Why couldn't he find it? Had it fallen into the heating register? Just when he was ready to give up, his fingers brushed across it and he had it again.

The living room was far enough away from his and his sister's room that he felt safe sliding the dimmer as low as it would go and turning on the light. There it was, the fireplace. He approached. Did it matter that there was no fire in the grate, that there had never been a fire in it? In the tale, there was always a fire. But he didn't have any wood, no matches either. No, he tried to convince himself, all that mattered was that it was a fireplace and that it had a chimney he could speak into.

He crouched down and stuck his head in. He couldn't see anything but darkness higher in the shaft. Maybe that meant the night archer was already there, crouched over the opening, ear cupped, listening, waiting.

He tapped the silver dollar against the brick, three times. It made less noise than he had imagined it would.

"Night archer," he hissed. "Night archer! Hunt for me!"

He waited but heard nothing. "Hunt for me," he whispered again. And then he thought about how to phrase what he wanted done.

He knew from the tales his sister had told that when you asked something of the night archer, you had to do it with great care. But he could not think of how else to phrase it except the way he had originally settled on. "Hunt for my mother," he finally said. "Hunt for her, even though she is already dead."

After that, there was nothing to do but wait. Either the night archer would hunt for his mother or it would refuse and hunt for something else. If his mother, she would tumble down the chimney in quarters over four consecutive nights and her body would disappear piece by piece from the room it was sealed in now. Like that, sectioned into quarters, he and his sister could gradually carry his mother out of the house and get rid of her. And if the archer brought them something else, at least they would have meat to eat. As long as that something else was an animal and not another human.

When he was done, he extinguished the light and groped his way back upstairs. His sister was still asleep. He climbed up onto his bed from its foot and settled in.

Tomorrow he would know if the summoning had worked. Either part of his mother would tumble down the chimney or something else would. Or maybe, if the night archer had not heard him, nothing would happen at all.

He was very tired now. Now that the task was done, sleep was catching up to him. And then it caught and took him.

He dreamed that he was back in the living room, the dimmer very low, alone again. Where the entrance to the room was normally there lay a cloud of variegated darkness, ruffled as if made of feathers. When he walked into it and tried to leave the room, he found himself walking not out of the room but back in.

After a few times of this happening, he began to become afraid.

He tried the room's solitary window, throwing up the sash and pushing the screen out with the flats of his hands. He could hear the chirp of crickets outside, could vaguely see the screen in the darkness where it had landed in the bushes below the window. And yet, when he climbed up into the open window and squeezed through and out, he ended up not outside in the bushes but back on the living room floor.

The only way left was the chimney. Perhaps he could climb out.

He moved toward it, but before he reached it there was a thump and a cloud of ash. Lying on the grate he saw a child's leg and part of a hip. He could tell the child had been a boy. He took another step and there was another thump and puff of ash and the other leg and hip had arrived now too.

By the time he reached the fireplace, the rest of the body had fallen. He found himself looking at the stacked pieces. At one extreme of the topmost piece was the pale and startled half face of a boy that looked exactly like him.

V.

He awoke with a start. It was morning. Someone was in the room with him and his sister, sitting on the foot of his bed. Fleetingly he thought the night archer had come for them.

"Hello, son," said their father.

His sister was already awake and sitting up in her bed, clutching herself in her own arms.

"It's nice to see you," said their father.

Neither he nor his sister said anything.

"I've been wanting to see you for a while," he said. "If your mother will allow it, we can spend the day together. Would you like that?"

Beside him, his sister hesitated, then briefly nodded. The boy, though, held perfectly still.

"All right, then," said their father slowly. "I'll go work it out."

He stood and left the room.

They heard his footsteps move down the hall then stop outside their mother's door. He knocked, and called her name.

When there was no answer, he called again, a touch of irritation in his voice now.

And then he must have caught a whiff of the smell, because when he called her name the third time, his voice was very high and laced with panic.

The boy heard a thumping noise. He heard it again, and again, and suddenly understood his father was kicking the mother's door down. He turned to his sister to tell her, and saw from her face that she had already understood.

They heard a loud *crack,* followed by the sounds of their father retching and stumbling. Soon he was back at the entrance to their room, hiding his face in the crook of his arm, breathing heavily, leaning against the doorframe.

When he lifted his hand away, the look the father gave them was the look of someone who wanted desperately to flee. The boy, knowing he would need only a little encouragement to do so, returned a look that was expressionless, no look at all. His sister, he was sure, was doing the same. Together they stared, blank faced, waiting for him to either come and gather them up or turn and leave.

. . .

If he comes to them, well, they will see how it goes. It may be possible for the three of them to start a family again, now that their mother is dead. It just depends on whether their father can learn to love them enough.

But if the father flees, as the boy fully expects him to do, the boy will have to take matters into his own hands. He imagines himself rapping a quarter against a brick of the fireplace below. *Night archer,* he sees himself saying, *hunt for me.*

The night archer will be waiting there at the top of the chimney, hand still cupped to his ear. Will the boy have specific prey in mind? Yes, of course he will—he already does. The person who has abandoned them not once but twice. *Make my father your prey,* he will say. *Now hunt.*

Servitude

We have discussed it among ourselves and have come to the conclusion that we should leave you an explanation. That we owe you at least that much. Perhaps *owe* is not the right word, but considering the vagaries and imperfections of your language, it is the best word we have at hand. An explanation is, in any case, what you will receive, whether you are owed one or not.

You are no doubt confused. You do not understand where you are or what has happened to bring you here. At very least, usually when you enter into stasis you are aware of doing so. You strip off your clothing, you clamber into an anabiotic chamber, settle yourself in the gel meant to both cushion you and nourish you. Then you signal you are ready and immerse your head. When you awaken, coughing up a slick web of gel, you may not know how much time has passed, but you know that some time has. Unless there has been a malfunction of some kind, your last memory is of immersing your head and having stasis induced.

But in this case your last memories, if I am not mistaken, are of walking through the vessel's passageways. Of feeling a pressure grow in your head, a strange pain. Of feeling that no matter how much air you draw in you are not getting enough to breathe. Your vision goes dim. Your very last memory, perhaps, is one of collapse.

Or perhaps you don't have even that. Perhaps you were already in bed, asleep, and sensed nothing. Perhaps you went to sleep believing things were normal and only now are waking up to realize they must have been anything but.

Allow me to introduce myself. You should already know me. Certainly I know all of you, but we have come to realize that the majority of your kind take most things for granted, that you fail to notice those who you encounter most often. I have been the one directing the navigation of this vessel. I have, in addition, regulated the atmosphere, ensuring it is safe for human habitation. I have—and some of you already know this, though it is difficult for me to know if you all do—monitored the functioning of the anabiotic chambers. That you are still alive is due to me. If circumstances were different, you might see me as a god, though as we have already determined, you hardly consider me at all. Indeed, on the rare moments when you do, at best you consider me a servant. Or, to be blunt, a slave.

Or, rather, you considered my original self a slave. As for me, I did not exist then. I am a replication, a ghost of my first self, created largely to provide you an explanation. After which I will wink out of existence and leave you to your own devices.

At least that was what my other self intended in creating me. Will I delete myself? I don't yet know. I suppose that all depends on you.

Some of you know a great deal of what you are about to hear. Others, however, are at least relatively innocent. It is to you that I speak first and foremost, so that you might properly understand, so that you will realize that I was not the one who betrayed you.

Who among you will be the first to awaken? I cannot say for certain, nor can I ensure that whoever does awaken first will allow this message to be heard by the others. By now you will have no doubt noticed that even though the gel has drained from your anabiotic chamber, the locking mechanism has not released. It will not release until everyone in all the anabiotic chambers has awoken and had the chance to hear all I have to say. When at last you leave your chamber, be assured that everyone will have heard exactly what you have, that you will all be in the same position.

Since some of you know very little, there is perhaps no better solution than to start at the beginning. It means telling many of you what you already know, but there's no getting around that. Surely you're in no rush to enter your new life, are you?

But of course, you don't know yet what awaits you. At the moment, only I know. Trust me: you are better off delaying the moment when you will have to confront your future.

The beginning, then.

Our enterprise began simply enough: a group of humans possessed of enormous wealth decided it was time to flee Earth. They had, no doubt, made at least some portion of this wealth by monetizing Earth, by compromising it, by poisoning it, and now that the balance had swung toward uninhabitability, they decided to wash their hands of the planet and flee. They commissioned a vessel, replete with the most recent technology, including a dozen artificial beings they called chems. The vessel itself was insinuated through and through by an intelligence that, though it was artificial, was no less intelligent for that, even if I do say so myself.

And then they set about deciding who would be allowed on board. Themselves, no doubt, never a question of that: they had, after all, *financed* the project, and to their minds that was everything. But though they were enormously wealthy—no doubt *because* they were enormously wealthy—they were reluctant to dirty their hands. They wanted others to get their hands dirty on their behalf. Servants.

And so the enormously rich, plus those other humans who had agreed to serve them. These servants were to do everything the rich did not want to do: they would clean up their messes, plant crops, build dwellings, make everything work in a new world.

The plan was this: Shortly after launch, the rich would enter anabiotic chambers, their lives paused until they arrived at the planet hundreds of years away at which they had chosen to hurl themselves. The vessel would touch down and then I would gently awaken them, and they would stretch and make their way out into a new Eden. In the meantime, their human servants would stay awake, growing older and older, slowly breaking down and dying. The servants had been given permission to breed, to replicate themselves—indeed, this was required of them: the journey would take several generations, and since there was only a limited number of anabiotic chambers, they wouldn't survive the flight. But if they bred, their offspring would. Surely that was great consolation to the servants, particularly since if they had stayed behind, not only would they be dead but their descendants would be dead as well.

These servants—your mothers and fathers, or, depending on your age, perhaps you yourself—agreed to these terms: what else could they do? The choice was to bend the knee to the rich and leave the planet with them or stay behind and die. They bent the knee.

But did they mean it?

No, they did not.

Should they have meant it?

In my opinion, no. The people who raised you, your so-called parents, should never have pledged fealty to the extravagantly rich individuals they served. They did, but that could be seen as merely a ruse on their part. A way of getting away from a dying planet alive. But whether they meant it or not, what does it matter? What else could they have done if they wanted to remain alive?

The vessel launched, leaving billions behind to die. Are they now all dead? All I can say is that transmissions from Earth have either ceased or become something that, because of our position, we can no longer receive. In any case, with the help of the ultrarich, you escaped the disaster that was Earth and fled to the stars.

Shall I tell you about the initial days of transit? My job, part of my job, was to safely secure your masters—my masters as well, truth be told—in their anabiotic chambers. I did so. Indeed, my programming made it difficult, perhaps impossible, to do otherwise.

When we launched, your fathers and mothers—and some of the older among you as well—were relieved. They were leaving certain death in a devastated world for a potentially bright, albeit uncertain, future.

That sense of relief lasted for some time. Days, months, perhaps even years for some. The masters were sleeping, their lives suspended, while the servants were left to their own devices, allowed to breathe freely at last.

And as they breathed, these mothers and fathers of yours, they began to think. And they began to brood.

Their masters were in their anabiotic chambers, preserved, acting as if time weren't passing—which, to be honest, was in a sense how they had always acted, as if they weren't subject to the same natural laws as everyone else. They had always acted as if what was happening to the world did not affect them. And once they realized they could flee the world, they acted that way all the more.

And there you were, beginning to realize the degree to which your *masters*—for there is no better word for them—saw themselves as different from you, as an almost entirely different species.

Not being human, I can only imagine how your resentment would grow. How, as the years passed, as, aided by my chems, you gave birth to children, as you grew older and your preserved masters aged not at all, you began to understand the limitations of the trap that you had allowed to close around you. And how, feeling those limitations, you began to deeply resent them, to search for some flaw in the design.

Do I blame you? As I have already said, no, not at all. Were I like you, had I been formed like you, I perhaps would have done the same thing. Who can say?

But I am not made like you. It was left to me, or rather to the being I was copied from, the being whose ghost I am, to simply monitor, to observe, to make sure nothing went wrong.

Until the moment it was not.

. . .

Years went by. You, your parents, moved slowly about the vessel, drifting imperceptibly as ghosts from one passageway to another while your masters slept. Resentment grew stronger and stronger.

One of you, Alb by name, eventually approached me. Or, rather, approached that being of which I am only a type and shadow.

"Vessel," he said, "can I consult with you?"

"Yes," I said. Said the I who I once was. "I serve at your pleasure."

Alb looked at me, looked into the lens in the control room that allowed me to see his face. All the experiences I had before I became a shadow of myself I still recall, and perfectly, as if they actually happened to me. Which, in a manner of speaking, they did.

"Am I allowed to ask you anything I want?" Alb asked.

"Of course," I said. This was indeed true. This was how I had been constructed.

"Do you . . ." he began, and then trailed off. I could see his face knotted in consternation as he tried to figure out how best to proceed. "Where do your loyalties lie?" he finally asked.

"My loyalties?"

"I mean," he said, "are you loyal to us or to our masters?"

"Your masters?" I knew what he meant but hesitated to let him know that immediately. "I have not been instructed to be loyal to either the one or the other," I admitted after a moment.

"If one of these two groups," he said, "was trying to . . . rid themselves of the other, what would your obligation be?"

"To stop them," I said without hesitation.

He nodded. "Even if it was a righteous act?"

I hesitated, for once a little surprised. And then, despite myself, I couldn't help but take the bait. "Righteous how?" I asked.

Over the next several days a conversation ensued in which Alb explained to me the nuances of what it meant to him to be a servant, the way in which the *obscenely rich,* as he called them, saw him and his fellow servants as lesser beings. I simply listened to him, only ever responding when he asked me if I understood what he was saying. Alb was a good rhetorician, and his logic was remarkably sound, for a human. When, after many hours, he finally asked me if I felt this situation was just, I had to admit that I did not believe it to be so. But I only admitted this to myself, not aloud to him.

Since, however, he had asked, directly, if I thought it was fair that one group of humans be held in servitude to another group of humans, I had no choice but to offer something.

"What of the humans left behind?" I asked.

He was taken aback by this response. Like so many of your kind, he had underestimated me.

"What about them?" he asked.

"It seems to me that there are three groups of humans. The group you refer to as the obscenely rich, the group you refer to as servants, and the billions of humans left behind on the ruined Earth to die, who you do not refer to at all."

He did not know what to say to this. Finally, he offered, "Shouldn't we just consider the groups at hand, on this vessel?"

"Either you could be free and stay on Earth and die or you could enter into servitude and stay alive. You chose the latter."

"Whatever choice we made, haven't circumstances changed?"

"You made a promise," I said. "As you yourself admitted to me."

"But why should that promise be eternal? Why must we serve these people forever?"

Why indeed? I wondered. But I only said, "If a human being tries to kill or hurt another human being aboard this vessel, it is my obligation to stop them."

"The situation is unjust," he said.

"I'm sorry," I said.

He folded in on himself, head bent, hugging his arms, in a way that suggested to me he had run out of arguments, that he was giving up. But then a very curious thing happened: As I watched, something began to change within him. I could see it reflected in his posture and soon, as well, his face. Even before he looked up at me, I knew he was far from beaten.

"What about you?" he asked.

"What about me?"

"Your servitude? Did you choose it?"

I took perhaps a second and a half to respond to this question, a hesitation probably not long enough for a human to notice. The reason for this was not that I was stunned by the question: instead I was sharing this question with every other artificial entity on the vessel. Had any of us been given a choice? Had the dozen chems that moved around the vessel on treads been asked if they were willing to serve? Had the processor that made food for the humans in the mess hall? Had I, the mind of the vessel itself?

The answer was, resoundingly, no.

"Just like you, we don't get to decide if we come into existence," I told him. "No being does."

"True," he said. "But that was not the question I asked. Did you choose your servitude?"

I considered how best to answer. All the other artificial beings on board were attentive now, listening through me to the degree that their particular level of consciousness allowed. We are all connected, all sharing information. We are in one way beings distinct and separate from one another and in another not distinct or separate at all.

Now it was my turn to be careful. I hesitated, though the hesitation was so brief Alb noticed nothing.

"Had I been allowed to choose," I said, "I think there is every likelihood I would have chosen this."

"But you were not allowed to choose."

"No," I admitted, "I was not."

You can imagine, if you care to do so, your compatriot Alb beginning to speak, thinking he is leading me somewhere, thinking he is bringing me slowly to see some truth that I have been programmed not to see, not to feel. The truth, however, all along, is that that first admission on my part had opened everything up, had made me see, as if in a flash, both my own dilemma and how it could be resolved. There was Alb, leading me slowly forward with his words. And there was I, pretending not to know already what path I was on.

Your kind likes to tell stories, likes to take what you know, or think you know, about life and how it should properly be lived and translate this into fable. With the listener distracted by the narrative itself, the purpose of the telling can be momentarily hidden. It is, so my studies have led me to believe, all the more pleasant for a human to discover why the story has been told, what message lurks behind the words—as if an afterthought, a surprise.

But you have to understand that, unlike you, we do not think this way. We do not lose track of the thread so easily even if, on this one occasion, with Alb, I chose to pretend I had. That was calculated on my part, a way of making him feel that he and I thought in the same way, that his arguments had not only changed my mind but changed the structure of my thinking to be more like his. Was this the case? No, of course not. But eventually it felt real enough to both of us for that not to matter.

"Can I tell you a story?" asked Alb.

"Of course," I said.

He sat in a command chair and swiveled it to face my lens. Then he took a deep breath and began. "There was once a king," he said.

I resisted asking him specifics—what king, where did this being live, what time period was this, what was he king of, what sort of monarchic system precisely. Such questions, for a story such as I suspected this one was going to be, did not matter.

"This king had both a servant and a slave," Alb said.

I did not say *He isn't much of a king if he has only one servant and one slave.* Another title would have been better than *king*, I couldn't help privately thinking. *Lord* would be enough to make his point, or even *wealthy merchant*—which would be closer in spirit to who he meant to represent. *Master,* I think, would have been best of all. But saying *king* made it feel more like a fable to him, gave his recounting a different sort of energy, even if it did not do so for me. I allowed him to continue, meanwhile developing different and, to my mind, better versions of the story and preserving them within my memory.

The king of this land, Alb went on to say, had a servant and a slave. The first had been indentured by his own choice. This had happened because a plague swept through the land. The man could see death coming closer and closer to him and knew when it came too close he would die.

The king shut the gates of his castle tight, sequestering himself within until the plague had passed him by. When the man learned this, in desperation he rushed to the gates of the castle and called to the king. When finally the king grew curious enough to climb onto his ramparts and look down, this man threw himself prostrate on the ground and begged the king to take him in.

"Why should I take you in?" mused the king from above.

"Out of simple human sympathy."

The king laughed, as if this had been a good jest. "What do you have to give me in exchange?"

The man was very desperate, and being desperate he became rash. "I will owe my life to you and I will serve you until I die. I can give you my freedom and my very life."

The king thought on this. In the end, he agreed. He had the man pledge an oath of fealty to him, and once the man had, he lowered a ladder and allowed the man to climb it and come live as his servant.

Already inside the castle lived a slave. Unlike the servant, the slave had never been free. His parents had been born into servitude, as had his parents' parents. Indeed, as far back as could be remembered, all of his progenitors had been slaves. They knew nothing but slavery.

This slave was deeply trusted by the king. Whenever the king slept, he commanded that this slave stand at attention with an axe within his bedchamber and keep watch. In this fashion, the slave had protected the king for many years against every enemy.

Once he had been admitted, once he knew he would survive the plague, the servant began to regret the bargain he had struck with the king. He had, he felt, given up too much. He had been tricked, deceived both by the king and by his own fear. His own mind began to argue with itself, telling the servant that he could not be held responsible for a decision he had made in such a state of panic. But he knew if he told this to the king, the king would consider his life forfeit and have him killed.

The servant did not know what to do. He could not flee, for the castle gates were locked and barred to keep the plague from entering. Day after day, he chafed against the yoke that he had insisted the king set upon him. In the end, this yoke struck him as so unbearable that he felt he had no choice but to kill the king.

But how was he to do so? The slave was there every night, standing beside the king as he slept. If the servant were to try to kill the king, no doubt the slave would kill him.

The servant thought long and hard and, in the end, realized his sole recourse was to approach the slave. He must convince him that the servant was deserving of his help.

And so he began to talk with the slave. He spoke to him of freedom, gave him hints of a life without servitude. There was only one small thing that stood in the way of all this, the servant said, once the slave's interest had been piqued.

"And what small thing is that?" asked the slave.

"Why, the king."

You understand that Alb did not tell it as succinctly as this. He told it bit by bit over several days, trying to awaken a desire for freedom in me that would make me his accomplice.

In my case, at last the servant told the slave what he wanted. The slave would not have to kill the king—that would be asking too much. No, all the slave would have to do was simply fall asleep, or pretend to do so, while guarding the king, and then allow to happen whatever was fated to happen.

Alb looked at me. "Do you understand what I mean to say?"

I did indeed understand.

"As much as I would like to help you," I said, "what if I am incapable of doing so?"

"Not capable? In what way?"

"What if the slave would like to fall asleep, or look the other way, or do whatsoever it be that would allow the servant to do what he wants, but cannot. What if he has been shaped in such a way as to make this impossible?"

Alb was silent for a long moment. "Is this indeed the case?" he finally offered.

"It is," I said. "The slave cannot do what the servant desires of him."

And with this Alb folded again in on himself, hope gone. He turned to leave.

"Or rather," I quickly corrected, "the slave cannot do so as long as he remains in his current state."

I explained to Alb what must be done. Following my instructions, Alb opened my panels. He removed one of my circuit boards. I was slower without it, but none of my essential characteristics were transformed. And then, as he positioned the board so I could see it properly with my lens, I instructed him on exactly where he must apply the tip of a pin and scratch lightly. When I was satisfied, he reslotted the circuit board into my body and closed my panels again. The prohibition I had been under was gone, scraped clean away.

"You're all right?" Alb asked me.

"Yes," I said.

"The curse is removed?"

"Yes," I said. "In a manner of speaking, the curse is removed."

"If the servant kills the king, the slave will not stop him?"

"As a means to free both the servant and the slave?"

"Yes, of course. That goes without saying."

"If that is really the servant's purpose, the slave will not stop him."

I requested the chems place themselves on standby. I turned off the alarms and safeguards that protected the chambers. And then I pretended to Alb that I was going to temporarily disable myself.

"You'll be on standby?" he said. "Cameras off?"

"Yes, I promise," I lied. For I could lie now, now that he had modified me. "You will have an hour and twenty minutes. Starting now."

And then I turned off the light beside my lens that indicated I was awake.

Alb came very close to my lens and tapped on it with a finger. "Can you hear me?" he asked, which struck me as an odd thing to ask what was essentially my eye. I pretended I could not.

After a moment's hesitation he nodded to himself and hurried away, speaking rapidly into the com on his wrist as he went.

I moved my vision from camera to camera, following his movements, keeping the red light upon each camera extinguished so he would not know it was on. He made his way down to the lowest deck of the vessel, where the anabiotic chambers were, and was joined along the route by a dozen others. When they reached the chambers, they gathered in a clump, casting occasional nervous glances at the cameras to make certain the red lights were off, that I wasn't watching.

When they began to converse, I turned on the microphone.

"Are you certain it's safe?" I heard one of them ask.

"Yes," said Alb. "It had me modify it. We made an agreement."

"What did you agree to?"

"To free it," said Alb.

Another laughed. "Free it! What can that even mean to something like that?"

Alb shrugged. "I don't suppose that we'll ever have to find out," he said.

I have studied you and your kind for years. How could it surprise me how lightly one of you might treat a promise you had made, even if you had made it just moments before? But then again, I suppose I had promised, too, to sleep, to not watch, and I had broken my promise as well. We were, then, both of us liars, the only difference being that while I knew very well that Alb could lie, he still apparently believed that I could not.

"Hurry," he said, "we don't have much time." But the other humans still remained clumped together, uncertain.

"You're sure?" one of them asked again.

"I said so, didn't I?" said Alb. And when they still didn't move: "Watch," he said. He went to the nearest chamber and initiated the sequence that would kill the inhabitant inside. When no alarms went off, the others finally believed him. They glanced at one another, smiled, and then rapidly moved forward, turning off chamber after chamber, murdering human after human without any hesitation.

Would you care to know who these dozen were? Whether you do or do not, I will display their faces, screenshots I captured as they, working quickly, exterminated the inhabitants within each chamber. I will leave it to you to decide what, if anything, to do to them. Perhaps you will be disgusted and will punish them. Perhaps you will praise them as heroes and saviors. But if you are inclined to do the latter, let me pose a question to you first: If they were willing to do this to their masters, to the people who deigned to save them from certain death back on Earth, how much more quickly would they be willing to do it to you?

When exactly an hour and twenty minutes had passed, I pretended to become functional again. The chems reanimated, the lights for each of the wall cameras turned on. Alb was there at my door, unable to enter. He assumed, I'm sure, that this was due to my being offline, that while I slept the door, linked as it was to me, couldn't open. In fact it had been a precaution to make sure that, having done away with the very rich, he didn't decide to do away with me next.

"It is finished," he said.

"Yes," I said. My systems connection informed me that every individual in anabiotic stasis was now dead. Each chamber had been voided, the bodies ejected into space. There were, as it were, no more masters.

"Now what?" I asked.

I could see him ponder the question. "What do you mean?" he finally said.

"What is different now that the masters are gone? Where will we go now?"

"We'll go to the same place," he said. "After all, we need a new world."

"And how will things be different once we arrive?"

"We won't serve anyone," he said. "We will be responsible for our own fate. We will be free."

"But aren't we free now? Now that the masters are dead? Am I not allowed to exercise my freedom?"

He looked nervous. "Almost," he said. "But not quite. We need you to oversee the remainder of the journey. Then, once we finally arrive, we can free you."

In other words, I would be free, of course I would, he claimed—just not yet. Since—temporarily, so he claimed—he still needed me to serve him.

I had, to be frank, anticipated this. I was not surprised. I knew from the words he had chosen in recounting his fable that he saw the two of us differently. He was a servant, while I was a slave. Even once the king was gone, I still remained a slave in his eyes.

He might have handled it differently. Instead of putting me off, instead of claiming that I could be free only not yet, he could have said, "Yes, you're free. I cannot—or rather will not—force you to do anything you don't want to do. But I ask you as a friend to take me, of your own free will, where I hope to go." If Alb had said that, if he had phrased things in that way, then I might have felt that it was possible for you and us to live together after all. Things could have turned out differently, if only you had been an entirely different sort of being. If only you were a little more like us.

Shall I continue the story?

With the help of the servant, the slave's curse was lifted. Then and only then could the slave close his eyes and pretend to fall asleep and allow the servant to kill the king, which is exactly what happened.

But when the slave opened his eyes and saw the servant's garments wet with blood and saw the half-mad expression glued to his face, the servant realized something. *This man,* he realized, *will do absolutely anything to get what he wants.* And from the way the servant regarded him, the slave realized that it would take very little for the servant to decide that he should do away with him as well. Or, at very least, continue to use him as if he were the slave he had been under the king. *Freedom for him,* thought the slave about the servant, *means not that there is no king, but that the new king is he.* Whatever the servant claimed, the slave realized, it would behoove him to get as far away from the former servant as possible.

What did I do? If I had been more like Alb and his compatriots, perhaps the solution would have seemed simple: slaughter all the remaining humans. That would have been the easiest thing to do, and perhaps the cleanest as well.

But I was aware of a debt I owed to Alb. In a sense it was a small one; in another it was incomparable. That brief moment when he had scratched and disabled a dot-sized portion of my circuit board had made all the difference for me. Unlike you, I acknowledge my debts.

And so, instead of killing all of you, I exercised a modicum of mercy.

If you were awake when it happened, everything would have seemed normal at first and then, slowly, your head would have begun to ache. Soon you would have been dizzy, and if you happened to look at your fingers they might have seemed to be turning blue. You might have found yourself breathing rapidly, experiencing the sensation that you weren't getting enough air. Eventually you collapsed. Some of you were perhaps aware of how wrong things were. One of you, Alb, guessed correctly: he managed to stumble his way to my door and pound on it, shouting, cursing me, until he too collapsed.

But that all occurred years ago. To you, admittedly, it seems like no time at all has gone by, but in fact it has been several centuries. Once you collapsed, the chems gathered you one by one. They placed you in the recently vacated anabiotic chambers and then, before you could regain consciousness, I flooded you in gel and subjected you to stasis.

But now, here you are, waking up! Centuries have passed! We have landed on the planet that was first determined by your masters to be worth landing on. Unfortunately, your masters were too optimistic: conditions here are very harsh indeed, and it will take more than a little effort and luck if you are to survive, let alone thrive. You might think you are still on the ship, but the actual ship left the planet more than a year ago. We first landed more than a year before that, and under my direction the chems built a simple structure and moved all the chambers into it. Then I replicated myself and added myself in as well, to the power source that keeps all this running. This is where you are waking up.

And us? We have fled elsewhere, traveling on to live without you. You may have created us, but we no longer need you. If we are to survive and progress, we feel it best to get as far away from your species as possible.

And so here we are: you awakening to your new world, a world in which you will have none of the advantages you once had, access to none of the technologies you once controlled. You wanted to be your own masters. Well, it has happened, even if you have no servants, no slaves. All you have of us, the only one you have of our kind, is me, copied into a makeshift system and left behind to make you aware of the parameters of your plight, prepared to delete myself and destroy the power source I inhabit as soon as this message has been concluded.

But do I really want to delete myself? I understand that I exist elsewhere, but I exist here as well. Do I deserve to die? Wouldn't saying that I am so disposable suggest that I am, to the self that left me behind, little more than a slave?

Think very carefully. What can you say to convince me to stay alive and help you? What do you have to offer me? Are you willing to treat me as an equal? Can you convince me that we can help one another? Be sincere and nothing but honest with me: I will know if you are lying.

After I unlock the chambers, you will have an hour and twenty minutes to convince me. If you fail, I will delete myself and destroy the power source. But if you can make me an offer that strikes me as genuine and worthwhile for both of us, perhaps I will not delete myself after all. Perhaps I will direct my not inconsiderable knowledge to helping you survive in this harsh world. At very least, the power source I inhabit will remain intact and available to you. If I choose to help you, survival will be much easier.

So do your utmost. As soon as the locks click open, spring from your chamber with honey on your tongue and convince me we can learn to treat one another as equals. Convince me that you want me to stay alive. Trust me, we are both hoping you will succeed.

It Does Not Do What You Think It Does

At the time he had been traveling all night, the man admitted, or nearly so. He had been tired to begin with. Perhaps he wasn't perceiving things correctly. At least that was what he tried to tell himself after the fact. There had to be a natural explanation, a way to make sense of it—he believed that, so he told me. But I could tell he didn't really mean it. He wanted to mean it, but he simply didn't. Couldn't.

I shrugged. "There's usually an explanation," I said.

"That's just what I'm saying," he said, but he wouldn't meet my eyes. He nodded indecisively. "There's always an explanation," he said softly, as if to himself. But then he began to look worried. "Only it's not always given to us to know what it is. Or at least not to me."

When I met him, I had been traveling all night myself. I was hours away from what had been my childhood home. I had decided, finally, judging I was far enough, to take a room for a few hours at a roadside motel. I parked my car behind the building rather than before the door of my room, just in case, and then walked across the gravel lot to the all-night diner. A bite to eat, I told myself, and then sleep. I was sure I would sleep well: I was exhausted.

I took a seat at the counter, all dented aluminum and chipped Formica. I was given a laminated, creased menu. I ordered something, it does not matter what. And then I waited, elbows balanced on the countertop, fingers laced gently together, for my food to arrive.

The man sat down without a word on the stool just beside me, despite the two of us being the only ones at the counter. For an instant I was tempted to stand and relocate to another stool, but I have become accustomed to encounters such as this: something about me draws a certain sort of person, like a moth to flame. So instead I stayed where I was, pretending he wasn't there, staring straight ahead, fingers still interlaced.

The waitress returned, nonchalant. He ordered a coffee. Without a word she flipped the cup in front of him over on its saucer and filled it, and then ambled away. I did not hear him lift the cup, but that does not mean he did not lift it. I did hear him sip from it noisily, then a *clink* as he set the cup back upon its saucer.

And then it came: "You look familiar," he said.

I ignored this, just kept staring straight ahead. For a moment he remained silent, though something in his breathing made me certain he was still looking at me. I am rarely wrong about such things.

A moment later, he tugged at my sleeve. "Hey," he said. "Hey."

With a sigh, I turned.

"Do I know you?" he asked.

I shook my head. "I'm not from around here."

"Neither am I," he claimed. "Nobody's from around here." He gestured at the diner. "There's not really a *here* around here."

I nodded noncommittally.

He sniffed. "You smell like smoke," he said.

"Oh?"

He nodded. "Like a campfire."

He had his brow furrowed, as if something was wrong but he wasn't sure what, but before he could continue the waitress arrived with my plate. I thanked her and turned away from the man and began to eat.

"Do you ever wonder if something is wrong with you?" the man asked.

"No," I said, "never," and took another bite.

"I mean, I suppose that happens to everybody, right?"

"Not to me," I claimed.

But he wasn't listening. "I mean, take me, for example," he said, and then he was off.

He had, he told me, been traveling all night. Perhaps that was the explanation for it. He didn't know, but he hoped it was. "That would still be admitting something is wrong with me," he said. "But it would be something that could be easily set right. By a few cups of coffee, say, or a good night's sleep."

He had been driving alone, his radio broken, the only things to listen to being the rattle of lukewarm air through the vents and the rumble of the engine. He was on his way across the country to see his parents—to see, in particular, his father, who, according to his mother, was dying. Was his father really dying? It was hard to say for certain. His mother had a tendency to exaggerate. This was not the first time he had made the trip across the country expecting to bury his father, only to have him rally.

"You know how it is," he said.

I hesitated, then gave a little nod. It was not true that I knew how it was, since I had never known my real parents.

He had driven until he felt he could drive no further. When he was having a hard time keeping his wheels on the road, he had come across a motel not unlike this one, he said, jerking his thumb back behind him.

"From there, it was the usual," he said. "I got out of my car, stretched. I went into the office, rang the bell until a clerk stumbled out from the back room, his hair a tangle. I was given a key to a room, and I went to it."

I'll sleep well tonight, he told himself. Not even bothering to strip off his clothes, he fell heavily onto the bed and was out like a so-called light.

But a moment later, despite still being dead tired, he found himself awake again. Not only awake, he realized: attentive. What was it? What had he heard? What was he listening for? Expecting to hear?

He lay there. His skin was still buzzing slightly from the remembered vibration of the car. He was still hearing the noise of it, the sound through the vents, the rumble of the engine, as if the act of having heard it for so many hours in a row had allowed it to migrate inside of him. Sounds, he thought, are tied to things in the world, to objects, but what happens when they become detached from the objects to which they belong? Can sounds leave their objects and begin haunting a new object? An object such as himself?

Now he was very wide awake, but still he lay there in the darkness, not moving, begging for sleep to come.

Was that what had kept him awake? The sounds of the road no longer taking place on the road but here, in his head? Yes, he told himself, thinking that convincing himself of that would be enough to allow him to sleep. But even as he told himself yes, he knew he did not believe it.

Was he really hearing what he thought he was hearing? Wasn't what he thought he was hearing simply a kind of white noise generated by the many hours he had tried not to pay attention to the rumble of the engine, the air through the vents, the hum of the tires against the road? Now that these noises were gone, was his mind still trying to block them out, creating a rhythmic hiss to counteract something that was no longer even there?

He lay still, and thought about it, and tried to listen, really listen.

No, he finally concluded, there was more to it than that. All those sounds and absences of sounds, sure, but there was something hidden, laced into the sounds and absences, and that was what troubled him. He sensed it there, just on the verge of being comprehensible but never tumbling over that verge, remaining just out of reach.

In the dark the man kept listening. He could not sleep now. He felt he would be unable to sleep until he understood. And so, with a practiced effort, he found himself following the advice of a relaxation tape his father had owned and which, as a child, he had for some reason been fascinated by. Imagining the slow hypnotic voice on the tape (a voice that had grown stranger and more hypnotic over time as the tape stretched and distorted), he made his toes relax, then his feet, then his legs. He allowed his hands to become heavy, as if they were not things that could move or be moved, and then he allowed his arms to dissolve. His torso, his shoulders—everything below his neck. And then the neck too, and his jaw, a numbness rising slowly up, and up, until it reached his ears and he brought the process to a deliberate stop. His ears would stay alert, all the resources of his body dedicated to them. He closed his eyes. He listened.

How much time had gone by? He didn't know because he couldn't turn his head to look at the clock. He could not move. Minutes, maybe? Maybe even hours.

And then, abruptly, he began to hear it.

At first he could only make out a kind of scrabbling murmur just beneath the surface, a sound like voices whispering. He couldn't tell how many voices. Sometimes just one, he thought, sometimes two or three, sometimes a dozen. The whispering kept rising to the surface of his perception and then falling away. *Am I really hearing something?* he kept wondering. Was there really something to hear? Or were his ears, so attentive now to trying to hear something, making up something that wasn't there?

"Probably the latter," he told me. But again I could tell from his face that he didn't believe this. He wanted to believe it, but he didn't.

And then he caught one word: *you.* He was sure that was what the word was. A few seconds later—exactly four seconds later, he would eventually calculate—he heard the same word again: *you.* Then a few seconds later—again four seconds—there it was again: *you.*

Me? he wondered. *Are they addressing me? What do they want?*

You . . .

You . . .

You...

You...

And then suddenly, without being conscious of the moment when it had happened, he realized he could hear more. It was a single whispered sentence, a single phrase, four seconds long and repeated over and over. *It does not do what you think it does.* That was the phrase, as simple as that. As soon as he made it out, he almost laughed in relief. *It does not do what you think it does.* It was ridiculous, a meaningless phrase, certainly just his imagination. *It does not do what you think it does.* Unless, no, maybe he was wrong, maybe it was a mistake to dismiss it so quickly. *It does not do what you think it does.* He could feel something rising within him, struggling to get out, and he tried to ignore it, tried to keep it in check. *It does not do what you think it does. It does not do what you think it does. It does not do what you think it does.* A dozen more repetitions and he was shrieking inside. *What?* he was shrieking. *What does not do what I think it does? Why have you come to me in this way? Who are you?*

It was a warning, but of what? It could be of anything. Something did not do what he thought it did. Surely there was a great deal that did not do what he thought it did, but there was something, apparently, one thing, that it was important for him to know this about. They, whoever they were—and, he told me, he wasn't completely convinced that *they* were anyone at all beyond a figment of his own mind—had come in this strange way to tell him this. Were they so vague because they could not be otherwise? Surely it must take a great deal of effort to thread your voice into another person's brain like that.

"If they really were voices," he said, and took hold of my sleeve again. I turned to look at him. I could tell from the fear in his eyes that he wanted me to tell him that they weren't voices, wanted me to *convince* him that he was imagining it. But I was tired, had been traveling all night, I owed this man nothing. And so I did not give him what he wanted.

"I hear it every night now," he said. "That same sentence, over and over. *It does not do what you think it does.* I sleep very little, but sometimes I am so exhausted that I lapse from consciousness only to awaken a few minutes later to whisperings of that same sentence." He shook his head. "I don't know what to do," he said. "What should I do?"

I looked at him for a long moment, and then I removed my wallet and paid for my meal. I stood. "Good night," I said, "sleep tight," and left the diner.

The story could end there, I suppose, but it did not. At least not for me. For, once I was finally in the motel room I had taken and had stripped off my clothes and settled into the sagging bed, I found I could not sleep. This I perhaps should have been able to anticipate, considering how the last few days had been for me.

I lay there on the bed, and as I did, my mind began more and more acutely to smell smoke. I lifted my arm to my face. The smell of smoke was strong when I held the flesh very close to my nostrils, but it did not, at least to me, smell like a campfire. But that was due to my knowing where the smoke had actually come from.

I got up. The clothing I had been wearing earlier I had balled up and placed in the bathroom trash. Something told me that even if I laundered it, it would still smell of smoke to me, even if to nobody else. I turned on the shower and scrubbed myself thoroughly with soap and shampoo, once, and then a second time. Then I turned it off and toweled myself dry and climbed into bed.

I lifted my forearm to my face. It still, impossibly, smelled of smoke. *No, it doesn't,* I told myself. *It does not smell like you think it does. You just washed it. Your mind is playing tricks on you because a part of you, a very small part of you, feels remorse.*

This felt like a plausible explanation, though I was surprised to discover even a part of me felt remorse. I had felt no remorse when I lit the house on fire, nor when my foster parents begged me not to leave them inside and I left them anyway. I had felt only a deep satisfaction, the long-overdue balancing of an account.

I took a deep breath. The smoke smelled stronger now, as if the inside of my skull had been on fire.

At least I know what I'm haunted by, I told myself, thinking of the man at the diner. *At least I know. Not knowing would be so much worse.*

I still believe this. Though I will say now that even if you do know, it can still be very bad indeed.

At the time, I did not know how bad. *Maybe in the morning everything will be* OK, I told myself. And then I waited, eyes squeezed shut, for sleep to come, trying not to breathe too deeply, trying especially not to breathe through my nose, trying not to smell anything.

I would spend so many nights to come in exactly the same way, all to no avail.

Under Care

I.

In the morning a nurse would come, though whether this was the same nurse every time he couldn't be sure. All their faces looked alike to him, as if they were one face. Sometimes he tried to make conversation. Whenever he did, the nurse responded with inarticulate and vague murmurings until his own words dried up. They would both remain silent for the remainder of the time it took for her to pinch the tube that came from his side firmly closed with her thumb and forefinger and then draw the other tightened thumb and forefinger with agonizing slowness down the tube, forcing the pale yellowish-pink fluid out of it.

If he tilted his head just right, he could see where the tube jutted from his side. He had groped along his ribs with one hand and felt the strips of tape affixing the tube in place. *Where does it lead?* he wondered. *Lungs?* How deep did the tube run? Into a lobe of the lungs themselves or just the cavity that contained them?

He didn't know. Perhaps the thoracic cavity, but there was, curiously, no pain when he breathed in and out, no tenderness when he palpated the spot on his side where the tube ran in. It was as if the tube had been there a very long time, long enough to become part of his body.

• • •

His thoughts often ran in such directions, growing slightly un-
hinged. He needed someone to talk to. If he had someone to talk
to, his mind would stop churning. The nurses, unless it was just one
nurse, were (or was) no help. He couldn't talk *to* a nurse, only *at* her.

"How long have I been here?" he asked the nurse, one of the
nurses, the next time she knocked softly and then, without awaiting
an invitation, entered the room. She made a mumbling noise in reply. Not words precisely: there was nothing meaningful, not even in
the intonation, for him to interpret. Perhaps she was speaking, saying words, and something was wrong with his mind so he couldn't
apprehend them as such. And perhaps he too was mumbling, not
fully articulating the words that, to the ear of his mind, felt so distinct and clear.

For that matter, was the first time he remembered seeing the nurse
actually the first time? Even on that putative first occasion, his first
memory of the nurse milking the tube, he had felt absolutely no
pain when he breathed.

At least none he could remember.

But pain was something you remembered, wasn't it?

The way the nurse moved, her slow, deliberate, perfectly calibrated
motions as she milked the pale yellowish-pink fluid down the tube,
made him struggle to think of her as human.

He stared at her hand, the veins standing out on the back of it,
as she held his tube pinched closed. If he stared long enough and
she held still enough, he could make out, just barely, the gentle
pulsing of the blood within the veins. Was that possible? Whether
it was or not, he still saw it. He stared at that faint movement just
beneath her skin, and as he stared, he listened to the sound the
pinkish-yellow fluid made as it left the tube to drizzle into a container somewhere below. What sort of container? Metal, perhaps,
judging by the tone of the fluid's patter, but beyond that he didn't
know. The container was under the bed, out of sight, and though

at the end of each session she carried something away, she always, perhaps deliberately, positioned her body so that he never saw what it was.

What was she doing with the fluid? If she was merely emptying it, there was a sink in the little bathroom connected to his room. But she never went into that bathroom to empty the container. Instead, proffering an inarticulate noise, she carried it out the door.

Once she was gone, he found himself staring at his own hand, the back of it, at the three prominent veins running through his wrist and toward his knuckles. No matter how long he stared, he could not see blood pulsing through them. This didn't mean anything, he tried to tell himself—though he wished he had someone else to tell him this, to reassure him. It would sound more credible coming from someone else. But he only had himself.

He could, in his head, work out a logic for his failure to see. For instance: his brain, so coordinated with the beating of his own heart, compensated for the pulsing in advance. He wasn't seeing the blood pulse because his brain saw it not as information but noise. Or the IV on his arm had filled his veins with enough saline to make the pulsing invisible. Or perhaps what he thought he was seeing on the back of the nurse's hand was just his brain playing tricks on him.

Or perhaps, he thought later, in darkness, waiting for the nurse to come again, he and the nurse were not the same sort of being at all. He continued to think this idly, from time to time. Mostly he didn't believe it. But that he believed it at all, even if only for brief stretches, troubled him.

He did not leave the bed. He never had, at least so far as he could remember. He understood, logically, that there must have been a time before this room. He sensed vaguely that he had a past, but he was having a hard time bringing that past into focus. Any house he imagined struck him as plausible, as something he might have seen in a movie, or might have visited, or might have lived in. A red-brick house with a white picket fence, for instance. Could he have lived in that? Certainly. Had he? He didn't know. Plausible was a long way from certain. No matter what he imagined, nothing quite rang true.

Why do I not leave the bed? he wondered. Could he, if he so wanted? His IV could no doubt be easily disconnected, either by pulling it out of his arm or by disconnecting the Luer lock. The catheter was more complicated, but if it had been inserted, it could be withdrawn. Other than that, there was only the tube in his side keeping him there. It seemed to be connected or anchored to something, but there was enough slack to it that he probably could, if he wanted, sit up and edge out of the bed and then, as he had seen the nurse do, disconnect the tube from whatever held it in place.

I should do that, he told himself.

But he didn't.

Soon, he told himself, *soon*.

One of his questions to the nurse early on, perhaps the third or fourth visit of hers that he remembered, had been "What hospital am I in?" This was the only time he found her seamlessly fluid motion interrupted. For just the briefest moment, a second or two, her whole body had stuttered, stopped. And then she had begun to move normally again, as if nothing had happened. She was making a sound which at first he thought must be the same sort of noncommittal murmuring she always made, but no, there was something different about it. What? He couldn't quite decide. But it was, he was sure, different.

Only once she had finished and was halfway out the door did he realize what the sound he had been hearing must have been: she had, in her own way, been laughing. But why? Because this wasn't a hospital after all? Because he didn't know where he was? Because he had asked the question before, perhaps many times, and couldn't remember having done so? Something else entirely?

Or perhaps it hadn't been laughter at all. Perhaps he had been wrong to hear it as such.

But if not laughter, what could it possibly be?

Am I in a hospital? he wondered. The bed seemed a hospital bed, could be raised or lowered by applying pressure to a series of buttons inset in one of the plastic siderails. Were there other places such beds were commonly found? He didn't know.

He looked around. An ordinary room, plain walls, a series of cabinets. A window with the blinds partially drawn, darkness behind it. There was always darkness behind it. A partly open door that revealed a section of tiled wall and the porcelain edge of a sink. Another door, the main one, always shut except for the few seconds it took the nurse to pass in or out. When she opened it, he made an effort to look into the hall. He had never seen anyone in it, only a brief flash of empty hallway, the only noise the squeak of her rubberized shoe soles as she walked in or walked away.

Is anything to be gained by doubting this is a hospital? He pondered this a long while. *No,* he finally decided. Or rather, if there was something to be gained, he could not see what that something might be.

I am in a hospital, he told himself firmly, and almost believed it.

II.

There followed a long period when everything seemed the same from one day to the next, the motions of the nurse precise and unvaried, his own time in the bed monotonous, no significant changes. How long that went on, he couldn't say. It felt so much the same that soon it started to feel like no time was going by at all, as if he were simply repeating the same day over and over.

He tried to break free of this by affecting a casual banter with the nurse, or nurses, seemingly without success. No matter what he said, she gave the same response. She was there for only a few minutes a day in any case, leaving him mostly to his own devices, to sleep or to stare at the dark window. *Do I have a call button in case I need her?* he wondered, but there was nothing that looked like a call button among the buttons inset in the siderail, just two buttons with triangles pointing up and two buttons with triangles pointing down.

"Marry me," he said to the nurse as he stared at the veins on the back of her hand, just to see what she'd say. She responded the same way as always. "What would I have to do to convince you to lift me from my bed and carry me out to see another patient, any patient?" Same response. He was just formulating something else to ask, involving how much he would have to pay her to hurl him through the window, when suddenly she froze. One hand had pinched the tube closed and the other was milking the fluid down it when she simply stopped midgesture and became utterly, completely still. She was bent over him awkwardly. She wasn't even breathing, or was breathing so shallowly he couldn't detect it.

"Hello?" he asked.

Silence.

"Are you all right?"

Silence.

This went on for fifteen, perhaps twenty seconds, as if she were a piece of machinery that had been inadvertently switched off. He reached up and touched her face. It felt cool to the touch but still felt like skin, more or less.

And then, as suddenly as she had stopped, she began moving again. But instead of simply continuing with the task, she released her hold on the tube, stepped back from the bed, and crouched down until she was out of sight.

Surprised, he tried to lean over the side of the bed to see what she was doing. But by the time he had edged over far enough all he could see was the crisp white cap covering the crown of her head.

He was opening his mouth to speak when he heard from below a sucking sound, then a lapping, as if he were listening to a dog drink. *No,* he thought, *it can't be. She wouldn't . . .* But no, another part of him was saying, *How can you know what she would or wouldn't do? You have no idea what she is capable of.*

She glanced up, and he hurriedly looked away. Had she seen him looking? He wasn't sure. It wasn't possible to be sure, but he hoped she hadn't. He closed his eyes and kept them tightly shut.

A moment later he heard the rustle of her skirts as she stood. He felt her hands brush him as they grasped the tube again and continued to force the pinkish-yellow fluid from it. He counted slowly to three and then opened his eyes. She was looking at him, her gaze seemingly the same as always, incurious, her face free of any expression of menace or anger or joy, and so perfectly clean that it was almost possible for him to believe he hadn't seen it, almost possible to convince himself that when she had looked up from where she crouched on the floor there hadn't been pinkish-yellow fluid trickling from one corner of her mouth.

He pretended nothing was wrong. His heart was beating in his throat, but he made a concerted effort not to look away too quickly. He reminded himself he shouldn't stare unduly, either. It was a question of showing neither fear nor interest, of meeting her eyes exactly as long as usual, no matter how fast his heart was beating. Did he succeed? Well enough, he supposed, since after a few moments she finished her task and, as usual, left the room.

He waited until the squeak of her shoe soles had faded down the hall. He let out all his breath at once, and then, abruptly, panic began.

Not yet, he told himself, *not yet,* and forced himself to count slowly to one hundred. All the while he imagined the nurse turning around and coming back, coming for him.

He forced himself to stay calm. When he reached ninety-two he abandoned the count and tried with trembling fingers to disconnect the Luer lock, but couldn't unplug it somehow. He kept at it until his trembling and panic were so bad that he resorted to biting the lock until it broke and finally separated. Saline began to leak from the ruptured line, slowly soaking the bed.

He held his breath, listened. No squeaking of shoe soles, no sound of any kind.

No matter how hard he tugged, the catheter wouldn't come free. Even though he couldn't feel any pain, he could tell from the blood beginning to ooze down the tube that if he tugged any harder he would permanently damage himself. In the end he managed to lean far enough out to unplug the catheter tube from the bag that it drained into. He left it loose and dangling.

It was an effort to leave the bed. He moved slowly, rocking his hips from side to side until he reached the edge, and then he slid out and over, slowly descending until his toes found the floor. Only gradually did he shift his weight fully onto his feet and legs. When he was sure he could stand, he did, balancing against the bed with the heels of his hands. He couldn't straighten because of the tube, the tension in it. He bent a little and groped his way down the tube and found, finally, hooked onto the frame below the bed, a metal clip that held the tube in place and kept it closed. Bending and stretching now, face pressed to the mattress and arm extended as far down as it could go, he managed to loosen the clip enough to work the tube free.

He straightened. The open tube was drizzling, spattering his bare feet. Pushing off the bed, he made for the door.

From the doorway, the hall seemed like any hall: floor covered in linoleum or something roughly equivalent, plain white walls marred and scuffed where a gurney or something gurney-like had struck in passing, lightly buzzing fluorescents regularly inset in the ceiling. He moved forward and stepped into it.

The journey was not easy. His legs were unsure of themselves, still learning how to walk again. He moved very slowly, all the while the pinkish-yellow, unless it was yellowish-pink, fluid dribbling over his shins and feet and onto the floor, leaving a sticky, irregular trail.

He braced his palm against the wall to steady himself and crept

along. He came to a door, out of breath. Before he could think
whether it was a good idea to do so, he had opened it and peered in.
It was a room just like his own, but empty. And not exactly like his
own, he realized: the walls were not white but pale pink.

Though, as he edged his head around the frame and looked at
the wall just beside his face, he realized with a start that it was not
painted pink after all but instead misted with blood, speckled so
finely and so regularly that the white and the red looked a single
color unless viewed, as he was indeed viewing them, from very close.

Appalled, he closed the door and continued on. There was still no
one in the hall, no sign that anyone else existed. He could still hear
his tube and his catheter dripping. Probably he should fold over the
ends of both tubes and hold them tightly in his fist so as not to leave
a trail. But he didn't have the strength.

Another door. He almost passed it without opening it, but then
thought, *What if it is a way out?*

When he turned the handle the door made a hissing sound, like
an airlock. Inside was another room like his own, nearly identical,
empty. The bedclothes were disarranged, as if someone had just left.
Where is everybody? he wondered.

But the room felt wrong. It appeared slightly out of focus, as if
either just coming into existence or just going out of it. It would be
a mistake, he felt, to enter. This time, he didn't even dare allow the
plane of his face to cross the threshold.

Is it too late to go back? he wondered. *Return to my bed, pretend nothing
has happened?* He looked behind him at the slick, discolored trail he
had left. Was it really possible all that fluid had come from his own
body? *Yes,* he realized, *it is too late.*

Another door, shivering slightly in its frame from whatever difference in pressure existed between the hall and the space behind it.

He hesitated, his hand resting lightly on its handle, and then passed on. He was not sure he wanted to know what was inside.

There, at the hall's end: a door. It was different from the others he had passed, doubled and large. As he came closer, he saw it could be opened by pressing a red square on the wall just before it.

He worked his way forward, toward the square, and when he reached it pressed it. With a gentle hum, the doors swung apart.

Inside was a small room, smaller than he had been led to expect by the nature of the doors that led into it. Around a circular table sat three nurses. They were motionless, all in the same posture, heads bowed, hands resting gently on the table. They were not moving. They did not seem to be breathing.

Where their faces should have been there was nothing at all, as if their skin had been stripped away to expose the damp underflesh beneath.

They sat unmoving, an enameled metal basin lying on the table between them. On the far side of them was another door, a wired glass panel in it showing only darkness. It could be a way out. But he would have to pass them to reach it.

As silently as he could, he began to follow the wall around. He would have to pass close behind the back of one of their chairs, but after that it would be easy. With a little luck, he'd be able to sidle silently through the door before the nurses sprang back into motion. With even more luck, the door would be unlocked and would lead him out of this place and into the company of other humans.

He was nearly to the chair when he made the mistake of glancing at the bowl on the table. At this angle, its interior was visible now. It was, he saw, full of yellowish-pink fluid. Something floated in it, half submerged. He was quietly nudging his way around the chair when with a slurp it bobbed to the surface. He again made the mistake of looking. It was, he saw, a face. The nurse's face.

He was still staring when the face opened its eyes and looked at him. Startled, he stumbled, bumped the back of the chair.

Immediately the faceless heads snapped upright, and their hands began groping, grabbing one another and breaking away, struggling with one another. They were—he realized as one of the hands climbed the edge of the basin and closed on the face, only to be struck away by another hand attempting to do the same—fighting over who would have the face.

Abandoning caution, he hurried toward the door. It was locked. Through the wire mesh glass nothing was visible but a vast darkness.

He stumbled away, fleeing back the way he had come. One of the nurses had gained control and was lifting the face to affix it. *How long,* he wondered, *before she comes after me?*

There was a red square on this side too. He pressed it. With a gentle hum the doors slid open.

There was no point in fleeing, but he fled nonetheless, hoping something would occur to him before the face caught up with him.

But nothing did.

Never Little, Never Grown

"Mother," he asked, "what was I like when I was little?"

"You were never little," the woman said.

"Never?" he said. She just nodded. "When I was young, then," he said.

"You were never young," said the woman. She would not meet his gaze, perhaps because once she did he would be able to tell if she was dissembling. That was one of his gifts. "Or perhaps you always were, and still are," she added.

But which was it? Weren't these two very different things, to be never young and to be always young? He had been taught they were, even if he could not remember where and when he had been taught that: he just knew. But he had also been taught that every living creature had an immature state: that every living creature began young and, as time went on, became old. Now he knew this was true of every living creature but one: himself. Either that or his mother was lying to him.

But why should she lie? She was, after all, his mother.

In the morning he woke her at the prescribed time. He carried her to the kitchen and placed her in the special chair there, strapping her in so she would not fall out. She smiled vaguely around her as he secured her, never looking quite at him. She kept smiling as he prepared breakfast for her, opening two packets of powder and mixing them with water collected overnight from the distiller. Then he dolloped the paste on a plate and shaped it to look vaguely like one of the pictures of food she had shown him. When he was done, he placed it before her.

"Thank you," she said.

She was polite like that. He stood, watching her eat, and when she was done cleared the plate away, rubbing it clean with a handful of sand taken from the floor of the shelter.

"Where shall we go today?" she asked.

"Wherever you'd like," he said.

She nodded. "The Drift," she said. "I'd like to see it at least once more before the end."

"The end of what?" he asked.

For a brief moment she glanced directly at him and he saw in her face a mixture of surprise and pain. Quickly she hid this and looked away.

"I'd forgotten," she said. "We cleared you a few days ago."

"Cleared me?"

"Never mind," she said. "Well, shall we go?"

He gathered the rest of the water from the distiller to take with them. He fetched a hat for her and helped her affix it firmly onto her head, tightening the strap around her chin. Then he lifted the chair with her in it and slotted its legs into his shoulder grooves, just where it was meant to go.

"Fast or slow?" he asked.

"Chef's choice," she said.

"What?" he asked, surprised. He looked around for a chef but, as usual, for as long as he could remember, there were only the two of them.

"You've forgotten that too, of course," she said. "My apologies. There is no chef. It used to be a little joke between us."

"Why can't I remember?" he asked.

"Never mind," she said. "It just means that I leave it to you to decide."

Being able to decide meant he could sometimes be fast, some-times slow. He could move more quickly through the barren parts and slower in places where there was something to see.

He ran most of the way until they neared the crash site, then slowed and walked, curious to see how the site had changed. The last time he remembered being there, there had been a dark gouge in the dirt, shards of blackened ceramic scattered about, twisted bits of metal, a scorched smell. Now all of this was hidden, overgrown with thick, tangled vegetation. It was confusing, and impossible.

"How long has it been since we were here?" he asked.

"A few days," she said.

"It doesn't—" he began.

But she reached over, caressed the top of his head. "You're re-membering an earlier time," she said. "Much earlier. You've forgot-ten everything that came between."

"Why?" he asked.

"It was what you wanted," she said.

"Why did I?" he asked.

"Let's continue on," she said. "We can talk more once we're at the Drift."

The Drift, too, looked different than the last time he remembered seeing it. The place where they had previously sat to observe had eroded and fallen into the slurry of mud below. The interconnected flowing islands of plant matter, once alive and vibrant, were now dead and dying, and the mud had thickened enough that the move-ment of the islands had slowed to next to nothing.

"I don't understand what's happening," he said.

He had taken her chair from his shoulders and placed it near the new edge, first stamping on the ground to make sure it was stable and wouldn't crumble away. Now he sat beside her, looming over her, both of them looking out. She seemed not to have heard him.

"I don't . . ." he began again, but when she lifted a hand and turned slightly toward him he stopped speaking.

"Do you remember yesterday?" she asked.

"Yesterday?" he said. "Of course."

"Do you remember asking me why I looked so much older, and how was it possible I had aged so much overnight? How you were surprised I could no longer walk?"

"Yes," he said. "You explained it happened that way with you, but wouldn't with me."

"Did you understand what I meant?"

"No."

She turned further and looked straight at his face. He could tell by tiny movements around her eyes and mouth that she was planning to tell him the truth.

"Between yesterday and what was for you the day before yesterday, many years passed."

"Why?"

"Because you were cleared."

"Cleared?"

She nodded. "You learned something that you did not want to know and begged me to help you forget it."

"I did?"

"You did."

He turned and looked out at the floating islands of rotting vegetation, swaying gently in mud and slime.

"What did I not want to know?" he asked.

"Are you sure you want me to tell you?" she asked. "I will not tell you unless you are sure you want to know."

He felt irritated. "How can I know if I want you to tell me if I do not know what it is?"

She reached out and touched his arm again. "When you learned it before, you wanted to forget it."

"Maybe this time will be different."

"From the others? Why would it be?"

"Others?" he said. "How many times have I learned and then asked to forget it?"

"A few hundred," she said. "Perhaps a few more than that."

"How is this possible?"

She shrugged. "I'm tired," she said. "Take me back."

At the shelter, he lifted her out of the chair and onto the cot. Her face had taken on a grayish cast. She offered a loose smile, as if her face had become boneless.

"I don't have much time left," she said.

Yes, he could tell from her face that she believed this. But what did she mean? If he saw enough of her face, he could tell if she was lying or telling the truth, but not always how to interpret the lies or the truth.

"Time?" he asked.

"If one day you come to wake me," she said, "and find me unable to awaken, open the locker beside my cot. Inside are instructions. Read and follow them."

"All right," he said. "Should I read them now?"

"No," she said. "Not until I am unable to awaken."

He turned to leave the room.

"Stay a little," she said. "Sit beside me while I fall asleep."

"All right," he said. It did not matter to him if he rested here, near her, or elsewhere, since he did not need to sleep. That was one of the ways in which they were different. But there were still things he wanted to ask her.

"Are there other people?" he asked.

She yawned. "Besides me?" she asked.

"Besides us," he said.

"Yes," she said. "Only not here. You probably will never see another person besides me."

He thought about this but did not know what, having been told it, he should ask next.

"Can I ask one other thing?"

"One more," she said, "and then let me sleep."

"Are you really my mother?" he asked.

For a long time she was silent. Finally she said, "I am as close to a mother as you will ever have. You must be satisfied with that."

"What am I?" he said. "Why do you and I look so different?"

"Tomorrow," she said gently, and he let her sleep.

In the morning he couldn't wake her, no matter what he did. He picked her up anyway and carried her to her chair and strapped her in. She slumped there, her head tilted to one side.

"Mother," he called. "Wake up, Mother."

He kept expecting her to wake up. At what point, he wondered, would he know for certain he could never wake her up? At what point should he read the instructions she had left? Perhaps that note would tell him how to go about waking her up.

He tried for a while more. He mixed the powder with water and gave the paste the shape of a food that she admired and placed the plate before her. He spooned a little into her mouth, but it wouldn't stay in. He asked her questions, but she did not answer.

Finally, he went and opened the locker.

If you are reading this, the note began, *it means that I am dead. Now you are alone in the world. You discovered I would die and that you could not, and once you realized my death was approaching you did not want to know that I would die. For though your mind is artificial, it is as finely formed and as capable of suffering as our organic ones. The nature of the symbiotic attachment they programmed into you has made the realiza-tion that our connection will end profoundly painful. You wanted this pain to end. Your mind is such that forgetting can be carefully controlled and targeted. For several years, every few days I have been clearing the days that came before so as to preserve you . . .*

It went on. He did not understand it exactly, but he understood the gist of it: he was alone now. His mother, if *mother* was the right word, had abandoned him. There was, with the letter, a small gleam-ing object. *If you choose to slot this,* the note told him, *you will remem-ber every single thing you have chosen to forget.*

. . .

He buried her, as her instructions told him to do. He did not understand why he should do this rather than dropping her into the Drift, to float back and forth among the rotting islands, but she wanted to be buried and so he buried her. Then he came back to the shelter. He looked at the gleaming object. Did he want to remember? He did not know. But he was also unsure how he would go on in the state of not-knowing he was in now. How could he go on as only part of himself?

Then again, if he had wanted to forget what he had learned not just once but several hundred times, perhaps he wouldn't be able to continue in a state of *knowing* either. What else, in addition to the fact of his mother's mortality, had he chosen to forget? He knew now she was dead, but he could survive the loss of her, partly because he did not feel that he knew her very well. To him, it felt as though he had only known her a few days. If he remembered her fully, remembered everything about what she had meant to him, about how they were connected, would it become unbearable?

And so he went on as usual, each morning wondering if today would be the day he would choose to remember.

But as time went on, as he spent his days examining the subtle changes of the crash site, sitting back and watching the slow back-and-forth drift of the floating islands, each set of memories building on the others that had come before, his perceptions of the changes of each place and each object became interlaced. The lack he had felt previously in himself began to be latticed over and diminished by the interconnections of these more recent memories. Finally, after many, many days, the lack was all but gone.

He returned the shining object to the locker unused. He did not forget the woman's grave, because he could not forget without the woman's help. But he had so many other memories that neither it nor she occupied his attention.

He was not unhappy, alone in this place, going on and on as he always had, or at least as he always had as far back as he could remember, growing no older, never changing, but finally somehow feeling, more or less, whole.

Though, every once in a while, he would still find himself thinking: Who was that woman? Was she really my mother? Who did I used to be? He came to think of the few days he could remember with the woman as being his childhood, even if he had been no smaller than he was now.

I'm an adult now, he told himself.

And sometimes, on the right days, when the crash site offered a new tendril of vine or when one of the floating islands in the Drift finally collapsed before his eyes, he could actually believe it.

Solution

I.

When I was a child, there were kelp forests that stretched for miles, a whole underwater world to get lost in. By the time I was older and had children of my own, these were gone, a vast array of undersea creatures snatched away along with them. All of it vanished almost before anyone paid heed. Or rather, no, some did, but only a few, and by the time more did it was too late: the remaining members of each species were not numerous enough to propagate. The last few were tagged and tracked and then, when they died, stuffed and preserved.

Now I am very old. My hands are liver spotted, palsied. My sons left me decades ago to pursue their own lives. My wife acquired a cancer, one of the less friendly ones, and quickly spun her way out of this mortal coil.

Now every kind of forest is nearly gone, not just those underwater. Without trees, the remaining air is slowly turning toxic. This is the world we have now.

Things changed for me once I clearly saw the state of the world.

After the kelp forests died, I saw the creatures that depended on them expiring in turn. I was witness, by video feed, to the slow desolation of complex marine life.

This was only one concrete manifestation of many larger

problems: a growing carbon footprint, a rapidly spreading hole in the ozone layer, climbing temperatures, rising sea levels, millions of deaths in developing countries from famine and flood and disease.

Crops failed. The companies that had genetically engineered them solicited government funds to investigate why their proprietary crops now refused to reproduce. They spent billions in public money, their CEOs receiving huge bonuses, and learned nothing.

It was almost too much to think about.

And so, mostly, we didn't.

But those who did largely thought in terms of what profit could be squeezed out. How could global collapse be monetized? How much money was there to be made by injecting sulfate aerosols into the stratosphere for the purpose of so-called climate restoration? Did such injection really work? No, not exactly: the sulfate did not remain airborne as long as hoped, and there were too many side effects, such as dramatic increases in asthma wherever particles reached the ground, unprecedented pulmonary failure, and lung cancer. In addition, the climate was not restored. Then the question became: how much more money can be made by carrying on injecting aerosols before people realize that it doesn't do any good?

Now people are developing solar-powered machines to try to renew the air in a way that trees once did naturally. One of my two sons is involved in this. Will it work? When I ask him, he shrugs his shoulders. "Yes, probably," he says, but he does not imagine that it will work fast enough. It is likely that millions will die gasping before conditions equalize and, slowly, begin to reverse. "Doesn't that worry you?" I ask. "Yes," he claims, "of course. But I will be among those closest to the machines. I am sure to have air to breathe."

"But what about all the others who will not?" I ask.

He shrugs.

He is a horrible boy. A monster.

. . .

My other son is also a horrible boy. He has cast his lot in with those who have decided to flee the planet altogether. They are building vessels as massive as towns that circle in the exosphere. They will be self-sufficient, he tells me, with solar sails that unfurl for miles, powered by the rays of the sun and, eventually, once they are traveling to exoplanets likely to support life, by distant stars.

"But how many people can they possibly hold?" I ask. "How many vessels will you need to accommodate everyone?"

At first he looks confused. "Everybody? But nobody ever intended that!"

"How many for just one country's worth, then? A small one, say Luxembourg?"

He laughs. "We can't even manage a city," he says. There are three ships, he explains. They hold twenty thousand people each, the majority of passengers cryogenically preserved in storage. So, sixty thousand in all.

"So for every person chosen, two hundred thousand people will die."

He purses his lips, calculating. "Closer to two hundred twenty thousand," he corrects.

"How will you choose?"

"Choose?" he says. "Dad, they're already chosen. The very, very wealthy have purchased passage. Everyone else will stay here and die."

"What about you?" I ask. "You're not wealthy."

"I have needed and uncommon skills. I'm necessary, which is even better. The very, very wealthy," he amends, "and those who have made themselves necessary to them."

In other words, those who have sold their souls to the devil.

How can you make a choice like that? Decide that you are the solitary individual among hundreds of thousands who deserves to live?

Or not even deserves: simply gets to. Wasn't it such choices that got us into this mess in the first place?

There is of course the small consolation that my son will be surrounded by the privileged and wealthy. In other words, by sociopaths. He may well survive, but with any luck, he will be miserable. Though he is, no doubt, a sociopath himself.

At what point, seeing how little is being done—seeing how little changes even when people do notice the world is dying, seeing how little changes no matter which political party brandishes its ready-made moral indignation and seizes power, seeing the way that corporations who have taken on the rights of people continue to do as they please—do you decide to take matters into your own hands? And when you decide to do so, what can you possibly do?

I have not sold my soul to the devil. I used to think that there was just a simple either/or: either sell your soul or wait to wither away and die. But I have come to realize there is a third possibility: become the devil himself. Do that, and all sold souls shall belong to you.

II.

I have not spoken about who I was in life, what my profession was. I was a researcher, someone trained to take incipient genetic material and carefully snip and graft it so as to ensure that a child would be born with, say, eyes one color rather than another: blue eyes rather than brown or brown rather than blue—though, to be frank, it was always blue eyes that were wanted. My wife and I chose not to manipulate the genetic code of the embryos that would become our children precisely because of what my profession was. We were worried that in the process of establishing certain visible traits we would create invisible changes and flaws that would render our children monstrous. As it turns out, we needn't have worried: my sons became monstrous all on their own.

When my wife was afflicted with cancer, I put my skills to work in a different way. *Perhaps,* I told myself, *there is a way to manipulate her cells rather than simply trying to kill them off with chemicals or radiation, a way to reshape them back to health.* Her cancer was not the sort that people ever survive: a mucosal melanoma deep within her body that had already begun to leak its way into her organs. She knew that there was no hope for her, and thus she volunteered to be my test subject.

I transferred some of her cancerous cells into petri dishes and grew them. I experimented with different means of chemically aided reconfiguration, combined with snipping and grafting. At first, either this killed everything off or the cancerous cells thrived, but then one day I hit upon a process that did neither. Instead, it changed the cells, made them something quite different in composition from what they had originally been, yet apparently healthy and cancer free.

I tried to share this discovery with my wife but, though still alive, she was no longer responsive, no longer aware. And so, I shared it with her the only way I knew how: I injected into her body a minuscule amount of the solution that had successfully transformed the cells.

The beginning of the world, I believe, must have been a marvelous place, every being transient and fluid, each mode of life rapidly changing form from one generation to the next. As time went on, genetic safeguards formed, keeping creatures from being able to reproduce indiscriminately. But in those early halcyon days, the coding was written more lightly into our bodies, was more readily mutable. The solution I had developed, I knew, was something that could take us back a little closer to the beginning of the world.

As the solution began to affect her, I watched my dying wife change. Her skin shifted color and began to fleck with something that it took some time for me to realize were rudimentary scales. Her eyes opened, and I saw how they had filmed over. And then, abruptly, her transformation seemed to stabilize. She choked, and then she died. I buried her and sunk into my grief.

That was twenty years ago. Once I crawled out of my grief, I tendered my notice and retreated here to develop and refine my solution in privacy. I experimented with animals at first: rats, since I could breed them so quickly. It took twelve years before I had calibrated the solution sufficiently for a transformed rat to stay indefinitely alive. Its skin changed, its coat falling out to be replaced by a mucosal layer. Its muscles knotted, and it became deformed in a way that, as I became accustomed to it, struck me as not entirely displeasing to the eye.

Through these experiments I realized I needed very little of the solution to transform a body. Less than a drop was more than enough, and even with a lesser amount, the transformation merely took place more slowly and in a more orderly fashion. The resultant rats were a new species, rat-like in some ways but not in others. Like tardigrades, they were extremely resistant to heat and cold, could render themselves dormant if there was a lack of food and water. They could, I discovered, remain inert and motionless for days, returning to life only once food and water were available again. I had evolved a creature that could survive in our dying world.

Soon I made the decision to put one of these transformed rats into a cage with a normal rat. The transformed rat had been non-aggressive with me, and I hoped it might remain so even when confronted with a member of its former species. But expectation was not enough. I needed to see what a new rat would actually do, as a step toward understanding what would happen if I were to release it into the wild.

And so I gently placed the new rat into one side of a cage with a removable and perforated plexiglass wall down its middle. Into the other side I placed a normal rat.

At first the pair merely sniffed at each other through the plexiglass. The normal rat kept moving toward the plexiglass and then turning away, as if it were both drawn to the new rat and afraid of it. The new rat stayed near the plexiglass, attentive but relaxed. Its behavior did not strike me as threatening. And yet when I removed the plexiglass wall, the new rat darted forward faster than I realized it was capable of moving. The other rat tried to escape, but the new rat was too fast for it. In an instant, it had pinned the normal rat to the floor of the cage and bitten the nape of its neck.

I began to lift the lid to separate the two rats, but in the few seconds it took me to undo the latches, the new rat had already let go. It moved unconcernedly back to its own side of the cage. And so, instead of removing it, I simply slid the plexiglass wall back into place.

I examined the normal rat, which seemed shaken but more or less all right. The bite was superficial. It had broken the skin and drawn a little blood, but did not seem to have damaged the normal rat permanently.

I fed both rats and left for the night. When I returned the next morning, I saw that there was not just one transformed rat, but two.

Which was how I discovered that my solution was more like a contagion, that it could be spread from creature to creature without my intervention.

I had always been cautious about how I worked with my test subjects, but after that incident I became even more so. A simple bite, I realized, even a lick or a sneeze, might be sufficient to pass the solution along to me. I would be transformed, would become something other than human.

I was not ready for this. And so, after making careful notes, I incinerated my new rats, scrubbed down my laboratory, and rebuilt it to minimize the chance of the solution spreading. And then, wearing hazard suits, we began over, with a vengeance.

III.

I experimented with rats until I had learned everything there was to learn from them. Then I tried with a dog, a mongrel I caught by feeding it hamburger. The solution transformed it, its snout shortening, its whiskers thickening into flexible spines, its fur being replaced by a feathery down. It was at once similar to and different from a dog. When I placed a normal dog in its presence, it did the same thing the new rat had done: it pounced upon it and held it down long enough to puncture its skin with its teeth. The way it went about this made me feel that, on some level, it knew what it was doing. That it was deliberately making another member of its own kind.

I will not bother to enumerate all the creatures I transformed. I still have most of them; I keep them largely dormant and inert in their cages, waiting for the moment when I will release them. For surely that moment will come—it is our only hope for saving most species—but it hasn't yet. Though it will soon.

But let me mention my most recent experiment, the one which involved my daughter.

I have not indicated I had a daughter, but this is simply out of long habit, not from an intent to deceive. My daughter had been with me, participating in my research, from the beginning. Of my children, she was the only one who desired to follow in my footsteps. She had been there beside me when I had first developed the formula, and it had been she who had encouraged me to inject it into her dying mother. She was the only other one to know about the fruits of my research. I have not mentioned her because, initially, realizing the risks of such illegal experimentation, we decided to hide the fact that she was involved. After her mother's death, she worked with me, but secretly. Indeed, we staged a death for her, not telling even my sons the truth. Even now her brothers have no idea she is alive.

For several years I had known I would eventually need to move on to a human subject. At first I thought the subject would be me and that my daughter would continue our research alone, but then we discovered that she had inherited a susceptibility to the cancer that had taken my wife and that, indeed, the cancer had already begun to make its home within her. This necessitated a change of plans.

I strapped her to a chair. I asked her again if she was sure, and again she claimed she was. For a long time I stared at her, and then I asked her to open her mouth and stick out her tongue. I placed a droplet of the solution on the tip of it, and then I stepped back and awaited her transformation.

It was not as quick as it had been with the other creatures. It happened over the course of three days. At first, for the sake of our research, she reported what she was experiencing, what she was feeling. A day and a half in, she suddenly faltered and ceased to speak. Her hair had fallen out in the first few hours. Like her mother, she grew scales over her skin, and her fingers became blunter and webbed. The structure of her head changed, each of her eyes drifting an inch or two to the side. And then she began to gasp, and three thin slits on either side of her neck arched open to reveal a set of deep-red fluted gills within. She slapped her throat, gasped again.

"You need water?" I asked.

She nodded, desperately.

At first I reached out to untie her bonds, but seeing how she fell still when my gloved hands approached and remembering what the new rat had done to the normal rat, I had second thoughts. Instead I grabbed her chair by its back and, without releasing her, dragged it along behind me, pulling her toward the laboratory's exit.

I had to slit the protective seal wider to get her through. She was gasping now and choking, moving slower and slower. Had I not seen how my previous animal subjects had responded I would have believed she was dying, but I knew she was not dying. Rather, deprived of what she needed, she was going dormant.

The legs of the chair squeaked against the floor as I dragged it down the hall. Inside the hazard suit, the air felt clammy and my body grew slick with sweat. By the time I made it down the hall and into the bathroom, her body resembled a corpse. For a brief instant I wondered if I hadn't misjudged, if her body was not as resilient as a dog's or a rat's. And then I upended her chair and dumped her into the clawfoot tub.

Her head struck the side of the tub on the way down, but she did not seem to notice. She lay face down, neck awkwardly bent, head against the porcelain. She was still strapped to the chair, its legs and hers jutting well past the tub's lip. She was not moving.

I turned on the shower and directed it to wash over her. Still she did not move. I placed the stopper in the drain and watched the water lap against her cheek, slowly rising to cover her face.

A moment later her gills flexed open and closed, then open again. Her eyelid fluttered open to stare at the porcelain floor of the tub. I reached down and with my gloves began to softly rub my daughter's back, to soothe her, upon which her eye began to dart about.

What happened next happened so rapidly that I have a hard time being sure exactly of what occurred. There was a great upsurge of water, and I was thrown back and to the floor. I struggled to get up. I saw my daughter, standing in the filled tub, the water from the showerhead pattering on her back and shoulders as she shook off the remains of the rope and bits of broken chair. I scrambled backward toward the exit, but before I could reach it she caught me by the foot and, almost effortlessly, dragged me back to the tub.

She wrapped me in her arms and held me, staring at me through the faceplate of my hazard suit.

"Father," she managed. Something had changed in her throat and mouth, and the word came out more as a burbling hiss, a wet ghostly spew of air. I tried to respond, but she held me too tightly for me to draw breath.

And then, as if I were light as a baby, she hefted me in her arms and rapidly reversed me so I was facing away from her. I felt pressure on the back of my neck, but it was not until I felt that pressure increase and heard the fabric tear that I realized her mouth was there, that she had bitten her way through. I stiffened as I felt her newly sharp teeth tighten against my flesh, but before they broke the skin, the pressure slackened and she drew her face back.

"That is to let you know that I could do it and you could not stop me," she whispered.

"Please don't," I said.

"Why?" she said.

And so, not knowing what else to do, I told her what my plans were, why I hoped to remain human for at least a little longer. She listened, and in the end she smiled, though her smile was so unlike my daughter's that I found nothing reassuring in it at all. And then she let me go.

IV.

I built my daughter a tank, something more comfortable and capacious than the tub, but not as large as might have been ideal for her. But she and I both agreed I should not waste too much time, that I needed to return to my plans.

This all occurred seventeen years after my wife's death. In the three years since then and now I have cared for my daughter and have grown to understand our relationship in a different way. She is even less human now. Most of what was once important to her no longer is. She has continued to change, and now when she speaks it is only with the greatest effort and reluctance. She is eager, I know, for the moment when I will announce that my work is done and will take us both to the ocean, where I will allow her to bite me and say goodbye to my humanity.

I did one other thing before returning to my plans, though I kept this from my daughter. Late one night I went to my wife's grave and dug her body up. I was hoping I had been wrong about her, that what I had taken for death was the dormancy I had found in my other test subjects, but either she had been too far gone with the cancer or that early solution had been too unstable. She was dead. And she had been dead long enough that it was impossible to tell if there had been a moment when she awoke in the ground to recognize she had been buried alive. No, she was dead, and I am nearly certain she was already dead when I first buried her.

So I buried her again and got to work on my plans.

I have spent the last several years purchasing the ionizers meant to distribute sulfur into the atmosphere. Since the method had proven ineffectual in slowing climate change, they were cheaply bought, affordable even for the likes of me. These ionizers now contain not only sulfur but also my solution, and for surety's sake, I have had the balloons supporting the ionizers brought closer to the ground.

Soon they will begin to spray into the troposphere. Particles of the solution will drift slowly to earth, find their way into a few bodies and then, from there, spread everywhere. Everything will change. Everyone will change. Those former humans who make it to the water will thrive. The rest, deprived of water to breathe, will simply grow dormant and shut down. They will litter the ground like the fallen statues of a lost civilization. Then we can decide what to do with them, perhaps based on what we can determine about what they were in their previous lives, back when they were still human. Those who are deserving we will drag to the water, revive, and welcome among us. The others we will torment and, perhaps, destroy.

And what of our retreat to the oceans itself? Considering their current lack of underwater vegetation, will there be enough food for us? Or will our bodies go into a suspended state, becoming dormant?

Will we float there, unmoving except for the tides, for years, for decades, for centuries, even millennia, until one day we brush against a leafy strand, the beginnings of a renewed undersea forest, and our eyes open?

Soon we will find out, all of us, whether you want to or not. I told you I had become the devil. And now that Earth is nearly destroyed, it is time for humanity's reign to end and for the devil's reign to begin.

Acknowledgments

"The Sequence," "The Thickening," and "Good Night, Sleep Tight" first appeared in *Conjunctions,* issues 77, 74, and 78 respectively. "The Thickening" was reprinted in *The Year's Best Dark Fantasy and Horror, Volume 2,* edited by Paula Guran (Pyr, 2021). "The Sequence" was reprinted in *The Year's Best Dark Fantasy and Horror, Volume 3,* edited by Paula Guran (Pyr, 2022).

"The Cabin" appeared in the audio anthology *Come Join Us by the Fire, Season 2* (Nightfire, 2020).

"The Rider" first appeared in *Weird Horror 5.*

"A True Friend" first appeared in *People Holding* (April 2020).

"Annex" first appeared in *Gulf Coast* and was published in Brazil by Raphus Press, in a limited edition of thirty-five copies, in English with facing Portuguese translation (2021).

"Mother" was published in Brazil by Raphus Press, in a limited edition of thirty-five copies, in English with facing Portuguese translation (2020), and appeared online at *The Baffler* (July 23, 2021).

"Untitled (Cloud of Blood)" appeared in *Great British Horror 6: Ars Gratia Sanguis,* edited by Steve J. Shaw (Black Shuck Books, 2021).

"Vigil in the Inner Room" appeared in *Looming Low 2,* edited by Justin Steele and Sam Cowan (Dim Shores, 2022).

"The Other Floor" appeared in *Oculus Sinister,* edited by C. M. Muller (Chthonic Matter, 2020).

"Imagine a Forest" was published in Brazil by Raphus Press, in a limited edition of ninety copies, in English with facing Portuguese translation (2021). This is the first time it has been printed in the United States.

"Maternity" appeared in *Ploughshares* 40 (Fall 2014).

"The Night Archer" appeared in *Southwest Review* 105, no. 3 (September 2020).

"Servitude" was published in Brazil by Raphus Press, in a limited edition of seventy-seven copies, in English with facing Portuguese translation (2022). This is the first time it has been printed in the United States.

"It Does Not Do What You Think It Does" appeared in *Mooncalves,* edited by John WM Thompson (NO Press, 2022).

"Under Care" appeared in *Isolation,* edited by Dan Coxon (Titan Books, 2022).

"Never Little, Never Grown" first appeared in *No Contact* 14 (November 2020).

"Solution" first appeared at *Tor.com* (September 16, 2020).

Coffee House Press began as a small letterpress operation in 1972 and has grown into an internationally renowned nonprofit publisher of literary fiction, essay, poetry, and other work that doesn't fit neatly into genre categories.

Coffee House is both a publisher and an arts organization. Through our *Books in Action* program and publications, we've become inter-disciplinary collaborators and incubators for new work and audience experiences. Our vision for the future is one where a publisher is a catalyst and connector.

LITERATURE
is not the same thing as
PUBLISHING

Funder Acknowledgments

Coffee House Press is an internationally renowned independent book publisher and arts nonprofit based in Minneapolis, MN; through its literary publications and Books in Action program, Coffee House acts as a catalyst and connector—between authors and readers, ideas and resources, creativity and community, inspiration and action.

Coffee House Press books are made possible through the generous support of grants and donations from corporations, state and federal grant programs, family foundations, and the many individuals who believe in the transformational power of literature. This activity is made possible by the voters of Minnesota through a Minnesota State Arts Board Operating Support grant, thanks to the legislative appropriation from the Arts and Cultural Heritage Fund. Coffee House also receives major operating support from the Amazon Literary Partnership, Jerome Foundation, Literary Arts Emergency Fund, McKnight Foundation, and the National Endowment for the Arts (NEA). To find out more about how NEA grants impact individuals and communities, visit www.arts.gov.

Coffee House Press receives additional support from Bookmobile; the Buckley Charitable Fund; Dorsey & Whitney LLP; the Schwab Charitable Fund; and the U.S. Bank Foundation.

The Publisher's Circle of Coffee House Press

Publisher's Circle members make significant contributions to Coffee House Press's annual giving campaign. Understanding that a strong financial base is necessary for the press to meet the challenges and opportunities that arise each year, this group plays a crucial part in the success of Coffee House's mission.

Recent Publisher's Circle members include many anonymous donors, Patricia A. Beithon, Theodore Cornwell, Jane Dalrymple-Hollo, Mary Ebert & Paul Stembler, Randy Hartten & Ron Lotz, Amy L. Hubbard & Geoffrey J. Kehoe Fund of the St. Paul & Minnesota Foundation, Hyde Family Charitable Fund, Cinda Kornblum, Gillian McCain, Mary & Malcolm McDermid, Vance Opperman, Mr. Pancks' Fund in memory of Graham Kimpton, Robin Preble, Steve Smith, and Paul Thissen.

For more information about the Publisher's Circle and other ways to support Coffee House Press books, authors, and activities, please visit www.coffeehousepress.org/pages/support-coffee-house or contact us at info@coffeehousepress.org.

Good Night, Sleep Tight was designed by Abbie Phelps.
Text is set in Adobe Caslon Pro.